BELOW
THEM
THE
HORIZON

LAURA ALLNUTT

Woodhall Press
Norwalk, CT

Library of Congress Cataloguing-in Publication Data available

ISBN Paperback 978-1-949116-26-7

ISBN Ebook 978-1-949116-27-4

FIRST EDITION

Edited by: Colin Hosten

Cover design by: Jessica Dionne Abouelela

Formatting: Jessica Dionne Abouelela

Woodhall Press, 81 Old Saugatuck Road, Norwalk, CT 06855

woodhallpress.com

Distributed by INGRAM

To Sarah,
my oxygen when it's hard to breathe
and my light through the darkness.

1

Blue-green waters rolled over white sands, leaving the shore smooth and soft. Lucy felt her feet sink in.

Don't sink, she told herself. Look at the Gulf. It's cold and gray, and the gulls are crying. A pelican rocks on the waves. Does a pelican dream? Keep guessing. Keep thinking. Keep dreaming while the lights are on. Look at the Gulf. Count the seconds between the waves. You can't stop the tide; you can't hold onto it. All you have are the seconds between crashing waves and receding foam, seconds on the sands. They're ticking. It's calling you.

The water knew her, owned her. And she knew the Gulf and whom she had lost to it. She could hear her name on its waves. She was losing herself there, slowly, as the bank loses a single grain of sand at a time.

The Gulf is not the ocean. It's warmer, the waves, smaller. Under a high sun, it's bright and translucent, like liquid emeralds; under clouds and haze, it's gray and blue. It's vast and open, a habitat—sea turtles, sandpipers, dolphins, horseshoe crabs, shrimp—so much life that the tiny coastal fish don't flee when human feet tread the waters. They're used to it. So much life, but the Gulf doesn't care. Indifferently, it throws clam and conch shells onto the shore, pulls away from baby turtles scurrying to safety, shades the tiger sharks waiting for them. Tourists love it.

Lucy belonged to it.

And only Audra knew why she walked along the shore, why she collected broken seashells, why yesterday Lucy had called and begged her friend to come, though they hadn't spoken in months.

"It's calling me," Lucy said, "and I'm afraid."

It was all gray when Audra came—the sky, the sand, the waves. A warm October breeze whipped at the short, curly hair around Lucy's face as Audra walked to her side. The Gulf was rising, and Lucy was sinking, the hair on her arms standing on end.

"Hey." Audra gripped her elbow and shook her gently. "Come on," she said. "It's going to rain soon."

The grip on her elbow cost Lucy her balance, and she leaned against Audra, who was a head shorter than Lucy, to steady herself as she pulled her feet from sludgy wet sand.

"Come on," Audra said. She hooked her arm in Lucy's and led her up the soft damp sand to the little blue house. It, too, appeared gray against the stormy sky. They walked up the battered white deck stairs, and Lucy opened the door that led into the kitchen. She had to work the knob to get it closed.

"Sit. I'll make you tea," Audra said.

Lucy sat on the bay-window seat and looked out at the Gulf. Lightning flashed against the clouds on the horizon and thunder rumbled in the distance.

"You have to pump the lever on the faucet for the water to come," she said.

She'd fix it sometime. So much else needed fixing. But Audra knew that.

Though it was one of many in a long row of coastal homes, the blue house was one of the few lived in by residents rather than rented by tourists. Once, a realtor had knocked on the door and offered to buy it, but Lucy knew she couldn't sell this house that was not a home, and never had been.

It looked like an average dwelling, with its three bedrooms, bathroom, living room, and kitchen. It formed a perfect rectangle, like a shoebox storing old things that ought to be thrown away. A door at the front in the living room. A small kitchen. A hall to the master bedroom, with two smaller rooms at the center, directly across from each other. A carport and laundry room under the house. While all the pieces may have been there, it was still not a home.

"A castle on the sea!" her father had called it when he bought it for her mother, who was pregnant at the time. Her mother had insisted they hire an interior decorator. *It's 1990, and the house should look like it.* So they hired Dez, a designer of her mother's choosing, a wiry little man with long shaggy hair. He hung blue-and-white-striped wallpaper in the kitchen and yellow-and-green-striped paper in the living room. He ordered an ugly green couch, hung yellow curtains at the window, and laid out white shag rugs. He finished with a Picasso-like painting of what could be a crab, or perhaps a fat lobster, on the living room wall.

It's hideous, her father said, and her mother knew it, but said this house hadn't given Dez much to work with. She fired him before he could ruin the bedrooms, and painted them herself: yellow in the first bedroom on the left, the room that faced the beach, for the unborn Lucy; carnation pink in the room across from it, for a hoped-for second daughter. The master bedroom, she left unfinished. In the living room and halls, she hung large mirrors and sconces and pictures of painted birds and flowers, covering as much space as possible. At times, she had asked if they could sell it, but her father had refused, and Lucy was glad. As a child, she couldn't have imagined living anywhere else. She didn't understand that it was ugly—certainly not with the ocean in her backyard.

Nothing about the house had changed for as long as Lucy and Audra had known it—nothing except its age. Now, the wooden floors creaked, the white shag rugs were matted and stained. A brown tobacco haze discolored the walls, and the blue siding was spotted with mildew. A once-white shutter hung lopsided, and a few other shutters and some shingles had blown off with Hurricane Ivan in 2004, and never been replaced. The wood was rotting on the whitewashed deck out back and the stairs out front.

Audra put the kettle on a burner, and they waited silently until it hissed and steam clouded its sides. She pulled two mugs from the cabinet and prepared the tea, joining Lucy on the bay-window seat.

She handed her the steaming mug and patted her leg. "Calm down."

The touch was startling but familiar, recalling days of childhood giggles under thin sheets and salty skin on warm sand.

But they hadn't spoken in months, and Lucy wouldn't have called her back now if she hadn't been the only person left.

"It's really bad," Lucy said, finally looking at Audra.

Audra held her gaze and sighed. "It's always really bad when it's bad," she said. "It's calmed down before, and it will again."

"It's too strong this time." She choked on her words and wiped her nose with her thumb. "I can't leave this house anymore. I quit my job."

"Quit?"

Lucy nodded.

Yes, she had left her job at Blue Herons. All she did there was weigh fillets of fresh fish and pounds of Gulf shrimp for consistent customers, and sweep and bleach the floors free of scales, blood, and the occasional fish eyes. She had never cared that she carried the fishy smells home on her clothes and in her hair. She didn't even think about them after a while.

It wasn't the job itself. It was the people and being around them and the constant stress of survival. She thought only of making it through another day, escaping any conflicts that might spur another attack.

"You can't quit," Audra said. "How will you live? Call the Flynns; I know they'll take you back."

"I have my art." She could spend her days sketching at her desk or painting at her easel, making prints for greeting cards. The freelance life wasn't so bad.

Leaving Blue Herons was a small loss in terms of career. Making a living with pencils, acrylics, and watercolors was freeing. She could see past the stroke of a brush and the opacity of color to the fluidity of movement on canvas, how the paints swirled and blended and changed. Art was never wholly one thing; it was both abstract and literal, peaceful and disturbing, melancholy and hopeful. It deeply affected her, as music affected her father, because art gave her a sense of both control and surrender. The subject was hers, but its formation was organic, as if something else was controlling the brush.

She'd spent much of her childhood at the small wooden desk in her bedroom, tacky with age and cluttered with pads and pencils. Her sketches depicted hazy sunsets over ribbed seashells and glistening sandcastles; a pair of hermit crabs under palm trees, shrimp boats on the horizon. Later sketches revealed a half-smoked cigarette, a chipped teacup, a sandpiper.

But even her art didn't cool the burning in her stomach, the clench in her chest.

"Unless you're going to get really serious about it, you can't make a living on it. Not yet," Audra said.

Lucy shrugged, but her brows creased with worry. She put her face in her hands and tried to breathe. Breathing was the hardest.

Audra rubbed her back and brushed away her tears, as she had so many times before.

"Sometimes life just builds up." She smoothed back the rumpled curls from Lucy's face. "That's what Dr. Preston used to tell you, right? So, what's building up for you now?" A pause, and then, "Sip your tea," she said. "It'll help."

Yes, and rest would help, the doctors always said, and the pills. They should, but they didn't always. It was never gone because it had no cure, always resurfacing.

The wind blew then, and the house groaned against the force as if it might collapse in the storm. Lucy gripped the window frame as if to hold the place, and herself, together.

"Thanks for coming." Lucy took her small friend's hand and squeezed it, looking into her round green eyes. She should have looked sooner, for there was comfort in them.

"I always do," Audra said.

2

Florida rain had puddled in the uneven church parking lot before
her mother had sent Lucy to the car for Emily's diaper bag, warning
her to keep her white shoes dry.

As she strolled to the car, she waved to Jessica and Gina,
playing hopscotch on a patch of almost-dry pavement, holding
their white purses higher with each jump. They were both deacons
daughters, and hadn't cared for Lucy since they'd learned her
parents smoked.

"Smoking's of the devil," they chanted loud enough for Lucy
to hear, "and it makes you smell like hell!"

Lucy stuck her tongue out at them and continued carefully
around the puddles.

What was so bad about the smooth, earthy smell of
cigarettes? They smelled good to her, and smoking seemed to help
her parents whenever they got angry. Besides, her dad was better
than theirs anyway, because he was nice, and she loved him. He led
the high school band at Gulf Coast Academy, where she attended

elementary school, and though she was in a separate building, it comforted her to know he was somewhat nearby and that she could sometimes hear his band practicing during her afternoon recess. She loved that she was so like him in appearance—curly blonde hair, tall, lanky, awkward.

What Lucy didn't see on the way to the car was another girl, leaping from puddle to puddle.

"Hello," the girl said when Lucy neared her. The hem of her soiled pink jumper was inches above her red rain boots, exposing stocky freckled legs. Was there even skin under all those freckles?

"Hi," Lucy said.

She reached the station wagon without soiling her shoes and pressed both thumbs into the metal button of the car door to get it open, releasing the smells of must and tobacco. She lifted the diaper bag onto her shoulder and shut the station wagon door with her hip, as her mother did.

As she turned to walk back to the church, the girl in the pink jumper leaped into a nearby puddle, sending a splash of murky water over Lucy's feet.

Lucy stopped, mouth open, eyes narrowed at the freckled girl.

"Sorry." The girl shrugged and jumped into another puddle. Jessica and Gina giggled.

"Too bad it won't wash off that hell smell," Jessica said.

Lucy twisted her face at them. They could bug off.

But if she could, she'd push this puddle jumper into the biggest, grimiest puddle she could find, right on her butt.

"It'll wash off," the girl said.

"Shows what you know." Lucy's voice cracked, and her nose turned red. Her stomach knotted, and dread, a familiar companion, put a lump in her throat. She turned back to the church, the bag slung over her arm.

Her mother was uncovering Emily's dimpled bottom and didn't bother to look over at Lucy when she handed her the bag.

"My shoes got wet," Lucy said.

Her mother lifted her eyes, which were always distant, even when they looked right at her.

"Wet? They're drenched! Did you deliberately jump in a puddle?"

"No."

"They sopped up water from the air, then?"

"No." The lump in her throat felt thicker, and Lucy fought against it, her pride at stake. How could she walk into Sunday school with the sorry evidence of tears on her face?

"Then what did happen? And remember, you're in church."

She was innocent. She and God both knew it. But now the truth felt like a lie, and the lump was too hard to talk around. She opened her mouth, but her voice didn't come out. Then another voice did—or, rather, it came from behind her.

"I splashed her."

Lucy hadn't noticed the puddle jumper following her, and from her mother's expression, neither had she. But then her mother's eyes softened, and she came back to herself. She was actually there, the way she was when Emily cooed on her lap, reaching for her breast or catching her long blonde hair in those small, delicate fingers.

She quickly wrapped a fresh diaper around Emily and set her in a crib, then pulled a ribbon from her purse and tied back the freckled girl's short, sandy hair.

"You're Audra Clarke, is that right?" she asked.

The puddle jumper nodded, clearly uneasy with this woman fixing her hair.

"Hi there! My name is Linda De Rossi," she said, suddenly happy and graceful, "and these are my daughters, Lucy and Emily. Lucy, Audra is our new pastor's daughter."

Audra hung her head and didn't say anything. Lucy shifted nervously in her spoiled shoes.

"She's going into fourth grade, too," her mother continued. "Walk down to Sunday school with her."

Then the lump broke in Lucy's throat, and she covered her face to cry. If someone had asked her why, at this point, she was crying, she'd have said she didn't know—only that she was, and she felt the worse for it.

"Oh, for goodness' sake, Lucy!" Her mother pulled a baby wipe from the diaper bag and cleaned up Lucy's face.

Lucy pushed her away, and the distance returned to her mother's eyes.

"Hurry up before you're late," her mother said, before she turned back to Emily.

Lucy wiped her eyes with her hand and shook her head as if to shake off the moment, the tears, the memory. But she would not forget. She remembered everything. She sealed the memory with a long inhale and took Audra's wrist.

"Come on." She led her down a carpeted stairwell to the lower end of the split-level church. The halls smelled of musty books and sour-metal stair railings.

Entering the classroom, Lucy's stained shoes clicked and Audra's rain boots squeaked on the linoleum floor. There were only two seats left in the circle of children, and they were side by side. They sat, and Jessica and Gina pointed at them, whispering and giggling. Gina held her nose and waved the air away.

Audra glared silently, but Lucy crossed her eyes and stuck out her tongue—a mortal offense in fourth grade. Jessica and Gina gasped, looked at each other, and rolled their eyes.

When the lesson started, Audra pulled a peppermint from her pocket and placed it on Lucy's lap. Audra didn't smile; she was too hesitant for that, too unassuming.

Lucy smiled first, then Audra almost did, and Lucy forgave her for the shoes.

10

3

On the way home from church that Sunday, Audra fidgeted in the back of the family's Impala, next to her older brother, Levi. She preferred the driver's side of the car even though her imposing father pushed his seat back so far it rubbed her knees. Sitting behind her mother was even worse, because she had motion sickness and rode with her seat fully reclined. Besides, Levi liked to sit behind their mother and massage her temples or shoulders, or hold her hand as they drove.

When her mother became ill on the ride home, no one spoke, except her father, when he surprised them by ordering a bucket of KFC from the drive-through. Her mother started to protest when he pulled into the parking lot, but then threw up her hands in resignation. Audra hated these Sundays spent in silence, which occurred too often, especially after a move to a new state. By the time she was nine, Audra had lived in Iowa, Maryland, North Carolina, and now, Florida, each time so that her father could take on a new church. Each move left her feeling placeless, uprooted, and alone—things she often felt before she'd met Lucy.

When you're nine years old and you've learned how to say good-bye better than how to say hello, you don't make friends very quickly. You may even be quite bad at it.

Audra was not. She attracted friends in every state, given a few weeks, but she handled them carelessly because she knew they would not last. Her father would take on another church in just a few years, and then she'd have to say good-bye again. Her friends would cry, but not her. She assumed the same thing would happen with this new girl, Lucy, whom she hadn't meant to splash that day. She didn't care that the silly girl had gotten her shoes wet, but she did care that the girl was upset. There was nothing worse than making someone upset, and Audra could not abide tears.

Their new home was only minutes from the church, on the sound side of the water, but not on it. Most of their boxes still littered the halls and living room, but it wouldn't take her mother long to unpack them. Already the familiar smells of Audra's family filled the new spaces: her mother's convenience-store perfume, vanilla and sweet; her father's ever-ready coffee; Levi's leather baseball gloves; powdery fabric softener.

Audra decided to finish her room by evening. After that, she didn't know. In the other states, she had roamed the woods and fields, picking wildflowers and watching birds build nests high in trees and thinking about the sounds trees make when they think no one is listening. But there were no mountains in Florida, and in the Panhandle, most of the trees were draped in Spanish moss, which she was told not to touch because the little chiggers living in it would make a home in her skin. The ground was hard and often dry, and the heat kept her indoors.

"Change your clothes before we eat," her mother said to all of them.

Audra didn't need to be told. She didn't like the jumper she was wearing, or the rain boots. Both were hand-me-downs from a cousin she saw only at funerals and on a few holidays.

She changed quickly into a tank top and short coveralls and returned to the kitchen to claim a drumstick. KFC was fine, but she preferred her mother's cooking, and she knew her mother preferred doing the cooking. She wondered why her father hadn't thought to ask her mother about it first.

Her mother believed in filling people with more food than anyone could ever eat—chicken pot pies, pans of brownies, plates of cookies, chicken salad, deviled eggs—enough for an army. In most of their churches, she worked hard as the secretary and church events coordinator. Then she would come home to cook the kind of dinner that makes you ready for bed when night falls, full and warm and satisfied.

Her father often worked long hours, late into the evening, and rarely ate dinner with them. Sunday dinners were special because he was there. Other nights, he came home and went straight to his den to counsel someone over the phone. Audra enjoyed listening to him speak, his confident baritone quoting the King James version, as if he'd penned it himself. It made her proud.

They were good people, her parents. She reminded herself of that often through the years. They loved people, and people loved them. Had her parents seen her jumping in puddles, had they seen her splash Lucy's shoes, she'd have been forking over her allowance until Lucy had a new pair, but her parents rarely saw what she did. So it surprised her, as she bit into her drumstick, when her mother mentioned Lucy.

"You made a new friend your first Sunday here, did you?"

Levi snorted. "She always makes friends." He said the words contemptuously, jealously, but only Audra caught his tone.

Her mother smiled. "It's good to be friendly like that. You always draw people to you. That's good."

Her father nodded. "We're very proud of you, sweetheart."

Audra forced a smile. She caught Levi smirking; he knew that she didn't care at all about people and being their friend. She kicked him under the table.

"Why don't you invite her over?" her mom said. "You've got all summer now."

"I just met her, Mom."

They wanted her to feel settled. She knew the game. They wanted to make her feel as if this were home, as if this might be the place they would stay for the rest of their lives, as if they might not leave it in a couple years. Friends are the seeds which give us roots.

"I'll give her mother a call for you."

The first time Lucy spent the night, Audra's mom made fried porkchops and chocolate pie. Lucy ate three chops, two biscuits, a pile of green beans up to her nose, and a large slice of pie with milk. The entire Clarke family marveled at her.

"It's like a magic trick!" Levi said, alluding to her long, scrawny body.

Audra's mom delighted in shoveling pork and pie down a child with such a healthy appetite. She all but offered her a cup of coffee by the end of the night.

"I wish my mom cooked like that!" Lucy said.

They were in Audra's backyard, a small sandy lot surrounded by a privacy fence. There was a concrete slab for a patio with a few cushioned chairs and a spit for roasting marshmallows.

"You'd be tubby like me." Audra looked down at her protruding belly.

"My mom always cooks fish and peas. We're always going to the fish market."

Audra wished she could say what they always did. Sometimes she found herself wishing that her mother were home all day, like Lucy's mother—that she had a baby sister like Emily to dote on.

Levi lit the spit and handed them each a stick and a bag of marshmallows. Audra watched Lucy skewer a marshmallow and hold it directly in the flame. It quickly caught fire, and Lucy pulled it out, blew out the flames, and pulled off the charred outer layer to eat it. She repeated this, continually, patiently, until she couldn't pull off another layer.

Years later Audra realized that Lucy treated her as she did the marshmallows, slowly pulling back layers until there were no more layers to remove, until she had seen her raw, exposed. She did to Audra what she wanted someone to do with her.

But Audra did not want to be exposed. She liked her layers.

Nonetheless, Lucy was innocently intrusive, and Audra slowly accepted the intrusion.

During that first summer, Lucy taught Audra to swim in the Gulf, linked arms with her as they walked the shore, and draped her in necklaces of little white shells.

Before school started that fall, Lucy gave her a friendship necklace, a half-heart charm inscribed with *ST NDS*.

"Mine says B-E and F-R-I-E," Lucy said, spelling it out.

Then she held her half against Audra's and smiled.

"But together, it all makes sense."

4

Lucy claimed she didn't remember learning to swim; she'd just always known how.

Audra said she didn't believe her, because swimming was very hard.

So Lucy insisted on teaching her. They splashed in the waves, giggling and fussing, until finally Audra learned how to keep herself afloat and propel herself forward.

Lucy wished her mother would join them in the water. "Swim with us, Mom!" she always asked, even though she knew her mother wouldn't.

Audra used to tell Lucy to stop asking, since she always seemed to get the same answer.

Audra and Lucy splashed in the gentle waves, floating on their backs and peeking their toes up through the emerald surface. The salty water gathered around their skin, holding them afloat.

"Come on, Mom!" Lucy called.

"I don't swim, Lucy," her mother said. "I wade. And I don't want to today. Who would watch Emily?"

"Let her swim with us!"

"Not yet," she said. "Emily can hardly walk."

She walked along the shoreline with Emily in tow, keeping her eyes on the girls and the surrounding water, so clear that they could see down to the soft sand in the shallow areas. They hadn't yet learned to fear riptides; they hardly feared the sharks and jellyfish, even though they'd each been stung by the latter more than once.

Lucy's father left in the early mornings, walking two miles to his job at Gulf Coast Academy to rehearse with the marching band, and while the air was less hot, she, her mother, Emily, and sometimes Audra took strolls along the shoreline to comb the beach. They collected the white shells—big, small, cracked, chipped, coiled, flat—and put them all in a blue plastic bucket where they jangled like coins when the pail knocked against her knees.

Audra wasn't interested in shells. She preferred living creatures—sandpipers scurrying away from the trailing water, sea turtles lumbering along the shore, dolphins skipping in sync against the horizon.

When the sun became hot, they'd drive across the bay bridge into town for fresh fish. Lucy enjoyed the crossing, as if she were being transported from one life—with sandpipers and gulls, church and school—to another, where important people lived and worked—fishermen, doctors, department store clerks, and, by comparison, big buildings surrounded by lampposts, banners, and crepe myrtles.

Down a mile or so from the bridge was a dock where her mother purchased fresh fruit, vegetables, and fish from Joe's Fish Market. One of Lucy's earliest memories was the smell of brine and the bleach used to wash away the blood and scales. They bought cod, salmon, Gulf shrimp, and crawfish.

Lucy preferred the shrimp, but hated having to walk down the uneven cement to get them from their tub next to the squids

17

and octopuses, their tentacles suction-cupped to the glass edges, eyes willing her to dip her fingers into the water so they could suck off her hand and leave her with nubby arms. She had nightmares about falling into these bins and feeling them wrap their rubbery arms around her appendages to rip her apart. The creatures in the tubs were no longer than a hand's length, but logic escapes the fearful.

"You don't have to be afraid of octopuses," her father told her. "They're like the roaches that get in the house: They're just looking for a little food and water; they don't want to hurt people. Termites—now, those are scary."

But Lucy hated insects of all kinds as much as the octopuses.

On this trip, her mother chose the seafood, and the men and women behind the counter wrapped her order in thick brown paper.

"Wrapped them up with some garlic and herbs, just the way you like it, Miss Linda," a teenager said with a boyish grin.

"That's why you're my favorite," her mom said, winking.

Then she handed the packages to Lucy and Audra, rolling Emily's stroller around so that she could inspect the fruit and vegetable stands.

"Looking for something in particular?" another teen asked. He nudged the first boy in the ribs and came around the counter.

"Lemons, apples, and perhaps a watermelon, if they're good this year."

"I can help you pick a good one," the boy said. He chose a dark green melon with a large white spot, then knocked on it three times. "If it sounds hollow, it's good. This one should be just right!"

"You're so sweet," her mom said, and the boy blushed.

Lucy looked at Audra and shrugged, and Audra put the watermelon in the bottom of the stroller with the other fruit.

The boys didn't bother Lucy, though she couldn't figure out why they fussed over her mother so much.

But the policeman who always pulled up on his belt and fingered his gun—he made her wish there was another fish market,

"You need help carrying those, little miss?" Officer Bede asked Lucy, who was still holding the packages of fish. Harold Bede was the resident policeman that Joe had hired after catching customers pocketing food from the shelves. He looked down at Lucy with yellowish-brown eyes. His greased dark hair curled at his scalp, and a thin black mustache stretched across the center of his wide, freckled face, which was pink from the Florida sun. He appeared to be several years younger than Lucy's father, but shorter, wider, and fuller. When he smiled, his front teeth were gapped.

"I've got them fine," Lucy said.

Bede smiled and winked at her mother, who blushed. Lucy narrowed her eyes.

"Lots of men wink," Audra said quietly when she saw Lucy's reaction. "It doesn't mean anything bad."

"It means something, though," Lucy said.

Outside the market, a young couple kept a food truck that sold warm beignets year-round. When Audra came with her, she and Lucy always begged for one of the powdery pastries, but her mom rarely treated them to one. While many other children would leave the pier with powdered sugar and jelly coloring their chins and staining their clothes—it was easy for mothers to press money into small hands and send them out for goodies so they could shop in peace—Lucy and Audra would eat only three beignets throughout their childhood. The first was on Lucy's eleventh birthday, and the second, a few months later, at Audra's birthday party. They would eat their third on this day, at the market.

Joe, who wore a flat cap and white collared shirt, kept a land-docked fishing boat beside his fish market for guests to explore. He called it the *Lady Salt*. An elderly fisherman named Sonny, who had gray unkempt whiskers, frequently welcomed children aboard and offered them his lap for tales of Caribbean pirates and his hunt for a hammerhead named Fred. Most of the children gathered on his knees and around his feet with sticky fingers, but Lucy and Audra preferred to listen to Sonny's stories from the dock, with Lucy's mother and sister.

Lucy's mother stood a few feet behind them in her dark denim capris and peach polka-dot blouse. Blue veins, visible beneath her pale, taut skin, formed leafless branches on the undersides of her arms. She wore a musky rose perfume.

Officer Bede stood by her side.

"Go play on the ship," her mother told her.

"I don't like that man," Lucy said.

"Sonny?" Bede laughed. "He's harmless."

But Lucy didn't trust Bede or Sonny, and she wished her mother didn't either. Why did she let him stand so close and touch her hip like that?

"Maybe Lucy's right," her mother said.

"Right about what?"

"Sonny. You don't see anything fishy about an old man so enthusiastic about holding children on his lap all afternoon in this blazing sun?"

"Well, I . . ." He shifted uncomfortably.

"Really, Officer Bede, maybe I should be the one wearing that badge."

"Oh, she's too young to think like that. Sonny's fine."

Then Bede bought them their third beignets. Audra and Emily nibbled theirs eagerly, but Lucy only picked at hers until it was time to leave, and then quietly threw it away. She wished it was her father who worked at the fish market, who stood by her mother's side at the dock, buying them beignets.

5

For Emily's fourth birthday one hot July, Lucy helped her father stuff a pony piñata with candy and hang it underneath the house in the carport while her mother lay in bed.

"Mom's sick," her father told her on days like this.

"What does she have?" Lucy asked from the foot of a ladder.

"It's hard to explain," he said, looping the string through a hook and tossing it down to Lucy. "Nothing to worry about."

Some mornings, her mother woke with the dawn and met them all wearing red lipstick and heavy perfume. Other mornings, she came from her room long after Lucy and Emily had eaten their cereal, still wearing her robe.

"Do you need anything, Mom?" Lucy asked once.

But her mother waved her away.

"Mommy!" Emily, who didn't understand the difference between the two kinds of mornings, would run into their mother's arms, and Linda would pause, breathe, and scoop her into her arms, sometimes crying a little into Emily's golden hair.

Lucy would watch—what else could she do?—until Linda smiled a little and kissed Emily's nose before returning to her room.

She wondered now if her mother had remembered to buy a present—if she'd come out long enough to bake a cake. When it became clear that she would not, Lucy pulled out a box mix and prepared it herself. She was thirteen and knew how to take care of her sister. Only her chocolate frosting turned out lumpy and dry, and it tore at the cake when she tried to spread it.

"Go knock on her door, Em," Lucy said.

Emily did and soon returned, holding their mother's hand. Linda looked at the cake and frowned.

"Is there any frosting left?"

Lucy handed her the bowl, and her mother added some milk, stirred, scraping the sides of the bowl, and smoothed out the frosting on the cake.

"Now it's pretty!" Emily said, and Linda kissed her forehead.

"Not as pretty as you, baby."

"I did the best I could," Lucy said, angry, "because you weren't here."

Her mother's smile faded, and Lucy left the kitchen, letting the back door slam on her way out. She crossed the grassy dunes and stormed down to the Gulf, where she sat close enough for the water to poke at her toes. She didn't know how long she'd sat there before her father joined her.

"Have I ever told you how I met your mother?"

She shook her head no.

He lit a cigarette and puffed it a few times. "I'm a third-generation Italian American. Well, started off Italian—De Rossi—but you have German, Irish, who knows what else in you. With the Depression and the wars, I didn't have a big family. No siblings; just one uncle and a few cousins." He blew out smoke from his cigarette.

Lucy nodded, knowing only that her grandparents had died when she was little.

Her father motioned for her to wait. "My parents divorced, and I grew up with my grandparents. My grandmother made me help roll out fresh pasta, always to the Rat Pack. She told me, 'You find somebody to sing to,' so I went looking. Sang at clubs and weddings, dancing and charming the ladies along the way." He grinned. "But then I was getting to be an old man—forty! And I was singing at a little gig for Mardi Gras weekend. She was there— young, bright, with cool blue eyes, dark red lips, and strings of green and purple beads around her neck. I picked the confetti from her hair and asked her to dance."

Lucy could hear the smile in his voice as he scooped up wet sand and let it drip from her fingers into a stalagmite.

"We dated for three weeks and then got married." He sucked his cigarette again. "I told her all about my family, but she didn't want to talk about hers. Her father gambled and drank; her mother yelled a lot. I never even met them."

"Are they still alive?"

He shrugged. "She's hurt, Lucy—on the inside. I knew that the day I married her, but I'd found my person to sing to."

When Lucy said nothing, he sighed and took her hand.

"Forgive her, Lucy. She doesn't mean to hurt your feelings."

Lucy nodded and whispered, "Okay," but only as a comfort for her father, and because she couldn't do anything else.

He kissed her hand and told her he was running up to the store. She stayed on the beach until he returned with a poorly wrapped present and a bouquet of daffodils, then followed him back to the house.

"A present for my baby." He handed the gift to Emily. "And flowers for my love." He handed the flowers to Linda and kissed her cheek.

"You're a sentimental old fool," she said, but Lucy caught her smiling over them as she touched the smooth, silky petals, putting them in a vase on the table.

Emily opened the gift, a set of Tinker Toys, and blew out her candles while their father played on the piano and sang "Happy Birthday." Then they all swung at the piñata until finally its back broke, dumping colorful candies over the cracked cement.

Later that night, Lucy hadn't been in bed long before she heard the CD of Sinatra and her father's light steps as he danced her mother out to the back patio, leaving the door open for the sea breeze to carry the music. She watched from the open window in her bedroom, leaning against the creaking sill, the white curtain tickling her nose.

"Are you spying on them?" Emily had left her room as usual and crept into Lucy's, joining her at the window.

"Shh," Lucy said, not wanting to miss the dance.

Her mother had heard them and started to fuss, but her father reached his hand through the open window, pinched Lucy's nose, and winked before he pulled down the blind.

"Why do they do that?" Emily asked.

"Do what?"

"Why do they play outside like that?"

"They aren't playing." Lucy secured the blanket around her sister. "They're listening to music."

"And dancing."

"Well, it's none of our business what they're doing." Lucy settled down in the bed and rolled away from Emily.

"Why were you watching, then?"

Lucy pretended to be asleep and let out a slow breath. She couldn't tell Emily why their dancing sat heavily on her mind, not for good or bad, nor could she explain how it entered her dreams as butterflies drifting through the nebulous land of sleep, with music on their wings and bright purple spirals of smoke at their feet. The heavens were their backdrop, with diamond stardust to guide their way.

When Lucy awoke, she felt light and fluid, as if all the forces of the universe had joined hands and carried her overhead: Lucy, the champion of dreams.

But such nights were not the norm.

The day before school began, Lucy returned from the beach with Emily to find their parents at war. Her mother threw a soapy plate at her father, then a cup, then a pot. The pot hit the wall and sent the Picasso crab picture falling to the floor.

"Calm down, baby; it's all okay." Her father tried to take her mom in his arms, but she elbowed his ribs and slugged his jaw.

"Don't handle me!" Her clear blue eyes had shrunk, small and distant, as if they couldn't recognize the man with whom she danced.

Lucy had seen these episodes before, but because she was thirteen, and feeling more responsible, this time she tried to stop her.

"Calm down, Mom." Lucy reached for her arm. "You're just being crazy."

Her mom smacked her so hard that she stumbled to the floor. It was the first time her mother had ever struck her, and the only time her father locked her mother out of the house. He didn't say a word, only gripped her arm and led her outside. He locked her out and picked Lucy up.

"Mom's sick, Lucy," he said, examining the small scratch within the purple bruise on her cheek. "She doesn't mean any of it." He kissed her temple where her hair curled the tightest.

"You always say that, and it means nothing!" Lucy cried.

Emily had stood helplessly in the kitchen, and when she saw that the worst was over, began to cry as loud and long as a four-year-old can.

Linda pounded on the door.

"Let me in, Frank! My baby's crying! Let me in!"

Frank unlocked the door and Linda fumbled her way over to Emily, scooped her up, and held her on the ugly green couch.

"Shh, shh, shh, my darling. Mama's here. No more crying. Shush, shush," as if she hadn't caused the tears. She held her close to her breast and rocked her back and forth as Frank urged Lucy back to her room.

On those nights, Lucy sketched at her desk until her eyes grew heavy, falling into a heavy mist of sleep, rocked on a stormy sea with nowhere to go.

6

"She slapped you that hard?" Audra said when she saw the dark bruise with the small scratch.

Over the years Audra had spent with Lucy, she'd known that Linda was unpredictable—certainly nothing like her own mother. Lucy described her as crazy, throwing things and hitting her father. Lucy had long ago sworn her to secrecy.

"Don't tell anyone it was her. She didn't mean it. I'll just tell the kids at school that I . . . I fell when I was roller-blading."

"And only bruised your face?"

They both knew the kids in seventh grade would see past that one.

Lucy considered the logistics and nodded.

"You're right. Punch me in the arm." She closed her eyes tightly. "Do it hard."

"What?"

"Punch me. Go on." She squinted her eyes, preparing for impact, but she couldn't have prepared for how hard Audra would slam her upper arm. The punch was so forceful that she fell over to the grass and yelped in pain.

27

Lucy stood back up, panting and angry, and Audra considered running for her life.

"Sorry. You *said* hard."

"Do it again."

"Lucy!"

"This time kick my leg." She braced again and then added, "But don't break it."

So Audra kicked her, and Lucy winced and sat on the grass. She found a jagged rock and began scraping her knee.

"What are you doing?" Audra asked with alarm.

"It's got to be believable." She scratched until blood came, but Audra couldn't watch. She couldn't bear to see someone in pain, let alone inflicting pain on herself.

"You're crazy," she said.

Lucy shot her an angry glare.

In a few minutes, she had a few colorful bruises to match the one on her face.

When Audra's parents saw Lucy at dinner, they both grew anxious, doting on her and asking her uncomfortable questions she didn't want to answer. At least that's what Lucy told Audra.

Audra wondered whether Lucy intended to cover for her mom, or if she simply didn't want to get into any more trouble. Lucy had told her she never knew whether her mom was in a good mood or a bad one, and what—if anything—she'd done to provoke it.

"Looks like you got slammed!" Levi said, laughing, as if the idea of Lucy in a brawl were the highlight of his day. A look from their father silenced him.

Her mom stooped to eye level and wrapped her arm around Lucy.

"Do you want to talk about this, honey?"

Audra saw Lucy fight back tears as she shook her head no.

Later, Audra would look back on that moment and understand that it was not the question her mom had asked, or even the fact that she'd called Lucy "honey." It was the maternal, protective arm around her friend's shoulders, the comforting scent of vanilla and sugar that had brought Lucy to tears.

The truth—that Lucy was grateful for her mom's embrace— would cause Audra to experience a moment's guilt that she had so often felt her mother's touch with no such emotion. She saw it as familiar at best and patronizing at worst—as if her mom assumed that Audra couldn't take care of herself. And Audra could *definitely* take care of herself.

Later that night, in the darkness of Audra's small, lavender room, they lay in bed, the small fan in the corner blowing their hair back and making their eyes water.

"Your sheets always smell like baby lotion," Lucy said.

"It's fabric softener."

"My mom doesn't use that, I don't think." She let loose a long breath. "Sometimes I want to hurt her."

"Your mom?"

"No." Lucy remained silent for only a moment, and when she spoke, her voice was low and hoarse. "Emily."

The confession made Audra uncomfortable and slightly confused. She'd wanted to hurt Lucy's mom when she saw what she'd done to Lucy's face.

"Why?"

"I don't know. She just gets . . . everything. I mean, not everything. I don't know how to explain it."

"Well," Audra said, "sometimes I want to hurt Levi. He's a real jackwagon sometimes. That's what Dad says."

"A 'jackwagon'?" Lucy laughed, and Audra blushed in the darkness.

Pastors' kids have such dumb slang, Audra thought, and she made a mental note not to use it again. "Don't make fun of me," she said.

"I wasn't! I just never heard that word before."

"That's because your parents probably say the real word: *jackass*."

Lucy gasped. "Audra!"

"What? It means 'donkey,' really. I don't know what all the fuss is about." But she smiled, happy about the reaction she'd gotten, and pleased to have *jackwagon* off her tongue.

"Mom's never hit Emily," Lucy said in her low, hoarse voice.

"Oh." Audra shifted, unsure of what to say, so she said nothing. Instead, she slipped her hand in Lucy's.

Lucy had new bruises the last day they swam in the Gulf together.

They'd had a half-day one early October Friday, and after school, the water appeared as calm as glass, shallow for a mile from the dry embankment, and still warm enough to swim in. Emily was jumping the waves as they rushed toward her toes.

"Watch your sister," her mother had said. She had left the three girls there to swim and casually strolled back to the little blue house.

Lucy and Audra had drifted far beyond the bank, deep enough to brush against turtle shells and schools of fish, close enough to see when Emily chased after a glimmering conch shell.

"Don't go too far, Em!" Lucy called, then dunked her head below the water. She swam to Audra and grabbed her leg, getting the scream she'd hoped for.

"Don't do that!" Audra said. "I don't like being this far out. Let's get closer to shore."

Lucy checked for Emily, who was now knee-deep in the water.

"All right," Lucy said. "Sharks don't eat at this time of day, you know."

"Okay, but what's that?" Audra pointed to a dark shadow moving in the water.

Lucy squinted, watching it a moment. "Just a stingray." She had looked away for only seconds, but when she turned around, Emily was gone.

"Emily?" she called.

"Where'd she go?" Audra asked, trying to run against the water to shore.

"Emily?" Lucy called, spinning and searching the water. "Emily!"

They searched above and below the water's surface, calling in voices raspy with fear, so much so that Lucy's neighbor, Gladys Walker, a snowbird who was watching nearby, called 911.

Audra was crying, and Lucy could barely breathe by the time the paramedics arrived.

"Riptide," they heard a man say. "See that calm area where there are no waves?"

"You girls stay onshore," another ordered.

They tried to believe it was some other four-year-old carried ashore that day, lying on the warm sand as paramedics frantically worked oxygen into her lungs. They couldn't see her through the men, could barely glimpse her white-blonde hair clumping in the sand or her red swimsuit, Lucy's hand-me-down, with the loose drawstring around her pudgy middle. It could be any child in the world, they told themselves, but they knew it was Emily.

It was her mom whom Lucy didn't know that day. She hardly recognized her mother's voice as she ran toward them, half paranoid, half smiling, some otherworldly expression on her face as she approached the cluster of men surrounding Emily.

"What's going on?" Her voice was higher than usual. "Did my little fish swallow too much water again?"

Lucy didn't speak. It was too soon to wonder what had taken her mother so long to return to the beach.

After a moment, a paramedic approached them, a grim expression on his young face.

"Are you the girl's mother?"

"I—I am, yes—yes, of course. I'm Linda De Rossi—I'm her mother. She'll need ginger ale after all that salt in her stomach. She's always swal—"

"Ma'am—" He glanced down at Lucy and Audra and motioned for her to step aside. He spoke again, and Linda's fair skin turned ashen. She gasped and brought her slender hand to her red lips. Her shoulders trembled, and from her mouth came a strange sound, somewhere between a scream and a gasp.

"You were supposed to watch her!" She said, turning to Lucy. "Why didn't you watch her!" She gripped Lucy's shoulders and shook her so hard that Audra thought she'd snap her friend's neck.

"Stop it, Mom!" Lucy cried.

The paramedic quickly pulled her off. "You're in shock, ma'am. Let's get you to the ambulance."

As Linda let go of her daughter, she and Lucy both tumbled to the sand. Then Linda began to sob and moan. "My baby! I've lost my baby!"

Lucy shook until she vomited. Audra put her arms around Lucy's shoulders and buried her face in her friend's hair, full of salt and sand.

"I'm sorry!" Lucy's voice was not her own, but she wasn't crying. She was hardly breathing.

Audra was crying, her warm tears sliding onto Lucy's shoulders. She cried so hard she was shaking. Why couldn't Lucy cry? Even the gulls cried overhead.

"I'm sorry," Lucy said again. Still holding tightly to Audra, she looked up over the water, so deceptively calm and glassy, as if it had not just changed the rest of her life.

The funeral was two days later. They wore black dresses and black shoes to honor the girl who lay in a casket the length of a guitar case at the head of the church. Flowers arranged in hearts and bouquets around the altar had already wilted in the autumn heat, their bitter honey scent sticking in everyone's throat.

Audra stood beside Lucy, her head on Lucy's shoulder, freckles peeling from sunburn. Her father was giving the homily. "No one should ever have to lose a child," he said solemnly. "No one." He wiped his forehead with a white handkerchief and then blew his nose in it. He looked at Lucy and then at Audra.

Lucy saw him as a judge, declaring her the guilty sinner who had let her sister drown.

"We know that Jesus loves everyone," he said, "but we know that he has a special love for little children. Christ encourages us to have faith like a child, to see with a child's eyes and love with a child's unconditional love. We can rest in peace tonight, knowing that he loved this child with unconditional love, and her soul is forever with him."

Lucy didn't cry. She held her father's hand as he silently wept into the crook of his arm, and, once, she glanced at her mother, who sat straight and rigid, eyes empty and dark.

Later, when she saw the grave ready to swallow her little sister, she felt tears fill her eyes, but, even then, Lucy did not cry. She held it in, tightly clenched and swelling in the back of her mouth until the burial service had ended and the congregation had gathered in the reception hall for lunch.

Then Lucy and Audra hid in the basement bathroom, huddled in the cramped corner of the farthest stall. They held each other close.

"It's not your fault, Lucy," Audra said, wiping Lucy's cheeks.

Lucy believed that the words people said were like the sounds of the tide: full of force, but empty of meaning. Her father had told her that her mother loved her, but the force of his words couldn't make them true. They drifted meaninglessly on the tide of her mother's unpredictable moods.

Now her father and all the others would tell her that Emily's death was not her fault—that it was just a horrible accident—but she would recognize the emptiness of their words as much as she did the pity in their eyes.

Had she allowed her sister to drown?

Watch your sister, her mother had said.

Hadn't she? She wasn't sure anymore.

How could she not remember? Emily was there, and then suddenly, she wasn't. Was it her fault she wasn't? Was it wicked of her to hope that now, with Emily gone, her mother would love her, the only daughter left?

7

Lucy stayed with the Clarkes for many days after the funeral. Frank insisted on it, saying that Linda needed space to grieve, and Marion welcomed her with ready hugs and a full kitchen.

But Lucy didn't feel like eating. She hardly felt like talking. She longed to be with her parents, grieving with them. Why did her mother need space from her? Shouldn't she hold tight to the only living daughter? An unfamiliar feeling wormed its way into her stomach, growing heavily in the bottom of her gut. It made her uneasy as she walked the halls of school and sat over homework in the evening. As it grew, she became more aware of a sense of dread—dreading school, the trip to and from the building, the people there, getting attention from anyone but Audra.

Then one day, as she walked into her classroom, the desks and chairs and walls spun about her head like a mosaic on which she couldn't focus. Students pushed past her. The air felt too thin to breathe, her lungs unable to function. Her palms sweated, her chest pounded, then clenched. The pain shot down to her fingertips, leaving them numb. She knew she was dying.

"Lucy, come on," Audra said.

But Lucy heard her through a fog.

"The bell's about to ring." Audra nudged her a bit through the doorway, but Lucy turned and walked back out, sliding down to the floor and holding her knees against her chest.

"Lucy! What's wrong? Are you sick?"

Lucy could hardly work her own voice. She was outside herself, everywhere and nowhere, and the world was spinning too fast. Her heart was exploding.

"Lucy!" Audra gripped her shoulders and shook her a little. "What's wrong? Do you need the nurse?" She stood and called for their teacher.

Lucy began to cry strange, hot tears that she would have suppressed had she felt them coming. That she had not hidden them made her feel even more ashamed as people gathered around her. This was not how she wanted to die.

"Something's wrong with me," she whispered to Audra. She felt herself lifted back to her feet. "Audra, don't leave me." She clutched her friend's hand, but their teacher and the principal pulled them apart and led Lucy down the hall to the nurse's office. The pain in her chest tightened as she realized she would die alone, without Audra.

"Do you have asthma?" the nurse asked as she flipped through Lucy's brief medical records.

Lucy shook her head and lay back on the cot.

The nurse checked her eyes and throat, felt the glands in her neck, and took her pulse. "What's going on?"

By now, Lucy's heart was resuming a regular rhythm, a normal pulse, and no longer ached. "I—I don't know," Lucy said. Her focus was also returning; the sweat in her hands was drying. She was inexplicably and miraculously cured. "I think I'm better now. Just really thirsty."

The nurse cocked her head to the side. "Honey, you were just on the hallway floor, and now you're fine?"

Lucy blushed but nodded. "Yes, ma'am."

"You got a quiz today? Test? A paper due?"

"No." She knew it looked bad, and she felt ridiculous, embarrassed. "I felt bad for a minute, but I can go back to class now."

The nurse appeared skeptical but finally nodded. "All right, but if you feel bad like that again, you come straight to me. You hear?"

Lucy nodded and hurried back to class.

Audra was watching for her, her shoulders relaxing noticeably when Lucy entered the class and handed the teacher her note from the nurse.

"I'm okay," she mouthed to Audra, sitting down at her desk.

After all, she was okay—wasn't she? She hadn't died, and when the feeling had passed, she felt like her usual self, just more tired than usual. But maybe she'd left the nurse's office too soon, and there really *was* something wrong with her? What if the feeling came back?

It had been terrible, and so embarrassing. She felt like she had when Emily died—the world turning upside down all over again. What should she do?

Don't think about it, she told herself. Think about Mom and Dad back home without Emily. Why didn't they want me with them? I'm grieving, too.

But I hadn't watched her. Mom knows I didn't watch her. They know it's my fault, and now they don't love me anymore.

Why did her chest feel so heavy? Maybe she would have a heart attack. Maybe it was a tumor. Was it only grief? Was it guilt? It was too heavy.

"Are you sure you're all right?" Audra asked as they waited for her mother to pick them up when school ended.

Lucy nodded. She needed to pretend this was normal, that *she* was normal. If everyone made a fuss, she'd just feel worse and even more embarrassed. She had nothing to say to Audra's parents when they asked what had happened at school. She hardly knew herself.

"It must be the grief over losing her sister," she heard Marion whisper to Saul as they sat down to dinner.

Yes, perhaps it was. But why was her chest aching? Her palms were sweaty again, and the slices of honey ham and bowls of fried apples swirled and rocked back and forth. She couldn't breathe.

"Will you pass the tea, Lucy?" Levi asked.

Why did he sound so far away? Here's the pitcher. Swallow. Why is your mouth so dry? Clear your throat and sip your tea. Make it go away! Why couldn't she swallow?

"May I be excused?" Her own voice sounded strange to her, and she struggled to maintain eye contact.

"Are you feeling okay, dear?" Marion asked.

"Yes. Just tired."

Don't look at each other like that, she thought when Audra's parents exchanged a glance of uncertainty.

But Marion nodded and smiled. "Of course, honey. Let me know if you need anything."

Now up to Audra's room with the door closed behind her. Crawl beneath the covers and pull them overhead.

You're yards away from everyone, in the cool and silence of a solitary bedroom, breathing in the scent of the soft sheets. The pains are going away. Palms are drying. Breathing is easier. Now just so tired.

Audra came in and closed the door behind her. She sat on the edge of the bed, pulling back the blankets to see Lucy's face. "It happened again, didn't it?"

"Yeah." Admitting it made her throat tighten. She swallowed hard to make the lump go away.

"What do you think is wrong with you?"

Lucy shrugged. "Maybe I'm dying."

Audra's eyes filled with worry, and her brow furrowed with determination. "We'll have to get you to a doctor. It's probably something silly, like, maybe you're allergic to something."

"Maybe."

But maybe it was something far from silly, killing her from the inside out. Something wanted her dead—as dead as Emily. Perhaps she'd swallowed the Gulf, and now the Gulf would kill her too. Perhaps she was drowning on the inside, and no one could see the riptide gripping her soul, ready to pull her down.

By the time Lucy returned to the little blue house, her attacks had become a daily occurrence, usually taking place at school. The little blue house felt unwelcoming, as if it, too, blamed her for Emily's death. Her room was cold, and the roof above her dresser had sprung a leak. Her father promised to repair it, but in the meantime, he had set a bucket in place of her trinket box to catch the water when it rained. Steady drips plunked one after another. Some even slid down the wall like a long, sad tear. It stained the yellow paint a rusty orange.

"How's Mom?" she asked her father on her first night home.

"Quiet . . . for now. Just give her some time," he said, "and space." His voice became very serious. He seemed old and sad. Did he blame her as she blamed herself? He hadn't hugged her when she arrived. He *must* blame her; he must not love her anymore.

He flipped on the TV, and she left him to go outside, her first time back to the beach and the Gulf that had swallowed her sister. Now it was chilly, but she pulled up the hood of her jacket and sat on the dunes. No one, not even Lucy herself, noticed when she fell asleep there and didn't come back inside. As she drifted to sleep, she thought of Audra, of holding her hand and finding it warm and soft. Audra was her refuge at school. She held Lucy's hand, talked to her about allergic reactions and different responses to tragedy, listened to Lucy's descriptions of how she felt without criticism or judgment. Couldn't she just stay with Audra?

But as her thoughts turned to dreams, she became enveloped in dark clouds through which she couldn't see. She was falling, no, swimming in a dark, cold ocean. A small octopus latched to her ankle, but when she tried to push it off, another suctioned onto her hand, then another to her arm, her face, her back.

"Lucy!" she heard a small, distant voice, a voice she knew well—Emily's voice. But she couldn't swim because the octopuses pulled her down, deep into the ocean's dark abyss.

She woke when the sky was still dark, and she shivered from both the cold and the strange feeling of waking from a long but shallow sleep. A few houses down, someone had already strung Christmas lights, though Thanksgiving was still two weeks away. For the first time in her thirteen years, she couldn't feel excited about the holidays. Perhaps she would never feel happy again.

That was no way to live.

She slid off her shoes and pushed up from the sand. She couldn't see the water, but she could hear it, a great abyss under a dark sky.

Lucy.

Was someone calling her name, or was it the swish of the waves?

The first touch of her toes to the water made her draw her foot back. Keep going, the ocean inside her urged, connecting itself to the Gulf through her flesh, like a magnet drawing her forward.

She waded into the frigid water, though her teeth chattered and her eyes watered from the cool, salty air. Then the water was in her mouth and up her nose. The sky became the Gulf, and the Gulf became the sky. The world and the water became one, and she became one with the water.

8

Audra's mom pulled her out of school early, in the middle of an algebra quiz. With Lucy absent, Audra assumed the worst.

"What's wrong, Mom?" she asked when they got to the car. At thirteen, she knew well her mother's emotional cues—the deep creases between her brows, the way she bit her lower lip. "Is it Lucy?"

Marion nodded and took Audra's hand in her own, choking back tears. Audra felt the color leave her face and the strength leave her arms.

"One of her attacks?"

"They've stabilized her."

"What does that mean? She's—she's still alive, right?"

"Yes," Marion said, but from her tone, Audra knew something more serious was coming.

"Lucy tried to drown herself last night. Her dad checked her room and saw that she'd . . . she'd never gone to bed. He ran to the beach and was able to pull her out of the water—just in time, they said."

Audra searched her mother's eyes, green and round like

her own, for answers, but Marion only shrugged and began to cry. Audra didn't have enough air to cry. She looked out the rear window at their middle school growing smaller—with distance, and in importance.

Lucy had almost died. Lucy had tried to leave her.

She visited Lucy often in the weeks she was in the hospital. When she'd recovered from nearly drowning, they moved her to the psychiatric ward for careful monitoring and treatment. She was fairly doped up when Audra came the first time, but on Audra's second visit, Lucy smiled when she saw her.

"Hey," Audra said as she approached.

Lucy opened her hand, and Audra filled it with her own.

"How are you feeling?"

Lucy shrugged. "Been better." Her voice was hoarse from the oxygen tube that had kept her alive the week before. "They've got a name for what I've been going through."

Audra's brows raised expectantly. "What is it?"

"Panic attacks . . . anxiety . . . mental illness."

Audra grimaced, afraid, because she could see that Lucy was also afraid.

"How do you get rid of them?"

"You can't. I'm on pills," Lucy said.

"But the pills won't . . . they won't make you . . . better?"

Lucy shook her head. "Maybe better, but not cured."

What kind of illness had no cure? Cancers, tuberculosis, pneumonia—those illnesses made sense. But an illness that could make a person feel as though she were dying when everything else was fine—how could there be no cure?

Audra looked down at Lucy's hand, white except for the purple and green around the IV in the center, which looked painful, but surely not as painful as almost drowning or as hurtful as being left behind. She realized then that she had never been left; she had always done the leaving. She never wanted to feel that way again.

"Hey," Lucy said, but Audra didn't look up. "Say something."

Audra breathed in deeply, but the tears still came.

"Why did you do it?" she asked.

When she looked up, Lucy was watching her with a face as pained as the bruise on her hand. She didn't answer, and Audra knew that she couldn't.

The school hours dragged without Lucy there to pass notes to or chat with in the hallway or at lunch. A small group soon absorbed Audra as one of their own, but while she was grateful for the companionship, she didn't yet care for gossip about boys and boring teachers or what movie was playing that weekend and when the middle school dance would be. Her best friend had tried to take her own life, and the pills could not cure her.

Adding to her concerns about Lucy were her dad's weekend trips to Atlanta for preaching engagements. Though her mother shrugged off their questions, Audra and Levi knew the signs. They'd been down this road before, but this was the first time it made her angry. She knew Levi was angry, too.

"He's candidating at another church again, isn't he?" Levi said from the table.

Marion pulled a tray of biscuits from the oven and set them on the counter. "Watch your tone. He's your father, and he does what he thinks is best."

He slammed his book shut. "Do you think he even cares about what *we* want?"

With easy strokes, Marion sliced a stick of butter and smoothed each slice over the biscuits.

"What about Lucy?" Audra said. "She needs us."

Marion stopped, inhaled and exhaled long and slow, her face

showing more tension than Audra had noticed before. "I know she does."

"Then . . . then why don't you tell him we have to stay?"

The look in her mother's eyes told her that she had told him, or maybe suggested to him, that they stay, that they stop uprooting every three or four years, that perhaps his children needed stability.

"Why does he do this? What's wrong with him?"

"Audra!" Marion slammed the knife down on the counter, but then she took another deep breath. "Enough."

Audra turned to Levi, who rolled his eyes, and then she hurried up the stairs and slammed her door in response.

She threw her pillow against the wall and plopped on her bed. She didn't want to pack up and leave again. She had grown so much since her nine-year-old self had first splashed Lucy's shoes. Now she was a teenager with routines, schedules, and friends—a best friend. She didn't want to leave, but she also didn't want to be left. Since Lucy had walked into the Gulf that cold morning, Audra doubted the legitimacy of their friendship. Who knew if Lucy would try to leave her again?

The question put a pit in her stomach. It made her feel that she was not good enough for Lucy; if she had been, Lucy wouldn't have wanted to leave her.

She scooped up her pillow from the floor and hugged it to her chest.

9

It snowed in Florida the weekend Lucy came home from the hospital. Flurries fell on palm trees insulated by large black tarps and then disappeared on the sandy white shores along the Gulf. Gulls cried, high on damp winds, and pelicans and cranes settled sorrowfully on sea posts. Throughout surrounding counties, schools and businesses closed, unprepared and unable to push the snow and ice from roads and bridges.

Had Emily been alive, she and Lucy might have stood at the bay window in their small kitchen where the blue-and-white-striped wallpaper now peeled from the walls and watched the flurries for hours, hot chocolate in hand. They'd have called Audra to come over, and together they would have admired this powdery substance Lucy had seen only in pictures. They'd hope for enough to build a snowman, even though the snow turned to ice when it hit the ground.

But Lucy wasn't at the bay window.

After a week in the psychiatric ward, talking to psychiatrists about the way her heart raced and her palms sweated and her lungs couldn't catch a breath, she was done talking, done listening to people who thought they had the answers, who so confidently diagnosed her with mental illness. Confidence eluded her. Who has any answers?

She felt condemned by the mental illness she now endured as she stumbled once again toward the Gulf. There was no escaping an attack, the earthquake inside that made her head ache and spin, her heart race. It was as if she was alone in a dark house and heard the shifting of weight on a wooden floor, an almost quiet breath in a room where she wasn't breathing, motionless so she could listen for the sounds of intrusion. She lay still, unable to breathe, listening for the next sound that might warn her of danger, eyes wide but seeing nothing, heart beating so hard she could feel it in the top of her head. Why wouldn't it just show itself and get it over with? Why couldn't she fight it?

Her toes white from cold, she stood at the shoreline, feeling the Gulf's icy hand gripping her ankles. With outstretched arms, she stepped in deeper, so cold that she gasped, and prayed in words she couldn't fully form. As the water numbed her limbs, she kept her eyes on the horizon. The moon hung in the gray evening sky like a hologram between the heavy clouds. She barely saw its face before the sky masked it with clouds.

She sought the answers drifting toward the horizon. Into the low, rolling tide she waded, the waves and wind knocking her from side to side.

Lucy.

She heard her name above the sound of the waves—surely, it was her sister calling.

"Lucy!"

She stepped farther into the water, eyes on the fading horizon.

"Lucy!"

It was her father, splashing into the water and pulling her out.

"It's too cold to swim today," he said. He led her across the ashy sands to the little blue house overlooking the Gulf like a lighthouse with no light, no warning of the dangers in the sea. It was a weathered structure sheltering its own storm inside. She didn't want to enter, though her toes felt numb and her teeth chattered so hard she nearly vomited.

"Audra is here," her father said as they entered the back door. "You don't want to swim today."

Audra was there.

"Take a hot shower immediately."

Audra was waiting for her on the ugly green sofa in the living room, smiling nervously. She waved, and Lucy's eyes implored her to follow.

The wooden floorboards creaked under Lucy's light weight, and the white shag rug inside the small bathroom held her wet, sandy footprints. Audra followed her in and sat on the closed toilet seat.

"Hey," Audra said.

"I'm glad you came," Lucy said.

"Me too." Audra took a deep breath. "What were you doing on the beach?"

"Just looking."

"Lucy."

Lucy hung her head. "The water calls to me now."

"Don't listen to it."

"I wish we could go back."

"Me too . . . but we can't. You can't do it again, Lucy. Promise me."

But Lucy looked to the cracked tile floor where mold lingered in the grout.

Audra took her hand. "Lucy!"

A tear escaped the corner of Lucy's eye and burned her cheek as it dripped to the floor. "I feel like I'll never be happy again."

"I know."

Lucy sniffed and sat on the edge of the tub, then leaned forward to rest her head on Audra's shoulder. She could smell her home—vanilla and sugar, old leather, fabric softener. What was her own scent? Brine, fish, tobacco, mold.

Audra took her hand and held it in both of her smaller ones. "I need to tell you something—something not good."

Lucy looked up. "What?"

"It's going to sound really terrible, and it is terrible, but we're going to work it out."

"You're leaving, aren't you?"

"How did you know?"

Lucy shrugged. "I just did. I always figured you would, knowing your dad." Then she began to cry. The familiar anxiety welled within her, and she let it happen, because Audra was there, and Audra wouldn't mind. Knowing that made it easier.

"Don't get worked up," Audra said, leaning her head against Lucy's. "Dad said I can come back every summer instead of going to camp if I want."

"But why?"

"It's our family's curse—or my dad's." She spoke clearly, though Lucy could sense her frustration. "He never stays in one place for long. We've moved every few years my whole life."

"But *why*?"

Audra shrugged. "No clue."

Lucy wrapped her lanky wet arms around Audra's neck, wanting to keep her with her forever.

"Better get in the shower," Audra said.

Lucy let go reluctantly. Her soaked clothes pinched her skin as she rolled them off to the cracked tiles. The light hairs on her arm stood up from bright pink goosebumps as she closed the heavy white shower curtain. The shower trickled over her frizzy blonde curls, down her bony shoulders and shapeless form. She was ugly, and she knew it—ugly because of what her life had become, because of the intruder inside her that she couldn't fight.

"Did the hospital help?" Audra asked.

"I guess."

"Are you better?"

"Better enough."

Turning off the shower, Lucy pulled a tattered navy towel from a hook on the door and wrapped it around her. She exited the shower with red swollen eyes.

Her mother knocked then and set flannel pajamas and yellow panties on the sink.

"Audra," she said in her low, sultry voice, "will you be staying the night?"

"Yes, ma'am," Audra replied.

Lucy saw in her mother's hollow blue eyes that Audra wasn't as welcome as she'd once been, the way Lucy, too, was no longer welcome.

"Your father said you were swimming," her mother said, her blonde hair falling in loose strands from her thick braid. She'd lost weight since Emily died; her cheeks were pale, her eyes, tired. She breathed heavily.

Swimming—that's what her father had said, as if Lucy were simply an idiot and not psychotic. But her mother knew that the Gulf called her, and Lucy assumed that perhaps she wished Lucy would have finished the task this time—that it should have been Lucy and not Emily in the first place.

"Linda, girls," Frank called from the kitchen. "I've got tea."

Her mother left, and Lucy dressed quickly. She couldn't find her wide-tooth comb, so with short, dripping tangles, she led Audra to the kitchen. The wallpaper peeled in spots along the walls, and Lucy wanted to rip it off, wrap herself in it, and hide against the wall. The silver kettle popped and shushed as her father moved it from the coiled burner and poured it into thin chipped cups with painted pansies disappearing from the sides. Lucy caught the subtle scent of chamomile as he carried the cups to the table.

He pulled out the chair beside her mom, and Lucy sat in it stiffly as he handed her a cup.

Her mother stirred honey into hers, the bent spoon clinking against the cup in a slow, even meter. She stood, still stirring, her thin pelvis jutting forward the way it does when a woman holds a child on her hip. She set the spoon in the sink and carried her steaming cup slowly back to her bedroom.

Lucy watched her leave, then swirled her own cup, searching its shallow depth.

"Snow won't stick in Florida," her father said. He talked because he didn't like silence, and he said anything that came to mind, even if no one cared to listen. He sat across from them, lit a Pall Mall, and placed his large hand on Lucy's. "How about some music?"

It was the first time he'd touched her, besides leading her from the water, since she'd come home, and his touch was gentle and warm. Lucy looked into his gray eyes and found them soft and full of love. She felt it through his touch and smiled a little. How dumb to think he'd stopped loving her.

He left the small kitchen and sat at the upright piano in the living room, resting his cigarette in a tray. He played softly, his smooth tenor voice carrying the strains of "As Time Goes By."

It's too cold to swim today.

Lucy wished it had been too cold three months ago when Emily had followed them into the water. They'd felt the cold in their chests when they saw her body.

They carried their tea to the bay window and watched the snow falling on the beach, frothy waves lapping on the shore.

It's too cold to swim today.

"Promise me you won't go to the ocean again," Audra said softly.

"I always go to the ocean."

"You know what I mean. Okay?"

"Yeah."

For Audra's sake, she meant it, but she still shouldn't have promised her.

There was a gulf inside her now; it called her to the water, now swallowing the snow and ice. The snow didn't belong there, nor the cold, but Lucy felt them calling to her, all the same.

10

The winter after Emily's death was long and gray and unusually cold. Lucy lived for the summer when Audra would return, easing her troubled mind with thoughts of afternoon swims and midnight giggles. School was lonely without her, but home was worse. Linda kept to her room and hardly spoke. She stopped attending church, but Frank still went every week, and Lucy went with him.

Sometimes, when a storm crept up from the horizon, she thought of the Bible story of Jesus calming the sea, walking on troubled waters, and she imagined herself as the Apostle Peter: "Let me come out with you!" Then she stepped out of the boat and felt the water smooth and solid like glass beneath her bare feet. She imagined Jesus holding out his hand as she staggered forward. But even with his hand of mercy outstretched, she would suddenly doubt, because that same man didn't keep her sister from drowning. Then she began to sink, legs breaking through the glass.

They sat in the back pew, neither pitied nor ignored, simply there. Lucy was glad that people generally left her to her thoughts, that the new pastor—what was his name?—didn't offer grief counseling, or even treat them any differently than he did most of the others, which was indifferently. If he knew about Emily, he clearly pretended not to.

"He's a different sort," her father told her on the drive home one Sunday. "Not the friendliest I've known."

"Pastor Clarke was friendly."

"This one probably won't last too long; doesn't seem to be too interested in people. God's work is always about people."

What about the people God allowed to die, Lucy thought, or, worse, the ones he left behind? She didn't say this, though, even to her father, because she knew her father's faith was stronger than hers, and she didn't want to let him down or cause him to worry that she was on her way to hell.

"I'd like to sing in the choir again when things settle down," he said.

Maybe things at church would settle down. Her dad would sing in the choir again, and she would join the middle school girls downstairs. Maybe, with time, people would stop looking at them as the family who had lost a child to the Gulf because the child's mother had gone inside and her sister had let her drown.

But what about her mother? Would time heal her of wounds that had existed long before Emily's death?

"What about Mom?" It was the first time she'd risked asking about her mother, and she could tell that it made her father uncomfortable.

"Mom is sick, Lucy," he said with severity. "You must remember that."

But Lucy was also sick, bearing the weight of her anxiety every day, alone. She was sick, and she wanted something from her mother that she could not name, something to make her believe that life would be okay, because her mother had learned to be okay.

But perhaps Linda, too, was sinking in a Gulf where her faith had wavered.

Lucy kept her sketchpad with her to doodle and draw and scribble in during dry church services and the long, lonely school hours.

Only a new student named Shawna James had anything to do with her these days. She had transferred from Maryland that February and knew nothing about anyone in town. She was a tall, dark-skinned girl with dark curls and square red glasses that were much too large for her slender face.

"Sure is warm here compared to my old town," she told Lucy at lunch one day. "Mind if I join you?"

Lucy shrugged. "It's actually colder than usual."

"Baltimore is super cold right now," Shawna said, with crumbs on her lips. She licked them off and swallowed them with milk. "Have you lived here your whole life, or did you move here, too?"

"I've lived here forever."

Thirteen—soon to be fourteen—years is a short time, but Lucy felt as if she'd lived forever.

"Do you have brothers or sisters?" Shawna asked.

"No," she said quietly.

It wasn't your fault, the psychiatrist at the hospital had told her. *Emily should never have been in the water without an adult present.*

But I was supposed to look out for her, Lucy thought. I was my sister's keeper, and when God asked *Where is she?* she didn't make excuses. *I didn't watch her, Father*, she said in the dark loneliness of the hospital.

Lucy finished off her cornbread and opened her milk. The cafeteria carried the energized buzz of adolescents with many important things to say: gossip about teachers, classmates, and crushes. She sat at the end of one of the long tables, near the mural of the school mascot (a dolphin in football gear), to avoid them all. She didn't mind. She was better alone with the dolphin and her thoughts, always mentally drafting letters to Audra or painting images on the canvas of her mind—a seagull blurred by fog in gray and blue and green, a half-smoked cigarette still letting off wisps of swirling, sparkling smoke against a green backdrop.

"I have a brother in high school." Shawna continued, despite Lucy's reticence. "You an only child?"

"No—yes. Well, now I am."

I hate school without you, Lucy drafted to Audra. *Sometimes, I hear no one around me for days—nothing but the beat of my heart in my ears. The room spins like a carousel, and all I can see are the colors mixing and bending and shaping into things they aren't, and I can't breathe. It feels like I'm walking with Death and no one can save me.*

Shawna peeled an orange and handed half to Lucy.

Lucy took it, and as she did, she felt a cramp deep inside her.

When she was at the hospital, she'd begun learning what it means to become a woman, and she'd wished Audra had been there. She woke in the night from a dream: Emily was crying for her, tossed on a sea that slowly filled with blood. Lucy felt the sharp clamp of jaws around her abdomen. It was her own blood filling the ocean. She was dying, and when she woke, the blood and pain woke with her.

"The curse gets us all," said the nurse who gave her pills, a hot water bottle, and a cup of raspberry tea. "Didn't your mother warn you this was coming?"

"No." She wondered if Audra had gotten her curse yet, and if Marion had told her all about it.

"Well, you can expect some other changes, too—some not so bad."

Lucy couldn't figure out which ones weren't so bad. Certainly not the ones that ached on her chest every time her father hugged her tight or the unsightly hairs she shaved from her body.

"Do you have a . . ." she looked Shawna in the eyes for the first time and whispered, "a few quarters? For the vending machine?"

"You want a snack? I got these extra chips." She motioned to the potato chips on her plate.

"No. For the vending machine in the ladies' room."

Shawna laughed. "The other girls were right about you," Shawna said.

Lucy didn't want to ask what she meant by that, but her eyes betrayed her.

"They said you're quiet and strange."

Lucy gathered her trash and started to leave.

"Oh, don't be upset!" Shawna reached out and held her by the hem of her shirt. "I got what you need in my locker. Let's go."

She and Lucy returned their lunch trays and trekked to the lockers. Shawna unlocked hers with three swift turns, then dug out the item and passed it to Lucy like a secret agent with a bomb code. Lucy stuffed it in her pocket with less panache.

"Thanks," she said.

"Of course!"

Lucy fished a tin of mints from her pocket and offered one to Shawna.

"My sister died," she said, and popped the mint in her mouth.

"Oh. I'm sorry."

"Yeah." Lucy shrugged. "I don't mean to be weird. I guess I just . . . am weird."

Shawna laughed so hard the mint fell from her mouth. "I don't think it's a bad thing, being different. I'm about the only black girl in this school—certainly not like Baltimore!"

Lucy smiled. "Why did you move here?"

"My dad's in the navy."

The bell rang then, and Lucy went to her own locker to fetch her books.

"I'll find you again tomorrow," Shawna said. "You're a good listener. I like you."

Over the next months, Lucy watched as her parents changed. They had stopped dancing together. Her father's music was slow. Her mother kept to her room except for her weekly trips to Joe's Fish Market—trips she took alone. Then weekly trips became twice a week, and twice a week became almost daily.

As winter turned to spring, she went out with painted lips, her only string of pearls, and a palm green cardigan draped over her shoulders, leaving behind the bitter scent of aged Coco Chanel perfume, which stuck in Lucy's throat and made her long for vanilla and sugar. She came back later than usual, too, long after Lucy had returned from school each day. Eventually, she came back so late that even Frank arrived home from band practice before Linda returned with fish for dinner.

"She won't be much longer." Frank reassured them both with words as hollow as empty clamshells. "Mom's always careful to get the best fish." He pulled a deck of cards from a kitchen drawer and dealt them a hand of Go Fish. Linda came back halfway through the second round when Lucy was collecting a set of queens.

"We were getting worried," Frank said with a smile that seemed both relieved and forced.

"You shouldn't have." Her alto voice snapped as she hung up her cardigan and then wrapped the old apron around her waist. "Lucy, set the table. Do I have to tell you everything?" She chopped the potatoes vehemently even though she hummed and sighed.

The fried fish and chips sat heavy in Lucy's stomach when the meal was over, and Lucy decided never to wait that long for dinner again.

I've started cooking dinners now, she wrote to Audra. *It's fun, and Mom doesn't fuss over my shoulder since she's hardly here to notice anything. I get better every time, too. I know because Dad doesn't just thank me; now he compliments me, too. He likes the baked fish best, with the lemon and pepper and butter. I don't fry fish very well. It always turns to mush. When there's no meat, I make biscuits and gravy. I've learned that with enough salt and butter, anything tastes good.*

Two weeks before the end of spring, Linda came home without any groceries. Lucy watched her from the living room window as she skipped up the walk from their clunky old car, her hair glowing in the late afternoon sun.

Lucy felt the familiar ache in her chest, the dizziness and shortness of breath. On any other day, she'd have waited it out in her room or busied herself in the kitchen, but she couldn't today. Maybe because she'd become a woman, Lucy sensed more than she knew; maybe being a woman now made her braver, even for just a moment.

"We don't have anything for dinner," Lucy said when her mother entered.

"Really, Lucy, I haven't even taken off my shoes."

"Does Dad know?" She followed Linda to the hall closet beside her bedroom.

"Know what?" Linda laughed as she hung up her scarf and coat.

"That you're whoring around?"

Linda slammed the closet door and slapped Lucy's face. Her sharp blue eyes grew small and defiant. "How dare you?"

Lucy felt heat rising on her cheek, but she stood her ground and narrowed her eyes. "Aren't you?"

"What do you even know about *whoring*?" Her mother turned to go to her room, but Lucy caught the bedroom door to prevent being shut out.

"I know enough! I know what I see. I see your smudged lipstick and the spots on your neck."

Linda looked as if she might strike her again, but then she sat on the corner of her bed and leaned back, her eyes shining in a way Lucy hadn't seen in a long time, her hair long and straight down her back, silky and blonde.

Seeing her there, dreamy and wistful, reminded Lucy of the way she'd looked when Emily once crawled into her lap with a storybook and noticed her mother crying.

"Why are you crying, Mommy?" Emily had asked, wiping the tear from Linda's cheek with her small, pudgy hand.

Linda had kissed her hand and forced a smile. "I'm crying for you, baby—happy tears, because your life will be so good." Whether or not Emily understood her mother's words, she rested her head against her mom's chest, not to be held, but to hold. Lucy had watched them from the hallway, alone, knowing that although her mother's words may have had truth fettered to their ends, she had lied to Emily about her tears. Lucy knew they'd held no such happiness. Unlike Emily, Lucy had not been able to comfort her mother. She'd only seen her pain, absorbed it, and sent Emily to do what she could not.

Now her mother sat again with tears on her cheeks. Neither of her daughters could wipe away her pain.

"Harold makes me feel alive." Linda's voice was soft and deep. She pulled a cigarette from her purse and lit it with a tarnished lighter in a trembling hand. "He loves me, Lucy."

"Dad loves you."

"Your father loves everyone. He'd love a dog that bit him."

"He loves you more than anyone. You know he does."

She fell back fully on the bed, puffing her cigarette. After a moment, she propped up quickly on her elbows. "Are you going to tell him?"

"Don't you think he already knows?"

With that, Linda's face fell. "Yes." She looked around the room as if for help. "I have to get out of here." She moved to the closet and pulled out her suitcase.

"Mom, you're being crazy! Just tell Dad you're sorry; he'll forgive you—I know he will!"

Linda stopped. She left the suitcase on the bed and put out her cigarette in a dish on the dresser. "Don't ever call me crazy again." Her tone was severe, and Lucy lost some of her nerve. "Get out, Lucy."

"I won't let you go." Lucy stood in the doorway.

Her mother slammed the door, and Lucy jumped back to escape the blow. She heard the lock click from the inside, then she felt the grip inside her chest, the clamp on her lungs.

"Mom, open the door!" She pounded on it, feeling hot and cold at the same time, her mind emptying and racing at once.

When her mother ignored her, she started pounding again, but stopped after one fist on the door. She knew her mother's stubbornness, and she knew that she herself was not the cure to her mother's ills. The knowledge made her angry.

"Fine! Stay in there!" She went to her own room and slammed the door.

11

The Clarkes had settled in the suburbs of Atlanta, moving into a house much like the one they'd left on the Gulf. The church already had a secretary and an events coordinator, leaving Marion to run the nursery. It was a thankless job, but to ease her load, Marion recruited Audra's assistance.

Every Sunday morning, the two Clarke women wiped the nursery down with disinfectant, inspected the tub of used toys for broken or hazardous parts, and turned on a cassette of lullabies. It was the best part of the morning, the part when the babies had yet to arrive and the blue walls with the Noah's Ark mural appeared so peaceful that Audra just wanted to curl up in a rocker and fall asleep. Unfortunately, the babies rarely slept. They came in, noses running, mouths dripping, diapers overloading.

"He just pooed when we parked the car," one mother said. "His bag has diapers."

"We brought her straight from the crib," another mother said. "Her comb and dress are in her bag."

"Here's her bottle. She'll be hungry in about ten minutes."

Audra soon concluded that church mothers considered Sunday mornings their break for the week.

"How hard is it to wipe your kid's snot in the morning?" Audra said, much too loudly, but the crying infants and toddlers drowned her words, so only Marion heard them.

"Audra Gail!" Her look said the rest.

Audra turned and rolled her eyes.

"We're providing a service here, Audra," Marion said. "We're a blessing to them."

"Well, who's a blessing to us? When do you have a morning off?"

Her mother hadn't had a day—let alone a morning—off from the demands of family and church since Audra was born. She made their meals, washed the dishes, cleaned the house, patched their clothes, served the church, and ran any errands Audra's father asked of her. She woke the earliest of any of them and went to bed last. And instead of admiring her, Audra considered her a fool.

Marion looked at her a moment, as if reading her daughter's thoughts and reconciling them, and handed her a warmed bottle. "Feed Michael Smith," she said. She scooped up another child and bounced him on her hip.

It wasn't fair, the things Audra thought about her mother, and she knew it. Her mother hadn't wanted to leave the Gulf Coast any more than she and Levi had. Her mother knew that the people there needed them—that Lucy needed them, and Audra needed Lucy—but even so, she'd let Saul move them five hundred miles away.

Whatever resentment Audra harbored toward their mother, Levi dealt double toward their father. Saul was never one to sit at home and watch a football game or spend long, lazy hours over a meal. When he was home, he sat in his study preparing sermons or counseling someone over the phone, always with a cup of over-brewed coffee at his side. Occasionally, he'd call Levi or Audra in, if time allowed, to ask about their day, what they'd been reading, and if they were proud of the decisions they were making.

When Audra was young, he was easy to respect, even revere, as a man of God; he was almost like God himself to her, the omniscient father who wanted only the best for her. But now, as a teenager who'd lived in too many places and seen too many failings, she considered him detached and, at times, even cruel in his disregard for her and her family's needs.

Saul called Levi into his study one late spring evening, and Audra listened from the hallway.

"What are you reading?" Saul asked.

"*Catcher in the Rye*," Levi answered.

Saul mused over the answer and sipped from the mug of coffee Marion had placed there over an hour ago. "What are you learning from it?"

"That being a teenager sucks."

Audra could almost hear her father's knuckles cracking as he tensed a tight fist. He hated the word *sucks* and all other such slang and profanity. After a moment, he spoke again.

"What decision have you made this week that you're proud of?"

Levi shrugged. "I matched my socks."

Saul rapped his fingers on the table and adjusted his large, thick-lensed glasses, the ones with bifocals that magnified his eyes. "Send in your sister, Levi."

Levi moseyed to the doorway.

He seemed to get off easy, but Audra knew her father had stored the moment away. Why, she didn't know, nor did she care. Bearing her brother's badge of courage, she approached her father's desk, ready to keep it short as Levi had done, but her father's face relaxed when he saw her.

"Well, honey, guess you'll be leaving us soon," he said.

"Huh?"

"Aren't you spending the summer with Lucy?"

"Oh, yeah."

"We'll drive you down Memorial Day weekend. Your mother will enjoy seeing the water again."

Audra nodded and felt her shoulders relax.

Then her father pulled his wallet from the desk drawer and slipped out two limp ten-dollar bills. "In case you need anything. Don't waste it."

"Thanks, Dad." And for a moment, she forgot to be angry with him.

She was nervous on the drive back to the Gulf, even though Lucy had called her the night before to review all the plans she had for them. Although she and Lucy sent letters weekly, sometimes daily, much had changed for both of them since Audra had moved away, changes Audra could feel inside herself that she could not yet name, but saw regularly in Levi. Her brother had left for camp the week before, and he didn't hug their mother good-bye. When she'd hugged him, he stiffened and looked away, and Audra caught the sudden sadness, the misunderstanding in her mother's eyes.

"Make good friends," Marion had told him.

He said nothing, but Audra knew his thoughts: that a two-week camp provides only two-week friends, to whom he must say good-bye. He was tired of always having to say good-bye, just as she was. She dreaded seeing Lucy for this very reason.

"At least you'll be gone all summer," Levi had told her last night. "I only get two weeks."

"Look for a job to keep you busy. Atlanta has jobs everywhere."

He nodded and hugged her. She was the only one he'd hugged.

"It's really great that Lucy has a friend like you," her father said, when Georgia became Alabama and the peach trees turned to pine. "You're closer to her than a sister."

Audra didn't respond.

"Don't complicate it, hon," Marion said. "They were friends before the accident."

This brief and unnecessary conversation showed Audra that her father didn't understand friendships—that he perceived them only in light of what he himself was able to give. Friends were not *friends* to him; they were opportunities, projects . . . ministries. Audra understood his thinking—not because she empathized, but because contrary to what her mom had said, her friendship with Lucy *was* becoming complicated. While time apart had helped her to understand why Lucy had tried to leave her last winter, she still couldn't shake the feeling that if she, Audra, had only been a better friend—if she had been able to help Lucy through her attacks— Lucy would not have tried to take her own life.

She loved Lucy. Lucy understood her better than anyone else in the world, and Lucy needed her. But there it was again, the nasty word that crept into her mind whenever she thought about Lucy— *need*. No matter how much Audra gave to Lucy, somehow, it never seemed to be enough. Her father could thrive on being needed, but not her. *Need* was only part of the equation. Being *enough* to meet someone's needs was something else entirely.

12

When the Clarkes arrived, Lucy fell deeply into the warmth of vanilla and sugar. She became greedy for it, not wanting to let it go, but when Marion pulled her back to look at her, nearly an inch taller than before, Lucy's eyes had glossed, and her throat stuck. Marion didn't miss the moment and pulled her back into another warm embrace.

It was close to dinnertime, and only Lucy was home.

"My dad's working with the band for the summer baseball games. They'll be traveling some this summer."

"Where's your mom?" Marion asked.

Lucy cast Audra a sideways glance and said, "She's gone."

"Gone?" Saul said. He looked to Audra as if she'd forgotten to tell them. She hadn't forgotten. She'd simply chosen not to.

Lucy nodded. "She left a few weeks ago."

The silence was loud with unvoiced questions, but Lucy shrugged them all away because she didn't want to—couldn't—tell the story.

Instead, she invited them to the kitchen, where she poured them lemonade and took out the potatoes to peel and slice.

"Oh, let me do that, Lucy," Marion said. She was faster than Lucy at peeling, and she wasted less potato, carving off the skin in one long clean spiral. "How about some fried fish?"

Lucy smiled. "I picked some up just for today!" She pulled a package of cod from the refrigerator and rummaged through the cabinets for herbs and flour.

"Do you have a fryer?"

"Yes. I also got some string beans." Lucy dug the fryer out from a cabinet and handed her the oil. For a moment, everything felt right—a mother there beside her, showing her how to peel and fry potatoes; a father reading his sermon notes at the table; a sister setting out the plates and silverware. But her awareness washed away the moment and replaced it with emptiness, the more solid awareness that this was not her life, and never would be.

"We'd like to get back on the road by seven," Saul said. "It's about a five-hour drive."

It was six-thirty, and Frank had not yet come.

"We can go ahead and eat. Dad doesn't mind leftovers."

Saul prayed, and then they ate. Lucy reveled in the glorious crisp and crunch of breaded chicken skin and the sweet, juicy meat. She hadn't yet learned the art of fried chicken—or fried anything. The anxiety had left her, and once more she felt the kinship of family. It remained as they ate the meal they'd prepared together, and as they cleaned the kitchen, a fast job with four people helping.

But at eight o'clock, an hour past their desired departure time, Marion pulled her into one last hug, and the trance ended. All was almost as it was before, except that Audra was by her side, and that made it bearable.

Linda was sick. That's what Frank had told Lucy and what Lucy told Audra that night. For a week after Lucy had confronted her mother, she had come home from school every day with a knot in her stomach, wondering if her mother would still be there, until one Thursday afternoon when she'd returned to an empty house.

"Mom?" she had called from the doorway as usual. She dropped her backpack on the ugly green couch and searched each room, except for Emily's, because no one entered that one.

The suitcase was still in Linda's closet, clothes still in the drawers. Waiting anxiously for her mother to come home, she plopped on her bed and picked at the threads in her gingham quilt. It wasn't long before the sun streaming through her lacy white curtains lulled her into a warm nap.

Her father came home first, then her mother, an hour later.

When Lucy saw that her mother carried no bags, she opened a couple cans of tomato soup and made some grilled cheese sandwiches with dill pickles.

"Why do you go to the market if you're not going to buy anything?" Lucy asked.

Her father coughed, and her mother turned to her with sharp eyes. She opened her mouth to speak, but Frank interrupted.

"Not a good season for fish, Lucy."

Lucy forced a smile, plated the sandwiches, and ladled the soup. Her father asked the blessing for the meal, and in the middle of his soft-spoken prayer, Lucy felt guilty for causing him a moment's grief. Because she knew her mother was preparing to hurt him, Lucy wanted to hurt her mother first. It was addicting, the rush of anger and the false courage it spawned. While it was there, her anxiety didn't have space to rush in.

Her resolve continued the next day when she came home from school and found her mother's suitcase by the door.

Lucy picked up the suitcase. "I won't let you leave."

"Don't be a brat, Lucy." Her mother was attaching the clasp on her pearl necklace and slipping on her best dress shoes. The sight drove away Lucy's anger, leaving instead the familiar fear and sadness that welled up where passion ought to burn.

Lucy said nothing. She heard a car pull up to the house and hoped, even though she knew her father walked to work, that it was him to stop the madness. He wouldn't let her mother leave.

But when the door opened, it revealed not her father, but Officer Harold Bede.

"I'll take that, kiddo," he said, and tried to take the suitcase from Lucy. "You ready, babe?"

"As soon as Lucy gives me my suitcase," Linda answered.

Lucy gripped the handle with all her might. "Don't go, Mom. Dad loves you, and we need you. Please don't go!"

When Bede tried to take it again, she pinned it down on the floor with her body, but she wasn't prepared for Bede's strength. He gripped her arms so hard she winced. "Your mama's given you an order." His yellow beady eyes, his wide and freckled face, his breath smelling of decay—all repulsed her.

Why would her mother ever leave her kind father, who had a clean, woody scent and sang Sinatra, for this? If only she were stronger and could put up a good fight, she could bide time until her father got home. But Bede was pulling her off the suitcase, so she stood up and shook him off.

Bede walked out to the driveway, slamming the door on the way.

Her mother picked up the suitcase and smiled. Then she put her hand on Lucy's cheek and caressed her, as a mother would do to a daughter she's sending off to college, a daughter she cared about. It made Lucy calm, and she hated herself for it.

"This isn't about you, dear," Linda said.

Lucy pulled away. It *was* about her.

It was about her because she was Linda's daughter, because she was the last daughter. It was about her because if her mother left, what would become of her—of them? She needed her mother, had always needed her, and now she would need her even more. It was about Lucy because it was about Linda.

But she couldn't say those things. There was too much to say, and so she said what she felt and not what she knew: "I hate you."

The words had a stronger effect on her mother than Lucy had expected. She could see it in her eyes. But then the horn hollered from the driveway, and her mother hurried to the door, looking back at Lucy with something like hesitation, something similar to regret.

Lucy turned away, unmoving, even after the door latched and her mother disappeared inside a car Lucy had never seen before, with a man she never wanted to see again. Her final words left an imprint on her tongue. She could feel it in her taste buds, the flavor bitter and dry.

Her mother's presence still filled the little blue house. Lucy and Audra both half-expected her to walk down the hall at any moment, still planning their days so as not to upset the absent woman's moods.

"She was hardly here when she was here, but now she feels even *more* here," Lucy said under the covers of her bed that night.

Audra nodded. "Do you miss her?"

Lucy's lips tightened, and she pulled at a thread on her pillow. "I don't know."

"Has she called you at all?"

"No."

Audra searched the blankets until she found Lucy's arm and then linked it with hers. "I'm sorry."

"It's not your fault. It's mine."

"No."

"Yes, it is." She unlinked their arms and sat up. "If I had only saved Emily—"

"Stop." Audra sat up too. "Don't say that."

Lucy put her head on her bent knees, and Audra stayed quiet.

"Dad comes home later than ever now, and he hardly eats. You should've seen him when he got home that day and I told him Mom was gone."

Audra put her arm around her.

"I told her I hated her."

"Do you?"

Lucy sniffed and wiped her eyes. "No."

The truth was, she wanted her mother back more than she had expected. Well, maybe *back* wasn't accurate. How could she want someone back who was never really there? She simply wanted her to be her mother. What a hard word, *truth*. It didn't matter what was true when feeling dictates the contrary. Her anxiety proved it. There was nothing to fear, yet the panic rose in her chest and tormented her mind. There was nothing dangerous about her classroom, yet it spun around her head during social studies and sucked out her breath during math.

The truth was not that she hadn't watched her sister properly; it was that her mother couldn't forgive her, no matter what was—or was not—the truth.

The truth was, she didn't hate her mother.

She remembered being eleven and sitting at the table, piecing together a jigsaw puzzle while Emily played in the living room, pulling a wooden duck on wheels by a string. The string had caught on a metal ring under the glass coffee table, and Emily had toppled to the floor, immediately bursting into tears.

Their mother unhooked the string and dried Emily's cheeks with her long, slender fingers. "It just startled you," she told the two-year-old. "You're not hurt." Then she turned to go back to her bedroom.

Emily stopped her with three poorly pronounced words, "Love you, Mama!" and their mother remained in the living room for the rest of the afternoon.

If Lucy had said *I love you* as freely and often as Emily had, would her mother have stayed? Why was it so much easier to lie and say that she hated her?

Because she feared that her mother might not accept it or want it. The truth was hiding in the Gulf, the Gulf that called to her, and when she answered the call again, she would find it there, covered in barnacles and wrapped in seaweed, disfigured and disguised, but she would recognize it.

"She thinks she deserved better than all this," Lucy's father told her soon after her mother had left. He motioned to indicate the house and then looked down over himself. "I guess she's right." He didn't seem surprised when he discovered her absence, though his grief drew him to the back deck with a fresh cigarette. Lucy followed him out, and they both leaned against the moist wood railing, the Gulf sighing in long hushes upon the shore.

"I was never the man she wanted," he said, exhaling a long stream of smoke. "I was never . . ." His voice cracked. He coughed to cover it and didn't try to speak again.

He smoked a whole pack of cigarettes that night, and Lucy never saw him come inside.

Lucy sighed. "I got a letter from her last week. She's in Jacksonville. My dad's family lived there and owned a restaurant, but it's closed now. Most of them have died or moved on now. I don't know why she chose to go there. She said she would write me again soon. She said I could visit if I got money for bus fare."

Though she knew her father would pay the fare if she asked, Lucy knew she couldn't leave him to go and see her. Only a few weeks had passed when Lucy overheard a band member at school say, "I heard his wife left him. He seems to be taking it well." It was an ignorant but expected assumption. If he'd known Frank

De Rossi at all, he'd know he was only ever alive with the beat of the band, the soft jazz of a sax, or the voices of the Rat Pack, even when Linda was around.

People mistakenly believe that people's passions are their hearts, when really, passions give the heart a reason to keep beating. Lucy knew her mother was never Frank's passion; she was his inspiration, the breath that filled every cavity in his being. When she left, he doubled his smoking, and something clicked off in his mind that never corrected itself. He had always been eccentric, but his quirks grew worse.

Lucy released Audra's hand, and the little blue house groaned against the wind tossing sand against the siding. Lucy escaped the tangle of her sheets and tried to shut her window so the sand wouldn't blow inside, but it was stuck. She pulled harder, with her body weight, and finally it popped and slid hard to close, smashing her thumb. She cried and freed it quickly. Already her nail was turning blue; a cut bled above her knuckle.

"Are you okay?" Audra took her hand and examined her thumb, but Lucy pulled it away.

"Yes. Dumb old house!"

No wonder her mother had wanted to leave. Lucy sucked her bleeding knuckle and slid back in bed, nestling close to Audra so that her head was on her shoulder. "I'm glad you're here," she said. "Everything will be better with you here."

Audra said nothing.

They spent those summer days strolling the beach, walking to the pier for strawberry snow cones, and taking the bus across the bay bridge to see movies at the theater on Main Street. Sometimes Shawna joined them.

"If you feel an attack coming, just tell me," Audra said. If she could help Lucy, suffer through it with her, maybe it would lighten the force and keep Lucy from the Gulf.

So whenever the heaviness fell on her chest, Lucy took Audra's hand, and by the sweaty palms, the weak grip, Audra knew to grip her hand tightly.

"Let's just walk," she'd say. "We don't have to talk."

Sometimes Lucy focused on the sandpipers fleeing the water or the pelican soaring long and hungry over the horizon. Other times, she breathed, in and out, as if her lungs would stop without her determination. Each week brought new strength and fewer attacks until, by August, they hardly happened at all. Perhaps the hospital was wrong about her having an incurable mental illness. Look at how well she was doing after a day at the movies with Audra and Shawna, walking around town, the Gulf, the pier.

And now Lucy and Audra were sitting at the water, as calm as the shrimp boats drifting miles in the distance, crunching the ice of their snow cones.

"Do you ever blame me?" Audra asked as they watched the pale moon rise in a lavender dusk. "For Emily?"

"Never."

"Why? I was there, too."

Lucy scooped wet sand and let it drip from her fingers. "Mom told *me* to watch her, not you. You don't . . . blame yourself, do you?"

Audra shook her head. "No, not really. It was a riptide. Even if we'd been watching, we couldn't have saved her. You shouldn't blame yourself, either."

Lucy wondered if her father had used the same logic, and if that made it easy for him to forgive her for not watching her sister closely enough. Maybe she shouldn't blame herself, but as long as her mother did, it didn't seem to really matter what she believed of herself.

Looping their arms, Lucy sighed and rested her head against Audra's, feeling more relaxed than she'd ever felt since Emily's death and her mother's departure.

"I wish you could stay here with me forever," she said.

"Me, too," Audra said softly.

But Audra would be heading back to Atlanta at the end of the week, and Lucy wrestled with her impending absence. Who would she lean on when the attacks came?

She couldn't let the attacks return. She couldn't. She wouldn't. If she could feel better now, surely she could continue getting better.

"I don't think it's incurable," Lucy said, smoothing over her stalagmite of sand.

"What's not?"

"The attacks . . . my mental illness."

Audra slurped some of the sugary syrup left in her cup. "I don't think the doctor would lie to you."

"But I'm doing well. I feel a lot better."

"Hmm." Audra stabbed at the ice with a plastic spoon.

"What are you thinking?"

"I think I'm going to crack my teeth on all the ice I've crunched on this summer." She spooned another bite in her mouth.

"I want to feel like I feel right now forever. I never want to feel the other way again. You know?"

Audra said nothing, but the way she pursed her lips and twisted to the side told Lucy that she was thinking. "Why did you stop taking the pills?" she asked.

Lucy looked down to her cup of ice. "They made me dizzy and nauseous. I feel fine now without them."

"But you didn't feel fine all spring."

"That was different."

Audra dumped the rest of her watery snow cone into the sand below. "You know how to take care of yourself. If you think you can cure yourself, go for it."

Lucy smiled, feeling for the first time since Emily died, more like herself.

13

Lucy was determined to keep her attacks at bay as the new school year started. When she felt her stomach swim and the room start to spin, she looked for something, anything, to replace the space in her head that so easily caved in to an attack. She channeled the feelings into frantic activities—sudden chatter with Shawna, a run on the beach, a movie, and finally, her sketches. She discovered that her sketching served her best. What looked like nervous energy to everyone else felt exciting and necessary to her.

"Why don't you take an art elective?" Shawna asked her, when they were considering courses for the spring semester. "It's probably an easy A for you."

Lucy had never thought about taking her art seriously, or even calling it "art." It was a hobby, a needed distraction. What if the teacher hated her work and ruined it for her? Then what would she have? But she knew her GPA could use a boost after the previous year, so she enrolled in art for the spring and soon met Ms. Florence Hooper.

She'd never seen Ms. Hooper around the school, but Shawna explained that she was only part-time and worked at an art studio on Main Street across the bay bridge.

"She's legit," Shawna said. "If she gives you an A, you'll *know* you're good!"

Lucy feared her A would not come easily. Why had she ever thought it would? She was just a fourteen-year-old with a little talent, not a real artist. Ms. Hooper would probably laugh at her simple sketches and give her Ds, and then her grades would never improve.

When the spring semester started, Lucy ambled down the red halls of her middle school, up the stairs to a classroom on the second floor. It was twice the size of a normal classroom, with posters of famous paintings—*Mona Lisa, Starry Night, The Persistence of Memory*—hung on the chalkboard and cement-block walls.

Walking into the classroom, Lucy felt her breath catch in her throat. She couldn't focus on the tables, chairs, or easels. Why was the air so stuffy?

Get a grip. No, don't run, scream, quit. Darn Shawna for suggesting this! Just withdraw from the class. It's too stressful, and you don't need this.

"Sit at any available easel," Ms. Hooper said.

Just leave, Lucy told herself, but her legs carried her over to an easel, and she pulled out the chair with a sweaty hand. This couldn't be happening. It wasn't supposed to happen. She was supposed to cure herself.

She played with the neckline of her T-shirt and tried to cool herself under an A/C vent. Cool air always helped.

Ms. Hooper called the roll, then began her lecture.

"We're focusing on dimensions of basic shapes in the beginning: a sphere, a cylinder, and a cone." She showed examples, and Lucy tried to count to ten and breathe.

"With a light touch, draw a circle using wide, round motions from the shoulder," Ms. Hooper said.

Lucy heard the scratching of lead on paper as her classmates began, but her hand felt too weak to hold a pencil. Slowly, she positioned it in her fingers and began the light circular motion. She had made a perfect circle and started shading it when Ms. Hooper came to her table.

"Well done, Allison!" she said to the student next to Lucy. "Excellent rounding of the shadows at the bottom of the sphere."

Lucy thought she would pass out before the teacher ever got to her, but when Ms. Hooper looked at her sketch, all she said was "Mmm-hmm" as she passed by. "You're all doing great!" she said.

Lucy's heart rate slowed, and her breathing became easier. Just *Mmm-hmm*? So she was neither special nor terrible—she could live with that.

By the end of the class, Lucy was scolding herself for having an attack and determining not to have one again. Her sphere, cylinder, and cone looked just fine, she thought, and nothing bad had happened after all.

She enjoyed the class even more over the coming weeks, and developed much respect for Ms. Hooper.

"She just gets it," she told Shawna one day at lunch. "Like, she gets that we have individual styles—there's no one way to paint a bowl. That's the trouble with math. I can look at the equation and tell you the answer. Who cares if I don't know how I know it?"

Shawna frowned. "Math makes a *lot* more sense than art. 'Rules hold the world together.' That's what Mr. Spencer says. You don't understand stuff until you know *why* you know it."

Then Lucy frowned, sensing defeat from her smarter, science-minded friend. "Yeah, yeah." She knew she was idolizing, and stopped talking before Shawna could catch on and call her out on it. Audra had already done so when they were instant-messaging online the night before. But what other teacher wore jeans and bangles and rings on every finger, ivy-green eye shadow, and treated her long auburn hair like clay to be molded and shaped anew each day?

One day, she'd entered class with a large messy bun bedecked with butterfly and bug ornaments that other women stuck in their flowerbeds. And always she carried a large, clear tumbler holding what looked like liquid grass, which she sipped throughout the class. She was nothing like the collared, bloused, cardiganed, bow-tied, suited teachers with their school-mascot mugs of coffee.

"Being different doesn't make her better than the other teachers," Audra had said.

Sure, that was true, but Lucy liked the idea of being her own person, not conforming to what everyone else did. It made her feel better about being the only girl in school with a cloud of blonde frizzy curls. When she had to get glasses, she chose large round green frames instead of the dark rectangles most girls wore. She painted each fingernail a different color, and used her art brushes to swirl on rainbows, swirls, stripes, or spots. She wore big bright hoop earrings and floral tops with striped pants. One evening, she painted a mustache on the Picasso crab in the living room and then painted the chipped shells she collected on the beach and strung them like macramé on driftwood from the Gulf, to hang on her bedroom wall.

As the semester progressed, she fell more deeply into her art, in mind and body. When she earned her first A on a sketch of her little blue house, she thought she'd explode with happiness.

"Is that your house, or just a house you found along the beach?" Ms. Hooper asked, catching her after class for the first time.

"It's my house."

"Your sketch suggests it holds quite the story," she said.

Lucy pushed in the chair at her easel, mentally searching for words to say, and finding she had none.

Ms. Hooper was wiping a few notes from the chalkboard.

"That shows you're a true artist. Artists don't just copy things onto pages, even with their own twist. They're storytellers, through a single image."

Lucy thought of the house and all the stories she did *not* want it to tell.

"How does someone looking at the sketch—how would they know its story?"

Ms. Hooper started packing up her carpetbag, which she used in place of a briefcase. "That's up to the interpretation of the viewer, to some degree," she said. "There's a lot to learn about art philosophy and theory."

"Huh." Lucy wanted to ask more, but didn't want to be intrusive or annoying, if Ms. Hooper wanted her to leave.

"You must enjoy art, I'm guessing. Come on, walk me out."

Lucy held the door for her and then followed her down the hall, where students stretched out the final seconds before the next bell. She figured she was getting the chance to watch Ms. Hooper transition from art teacher, to artist.

They left the building and walked to a white Camry that seemed to have seen better days.

"Do you prefer teaching or working in your studio?" Lucy asked.

"I enjoy both very much," Ms. Hooper said. "Now, tell me, what does art mean to you?"

The passenger door moaned when Ms. Hooper opened it and set her carpetbag inside.

"Oh, umm, I guess . . . No one's ever asked me that before." She paused. "I guess, for me, it's like a place to go . . . to deal with things."

"You sound a bit like me at fourteen," Ms. Hooper said. "When my father died of cancer, I dealt with a lot of anxiety. Art was my savior." She shut the door and walked around to the driver side. "Let's talk more sometime. Thanks for walking me out!"

"Yeah!" Lucy said. She stepped aside as the Impala pulled out and drove away, feeling as if she were in a dream.

This amazing person had struggled with anxiety?

For over a year after her mother left, Lucy cooked mostly hot dogs and ground beef. She no longer visited Joe's Fish Market, because Joe and all the regulars knew her too well. She wanted neither their judgment nor their pity.

Then Shawna told her about another fish market a block down, Blue Herons, run by Henry and Beatriz Flynn. Their prices were close enough to Joe's that Lucy didn't need extra cash from her father for groceries, but she did get smaller cuts to make up the difference. They did not serve beignets.

To get there, she walked past the pier with the snow-cone stand and took a bus across the bridge, then got off on Main Street. From there, she went left at the intersection where the city had erected the statue of a large painted pelican. Blue Herons sat at the corner of Main and North E Street.

To escape the heaviness in her chest, Lucy began exploring the city she'd always loved, the city across the bridge. As an adjunct to a small beach community, it had no skyscrapers and few significant landmarks to attract tourists, so the responsibility of tourism fell to the beaches and seafood restaurants on the Gulf, where visitors could eat fresh flounder and watch the shrimp boats on the horizon. As with many cities in Florida, a Spanish influence lay everywhere—the red-clay-tile roofs, stucco wall siding, al fresco tacos on the street corners, the trees draped in Spanish moss.

Main Street was lined with old brick buildings and crepe myrtles on cracked sidewalks. Most stores had awnings to shade potential customers from the harsh sun and occasional downpours.

These were all things that Lucy noticed now—perhaps because she had developed a more observant eye, or perhaps because she now saw things that her mother had blocked or distracted her from noticing.

Now she felt emboldened by her small city. Strolling the sidewalks helped steady her mind, which had, over the past year, slowly calmed with the general lack of stress. Rather than turn inside herself, she focused on outward things like the markets on Main, the florist and local restaurants, the music store Blue Jazz that her father frequented, a few bars, Florence Hooper's art studio, and the upscale salon.

She was fifteen now, long and lean and developing, and she cared more about her appearance. A little eyeliner and mascara, some red gloss for her lips, a touch of blush. Not too much, though; not like the cheerleaders. Just enough. Sometimes she wore a headband or a handkerchief to hold back her curls, and her fashion preferences were always evolving. When a shirt became boring after a few wears, she cut off its sleeves or turned it into a scarf. Yet she was still awkward and clumsy, her eyes her truest beauty.

"You've got the kindest eyes I ever saw," Beatriz told her one day as she weighed fillets of flounder. "So big and blue and soft!"

It was one of the few compliments Lucy had ever received, and she wrote it in her journal.

Like the city, Beatriz, too, was Spanish. She told Lucy that her father had emigrated from Spain and met her mother in Mexico. They married and moved to the States, where they raised Beatriz and her siblings. Henry had grown up in New Orleans near the French district. They had one son, Charlie, whom Lucy had seen at school but never spoken to, like many of the students at her school. She finally met him one late-spring day at Blue Herons.

"It's Lucy, right?" he said with a wide grin. He shared his mother's dark coloring.

"Yes."

"I see you at school."

"Oh."

"I've started working here some afternoons after school. Help save for college." He walked along behind the counters, following Lucy as she inspected the displays of fish. "I'm Charlie."

"I know." She wouldn't look at him. "Your mom mentioned you a few times."

"All right, then, smarty," he said, laughing.

Lucy felt her face grow warm. "I mean, I know you from school." She backed up and moved slowly to the door, inspecting a display of garlic cloves to avoid looking too eager to leave. With a shrug as if to say the produce simply didn't satisfy her standards today, she said, "Have a nice day," and left.

She was halfway up Main when she heard the smacking of sneakers against the pavement in rapid succession.

"Hey, Lucy, wait up!" he called as he neared.

Refusing to turn, she heard a crash and then, "Oh, man, I'm so sorry!" She stopped, still not turning. That someone wanted her attention this badly sent her heart racing—and not in a good way. Just breathe. Don't think too much. It's okay. Turn now. Deep breath.

Charlie waved when he saw her turn. He'd collided with a man leaving the music store, knocking over the sidewalk sign in the process.

"Don't you know better than to run on sidewalks?" The man groused, brushing himself off.

"Yes, sir. Sorry." Charlie was the picture of humility, but Lucy caught the amusement in his dark eyes. He couldn't hide his grin as he closed the few feet between them.

"Hi," he said.

"Shouldn't you be at the store with your fish?"

"My dad's there. In the back."

They shifted uncomfortably, allowing others to tread by them.

"It's kind of hot out here," Charlie said. "You want to get a lemonade?"

No, she did not want to get a lemonade and submit herself to small talk. Her stomach dropped at the thought, and her palms began to sweat. But his unassuming eyes and boyish grin gave her the feeling of lazy summers and long, sunny evenings. So she hesitated, nervous, finally saying, "Just a quick one."

A quick lemonade became a weekly lemonade, sometimes twice a week, and Lucy soon found herself enjoying the small talk more than she had with anyone other than Audra, and sometimes, Shawna. She found herself forgetting that she was Lucy De Rossi, whose sister had drowned and whose mother had left, and whose mind was difficult to control. With Charlie, she was just Lucy.

"Don't your parents wonder what you're doing when you sneak out of the store?" Lucy asked one afternoon.

"Nah. They know." He grinned. "They let me get away with it because they like you."

He also started joining her for lunch at school, sometimes along with Shawna and her latest beau. It had been over two years since Emily died and Audra left, and Lucy realized that she was finally beginning to feel a sense of normalcy. She was a teenager with a boyfriend who grinned every time he saw her. Unlike other girls, however, her heart didn't flutter with glee, and she didn't spend time worrying that he'd grow tired of her, or fretting if he didn't call some evenings. She didn't expect her first love to be her only love, but she would enjoy their time together while it lasted. She liked him, but knew that if she didn't grow too attached, his leaving wouldn't be as painful.

It wasn't long before Charlie drew her in for their first kiss, pulling her into the doorway of an abandoned law firm downtown and pressing his lips against hers. His lips were soft, and hers were ready, but there was more spit than she'd expected.

"I really like you, Lucy De Rossi," he said, his mouth to her cheek.

Lucy smiled but said nothing. She couldn't, and she didn't know why. It was as if happiness eluded her in these moments when humans ought to be happy—Christmas, birthdays, first kisses—as if these basic emotions had been compromised ever since she'd stepped into the Gulf and nearly drowned. If she allowed herself to feel excitement, joy, or anticipation, it was quickly followed by a sense of impending loss. The path to peace was one of steadiness, the even-keel feeling of routine.

She knew by Charlie's eyes that he expected her to say something back, something to affirm her affection for him, so she did as she had seen her mother do when Frank had lavished love on her in doses too hard to bear: She rested her hand on his cheek, gazed into his eyes, and pulled his head back to hers. Kisses were free, and kisses could easily hide the truth. Sometimes they could even deceive. Humans have used their lips to lie without words since the beginning of time, but that didn't make her feel any better, and when he pulled back again, smiling, she felt a pit in her stomach that united her for the first time with her mother. It made her feel ill, and she started to cry.

Misinterpreting her tears, Charlie grinned, clearly proud of the effects of his kiss, and wiped her cheeks dry. "Don't cry," he said, and almost laughed.

"I need to get home. My dad will be there soon." She caught a glimpse of his confusion as she pulled away.

By the time she got home, she was angry. She wanted nothing to do with her mother—didn't want to understand her, and certainly didn't want to become her. Not after what she had done to her, and her father. Though he'd never been loquacious, he spoke even less than before, and what he did say came out in song or random outbursts. He made it impossible for Lucy to bring friends home—other than Audra—without embarrassing himself, and her.

Gone were the days of moonlight serenades on the back porch. Now Lucy watched him lean against the rotting railings alone, silently blowing wisps of smoke into the empty night, the music off. On those starry nights when her father smoked alone, Lucy painted stars above horizons of gold on oceans of blood, with a dark ship silhouetted against the sky. Her father was the captain of the ship, a slow vessel of the sea, searching the stars to find a way home. Her mother was the farthest star, the faintest speck of dimmed light on the canvas. This was the story in the painting, Ms. Hooper would say.

Lucy pitied the captain, yet she loved him, too. She loved him because he sailed to his own tune in uncharted waters. Because every now and then, when the clouds covered the stars and distracted him from the search, the captain would look to the horizon. Then, for an unmeasured moment, he would smile and wave and alter his sails west, toward her.

The night after she kissed Charlie, she blotted out the dimmest star.

14

By the time she was sixteen, Audra had packed up her clothes, trinkets, and picture of Lucy into boxes, once again to follow her father to Birmingham, Alabama. This time, they settled in a townhouse near the center of the city, far from the sounds of morning songbirds and evening crickets, but she was an hour or so closer to Lucy than she'd been in Atlanta, so that was a comfort.

Audra had learned after the move from Florida that her father would never put down secure roots, and with that knowledge she guarded herself against deep and meaningful relationships. She had Lucy, her always friend, whether it was because Lucy loved her, or because she needed her. Either way, Lucy filled the role of confidante that every person longs for, and Audra anticipated her summer visits with her, knowing she could be herself and say whatever she wanted, far from her parents' scrutiny.

In Atlanta, she had enjoyed sitting in the small woods on a patch of grass and trees behind her house. She'd sit there with a book or homework or a snack on this spot, like a square on a quilt, watching ants marching single file down the trunk of a tree, over its rugged bark, carrying snips of leaves and bits of wood. Onward they walked, fulfilling their one duty in life without complaint or worry. One day, she set a rock at the bottom of the path and watched them pause, assess the blockage, and reroute, plotting a new course over the roadblock without griping. It was this place and these insects that she missed the most when she left, far more than she missed anyone in her church or school or neighborhood. She had learned not to form attachments to people.

Levi had grown over the past three years. He was now well over a head taller than their mother. He'd always had Audra's coloring and features, but overnight he had traded in his freckles for whiskers and his baby cheeks for a strong jaw. He'd grown out his sandy hair so that it hung in his eyes. But more than physically, he'd grown angrier, and more distant.

"Why can't we just stay in Atlanta 'til I graduate?" he said when their father announced the move one evening over dinner.

"The church in Birmingham needs us now, son." Saul spoke softly and ate another bite of mashed potatoes.

"Right." Levi dropped his fork on his plate. "Because you're the only pastor in the world that can help them out."

Saul continued eating quietly.

"You've always got to swoop into the next desperate church so you can feel like a hero."

"Levi!" Marion started to scold, but Saul raised his large hand.

"Let him say what he's got to say," Saul said. "Go ahead, son."

Levi looked down and ground his teeth, chewing the words he'd now lost the courage to say.

"Go on, son. Get it off your chest."

89

Finally, Levi looked up at Audra, a plea in his eyes. You resent him, too, his eyes said.

Audra knew she ought to back him up. Would their dad respond better if they both charged him with his transgressions? She wanted to speak, tried to come up with some poignant defense for her brother, but her tongue stuck to the roof of her mouth. One look, and Levi knew he stood alone.

He pushed back his plate and stood. "You go to Birmingham. I'm staying here."

He left the house then, letting the door slam behind him. If he'd had a car and a license, their parents might have tried to stop him. As it was, they let him roam the neighborhood on foot, trusting he'd return.

Her father went back to his dinner. Audra noticed that her mother only pretended to eat hers.

"Your dinner's getting cold, Audra," Saul said.

She should have become angry when their father announced another move, when their mom had tried to silence Levi, when their father expected them to have good attitudes about it. But the fire didn't burn in her stomach in any of those moments, though they had made her uncomfortable.

No, her anger arrived with that simple sentence: *Your dinner's getting cold, Audra.*

Yes, dinners do that. But she knew what was implied: *Your dinner's getting cold, Audra. Eat it now, and don't worry about your brother. You be the good one I can always count on.*

As she picked up her fork she suddenly saw this moment as the proverbial fork in the road. If she ate her dinner now, quietly, and helped her mother clear the dishes, and spent the rest of the evening in her room, resigned to yet another move, and her brother's absence, she would remain the good one on whom her parents could always count. On the other hand, if she spoke up—if she threw down her fork, as Levi had, if she told her father that his resistance to establishing himself in one place was cowardly, that he had finally lost her respect—she would become the new Audra who would eat a cold dinner if she darn well pleased.

In standing up to her father, she would free her brother. Her parents could never win a battle against the two of them, and compromises would have to be made.

But there were ants in the backyard, fulfilling their duties and plotting their course around the obstacles of life. This was not the one to fight against, so she stabbed her fork into her potatoes and scooped up a large, deliberate bite. Her father smiled and winked at her, and she swallowed the potatoes without chewing.

This obstacle, she thought, would not be moved.

This time things didn't smooth over within a few weeks, as they had when they'd adjusted to other moves. They just couldn't seem to resume their normal roles. Levi, whom Saul forced along, rarely spoke at home without shouting, and he came home late, and irritable.

Audra marveled at her parents' lack of perception—that they never pressed him for answers about what he did in the late hours of the night when he wasn't home. Perhaps they assumed that because he'd been raised to know better, he would do better. Maybe they didn't want to know, because the truth could damage Saul's ministry. But Audra smelled his sins on his clothing, saw his red, distant eyes.

Saul also continually came home later than usual, long after their family dinnertime. Sometimes Audra went days without seeing either her father or her brother. Marion felt the strain, and it showed on her face and in the way she fried the chicken, which often came out dry, or even burned, and she didn't care. She served it with canned beans and potatoes, "to save time," but what she was saving time for, Audra didn't know. Her mother was working less now than ever before because the church in Birmingham had no open positions when they arrived.

"I'm going to take a job starting next week," Marion told her one evening. "At the department store up the street."

Audra was pulling at the meat on her drumstick but stopped at her mother's words, her uncharacteristic transparency.

"Does Dad know?" She didn't know why that was her first thought.

"He'll get used to the idea," Marion said.

"Are we hard up for money?"

"No." She chewed a potato long and slowly, and, for the first time, Audra noticed the lines around her mother's eyes and mouth, the slight sagging of her cheeks.

Marion shrugged. "What else am I going to do?"

What had her mother always done?

"We'll probably move again in a year or so," Audra said, as if that should give her mother some element of hope.

But to Audra's surprise, her mother rolled her eyes. "Probably."

"Why don't you just tell him no? Tell him you don't want to!"

"That would do nothing."

"Why?" Audra didn't need her mother to answer, but Marion did so.

"He's the head of the house, and his word is law. One day when you're married, you'll understand."

Audra gawked, shaking her head. "Umm, no. Not for any amount of money would I let someone control me the way he controls—"

"—all of us," Marion said.

Audra stopped. Her mother had spoken a truth she'd never consciously acknowledged before: Her father did indeed control all of them, including her. She silently promised herself that this would not be how she'd live her adult life.

"I would leave him."

"Audra!" Marion held her eyes for painful seconds. "When you love someone, you stick with him." She took Audra's hand and clasped it between both of hers, and Audra wondered if her mother ever regretted marrying at all. What could she have done with her life had she been free to live it the way she wanted?

"I'm so sick of moving," her mother said at last.

"Why does he do it? Why can't he just stay put?"

At any other time, her mother would have told her to respect her father, not to question his judgment, that he was doing the Lord's work. But now she was tired, and Saul was hardly there. Neither was her brother.

"Levi said it right, back when we were in Atlanta," said Audra. "He needs to be a hero."

"He's a good man," her mother said.

Audra feared that her mother was backtracking now—that their moment of open honesty had ended.

"But he needs to be needed. He wants to help people," Marion said. "He does too good a job, I guess. He gets hurting people back on their feet, and then they don't need him so much."

"But, no one is ever . . . nobody ever becomes, like, totally self-sufficient," said Audra.

And what about Lucy? Hadn't she needed all of them?

Her mother rubbed her hand, seemingly reading Audra's thoughts. "I know," she said. "I know."

15

Lucy visited her mother in Jacksonville only once, the winter after she started dating Charlie. Frank had to travel with the band over Christmas break, and he didn't want to leave Lucy home alone for three weeks, even though she was almost sixteen.

"I'll pay the bus fare wherever you want to go," he told her. "You can go to Birmingham to stay with the Clarkes, or to Jacksonville, to see your mother."

The idea of seeing her mother both excited and terrified her. It had been nearly three years since she'd last seen her, one year since she'd last received a letter. Letter writing allowed the comfortable space and distance that suited their relationship. The phone was too intimate, too immediate, too difficult to hide behind. It would unite them in the same time and space, their voices brushing too closely.

Her mother's letters maintained the rigidity Lucy had always known in her relationship with Linda: short, cryptic, and bearing a strange sense of obligation, as if she were trying to be a good mother and assuming that these letters earned her that title. Her house was small but perfect. Her life was simple but charmed. She missed Lucy and hoped she'd visit. How was school? Love, Mother.

Lucy had never called her "Mother." Ever. What was she thinking? Was she subtly distancing herself, or just being melodramatic? Either way, Lucy decided not to respond quickly, waiting at least a month each time before penning a reply. She was fine. Dad was fine. The house was fine. There was a storm. Yours truly, Lucy.

She had a steady rhythm to life now, so much so that she wasn't even sure that she missed her mother or wanted her back. None of her letters ever mentioned Charlie or Shawna or even Audra. Not school or her art. Not how many shingles had blown off the roof in the last storm, or how she'd become truly skilled in the kitchen, though she still couldn't fry. Why she bothered to write back at all, she didn't know, except that perhaps she wasn't ready to be rid of her mother for good.

The Christmas season certainly felt strange without her mother's attention to potpourri and dark pine wreaths. Lucy spent long evenings lying in bed, dreaming of white Christmases and telling her heart to be light while her father sat at the piano, planting his strong fingers into the melancholic chords of Christmas, releasing his soft baritone, then transitioning to the upbeat tunes.

"Sing with me!" he'd say. They sang about Rudolph, Frosty, and Dominic, the Italian Christmas donkey, who had always been Lucy's favorite.

She enjoyed the kitchen, basting the turkey breast, mashing potatoes, preparing green-bean casserole, baking the pumpkin pie for dessert. Bethlehem's star shone atop the small tree in the corner, next to the Picasso crab. It was a hideous picture, and, now that her mother was gone, Lucy thought about taking it down. She could throw it away, bury it, or burn it on the beach. Her dad wouldn't care. Her mother had hung it there and pretended to like it because Dez had said it was modern. Maybe her mother had no eye for good art, or maybe she was just sleeping with Dez, too—Lucy didn't care to know. She did know that removing it, or any of the other decor her mother had chosen, would be removing the last of her mother from the little blue house, and Lucy told herself that her dad couldn't handle that.

One evening at dinner, her father said, "So, I called your mom earlier, and she said she'd love to have you stay with her."

"That's a lie."

"She's your mother, Lucy. Not the best one in the world, but the only one you've got. Someday, you may regret not seeing her while you had the chance."

It was the voice of regret from a person who'd lost his own mother too soon.

Her visiting her mother meant something to him; she could tell. So the day after Christmas, on a chilly, sunny afternoon, Lucy kissed him good-bye and boarded a bus to Jacksonville. She'd packed a few sweaters and some jeans and socks, knowing the temperature might drop to the mid-thirties. The cold never lasted long, and it hadn't snowed since the winter after Emily died.

Despite the weather outside, she thought she might suffocate on the bus. Her knees pressed uncomfortably into the seat in front of her, directly below the tormenting drone of the heater. For most of the ride, she leaned forward with her head resting gently— hopefully unnoticed—on the seatback, eyes shut, forcing herself to take deep breaths through her nose and exhale out her mouth. An attack was forming, and already she regretted agreeing to this trip.

As the road rolled ahead in one long stretch of interstate between the two cities, she watched the sprawling evergreens blur by her window. Breathe, she told herself. Think of green. Grass is green. Think of cool droplets of dew dripping from each blade. Think of palm branches swaying in the wind. Think of jasmine tea in a chipped white cup. Think of them. Breathe them. Breathe.

She now rested her head against the window, cool and moist, a relief from the heat. Why hadn't her dad driven her himself? She wouldn't feel as nauseated, and maybe not so dizzy. He probably didn't want to see her mother any more than she did, probably because of Officer Bede. Certainly her father couldn't bear to see the woman he loved in the arms, or house, of another man. How would she feel when she saw her mother with Bede again? The last time she'd seen them together was the last time she'd seen her mother at all. She remembered the brief moment of fear in her mother's cold blue eyes, the tremor of her lips when she looked at Lucy one last time.

Now she had a new life. Perhaps, for the first time in her life, Lucy would see what her mother's eyes looked like when she was truly happy. Perhaps she and Bede spent long hours on their porch, sipping iced tea and counting fireflies.

Here she was, hoping for her mother's happiness. Had she forgiven her without realizing it? Could forgiveness come passively? When had she stopped hating her—or had she? She was just anxious, feeling the heaviness in her chest. There was no trusting her mind now. Besides, whether she had forgiven her mother or not, her mother could not be trusted. She had told Audra so the night before.

"If it gets bad," Audra had said over the phone, "you can still come here. We'll put our money together if we have to. I got a bit from my grandma for Christmas." She made Lucy promise to call her every night or instant-message her.

Lucy promised to call her on the new Motorola Razr phone her father had given her for Christmas. Charlie told her to call him, too. She hadn't decided whether or not to tell her mother about him yet, though she wanted to. She imagined them sitting at the kitchen table over tea, chatting like a *real* mother and daughter, confiding in each other about boys and love.

But her mother wasn't one for intimate conversation. After all, she'd never thought to warn her about her period. What could she possibly tell her about love?

Her internal questions quieted as the bus approached the city and groaned into the station to a slow stop. Lucy breathed deeply and had to force herself to exhale. She felt dizzy. She wanted to run all the way back to her little blue house, but she knew her mother would be waiting inside the station.

Lucy stepped off the bus, claimed her duffel bag, and followed the crowd inside.

She looked around but saw no one familiar. Then, a voice.

"Lucy."

She turned to see Officer Bede, alone, and not in uniform. Her mother was not there.

"Linda sent me to get you," he stated matter-of-factly. "She's not feeling well."

He took Lucy's bag and motioned for her to follow him. He led her to a tan Ford sedan with doors that squeaked when they opened and seats that smelled of must and old grease. He tossed her bag on the backseat and motioned for her to sit in the front.

She pushed aside newspapers and a sticky foam cup. The leather seat was cold.

"It's about a fifteen-minute drive," Bede said.

Lucy watched out the window as they turned deeper into the city, a real city with skyscrapers and heavy traffic. Immediately, she knew she preferred her Gulf town, its brightness and color, to this metropolis, and she wondered why her mother did not.

Bede said nothing on the way. Fine by her; she had nothing to say to him. But the silence made the fifteen minutes feel long and awkward, and Lucy played with her seat belt to busy her hands and slow her mind.

At last, they pulled onto a one-way street along a strip of houses and parked on the curb behind his squad car, in front of a brown house on the corner. Lucy heard sirens nearby, the rush of traffic, a door slam, and dogs bark, and she clutched her seat belt tighter.

Bede exited and retrieved her duffel from the back while Lucy pushed open the heavy, squeaky door.

"This way," he said, leading her up the few cracked steps out front and letting her in the door to a split-level house much smaller than she'd imagined. She set her duffel bag on the matted carpet, which covered every floor except in the kitchen and bathrooms, where the floors were linoleum. The white textured wallpaper bore more stains than any of the walls in her little blue house.

From her vantage point in the living room, she could see the kitchen with a small table and a few chairs, and a mirror on the wall. The only resemblance to her home was the strong smell of tobacco.

Then her mother came from an upstairs bedroom, wrapped in a robe as thin as she was. Her cheeks were sunken, and the skin below her eyes had darkened.

"Well, you're here," she said in her usual low, sultry voice.

Breathe. Run. Tell her you don't feel well and want to go home. None of this feels right. She clutched her chest, searched for words, but didn't know what to say or how to say it.

"I suppose you'll want tea." Her mother slowly descended the stairs.

"Yes, please." Lucy's voice was small and strange to her own ears.

Her mother hardly looked at her and didn't hug or touch her, as if Lucy had never been a part of her at all. She boiled the water in a pot and dumped it over chamomile tea bags, one in each cup.

"Where's your kettle?" Lucy asked, twisting her hands in her lap and trying to breathe.

"A pot does fine," Bede said. He sat across from her with the newspaper shielding his face.

Linda cast him a glare that he couldn't see and then spoke calmly and low. "Honey?"

"Yes, please."

Lucy stirred her tea and tried to ward off an attack by searching for what she could possibly say to this woman she felt she hardly knew, and the man she wanted to know even less. If she were at home with her father, they'd sit silently but for the sip and slurp of steaming tea, and the silence would speak of their familiarity and comfort, would say all the nothings that each felt and understood without saying. She would think about things like colors and how they appear where you'd think they wouldn't, how people describe clouds as white when, really, they're the brightest yellow, the coolest blue, and the softest gray. "*White* is a lazy word for people who don't care to look long and hard at the world to see it as it really is," Ms. Hooper had told her.

She would think about Charlie and how he'd turned their doorway kisses into a routine that she both enjoyed and hated. She would think about Audra and the summer and all the things they'd do together.

"How is school?" her mother asked.

"Fine. Same as always."

What a person knew about her would become a power to be used against her, and Lucy knew better than to pass such power on to anyone—anyone but Audra, the only person who knew Lucy's innermost darkness.

"You've grown since I last saw you," her mother said. "Still thin as a rail."

Bede looked around his newspaper at Lucy and eyed her uncomfortably.

Lucy shifted so that her back was toward him.

"Have you made any new friends?" her mother asked.

"A few."

Her mother frowned and lifted her eyebrows, as if shrugging with her face, as if to say, Of course Lucy didn't have many friends.

"I'm good friends with a girl named Shawna," Lucy said, and then wished she hadn't, because she'd only said it to prove that she did so have friends. She was not a loser.

"Do you still talk to Audra?"

Lucy nodded, swallowing the hot tea.

"Got yourself a boyfriend?" Bede asked over the top of the newspaper.

Lucy avoided looking at him. "Yes," she answered, looking into her cup. Even with tea, now her mouth felt too dry to swallow. She needed to change the subject.

"Do you have Internet here?"

Bede dropped the newspaper dramatically. "It's dial-up, and I don't need you tying up the phone line."

"Really, Harold." Her mother rolled her eyes. "I don't know why he doesn't just switch to broadband like the rest of the country."

Bede slammed the paper on the table so hard the cups rattled and spilled.

"You want it so bad, you call and get it installed! I'm not stopping you!"

"Calm down, Harold; you're embarrassing yourself."

He gave her a look that was both mean and frightening.

Lucy wanted to dump her tea and hide in her room the rest of the evening, but it only occurred to her at this very moment that her room was not here. She hadn't even seen the room she would sleep in.

Lucky for her, her mother stood, dumped her tea down the sink, and motioned for Lucy to follow.

"We have a computer in your room with dial-up. Just don't tie up the line when Harold is home," she said. "Come with me."

Lucy followed her upstairs to the small bedroom across from the master. Inside was a double bed, a window straight ahead, a small nightstand holding a lamp and telephone, and a desk with a computer along the opposite wall. Her duffel bag sat in the middle of the room.

"We typically just use this room for storage and using the Internet," Linda said. She sat on the bed and looked around the room as though searching for something to say. "How's your father?" She asked this so quietly that Lucy almost didn't hear her.

"What?"

How dare she pretend to care about the husband she'd left?

Her mother frowned and looked out the window to the alleyway below.

Lucy relented.

"He's fine. He's great, actually. He's been seeing someone."

Had her eyes not darted away when she'd said this, her mother might have believed her.

Instead, her eyes narrowed. "You're lying."

She gripped Lucy's chin to look into her eyes. It was the longest Lucy had felt her mother's touch in her recent memory, and though it was hard, she didn't want it to end.

Her mother's eyes searched her own. "You still hate me," she said at last.

Lucy pulled away from her touch. "Why shouldn't I?"

"I'd hoped you'd understand by now."

"Understand what?"

"You know your father isn't all there."

Lucy stood and slapped her mother's face, hard, the way Linda had done to her more than once. She felt the thin skin of her mother's face, the hollow of her cheek, the hard jawline. It stung, and the sting stuck to her hand and burned.

For all the times Lucy had fantasized about hurting her mother, she had never expected the regret that would follow. She looked to her hand, throbbing with anger, and her jaw fell open, waiting to apologize if only she could summon her voice.

"Mom," she said. "Mom, I—"

But Linda pushed herself from the bed and left the room, leaving Lucy with nothing but her empty, tingling hand.

16

The first week in Jacksonville passed with cold rain over a silent house. Linda hadn't spoken since Lucy had slapped her, and Bede worked several twelve-hour days, sleeping most of the days that followed. In the evenings, he drank beer from a can as he read the paper or flipped through television stations, without ever settling on a single channel.

Lucy read *To Kill a Mockingbird*, a required text for the coming spring English class, and sketched anatomy to practice for art class, focusing on hands. Linda knitted or stayed in her room. Once again, Lucy found herself making the meals, her mother's absence like the dense fog that lingered outside.

One evening as Lucy stirred a pot of tomato soup, Bede arrived home and came through the living room to the kitchen. He stood behind her, silent, his body so close that Lucy could smell the Jacksonville air on his skin, damp and sour. She continued to stir and taste and add some sugar, hoping that if she ignored his presence, he might go away. Then he slid his hands up her arms and began massaging her shoulders.

"Relax, Lucy," he said when she stiffened.

"I need to get the grilled cheese sandwiches on."

"Just relax."

His large hands worked her shoulders softly and rhythmically, up and down, squeeze and release. Finally, he stopped and pulled her into a hug that she did not return.

"You're a beautiful woman, Lucy, and you deserve to feel it. Don't let your mother tell you otherwise."

He let her go, got his beer from the refrigerator, and headed to his recliner in front of the TV.

When she finished the cheese sandwiches, Lucy excused herself to go to her room, trembling with fear and uncertainty. It was just a massage and a hug. She had not been groped or kissed or anything worse. This was just a hug. A massage. She couldn't define anything specific that made them wrong, but they felt wrong, and she didn't want to know why.

It felt the way the snow feels in Florida, she wrote to Audra later. *Like nature doing something wrong. I didn't tell my mom. She isn't speaking to me, anyway, and I don't know if she'd consider it a big deal. Maybe it isn't.*

But it nagged her into the second week, when she awoke in the night with Bede in her bed, caressing the smooth of her stomach. Her instinct was to scream, run, call for her mother, but she forced her eyes to remain closed and rolled over, as if disturbed in her sleep, so that her back was to him. She didn't know why she lay still as he worked his hand up her stomach to her chest, and she was ashamed of the fear that kept her in place and sealed her lips. In the darkness, death, loneliness, and fear were groping her, hungry for her, and their embodiment grew against her legs. Yet no screams—a gasp, tears on her cheeks as she felt herself bruising and ripping—voiceless.

105

Finally he climbed clumsily from her bed, leaving her trembling beneath the blanket. The door made a quiet click, and he was gone.

She was alone, hearing a creaky floor in a room where she wasn't walking, a breath in a room where she wasn't breathing. Were her eyes open or closed? There was only the dark and her heart beating so hard she could feel it in the top of her head.

Why hadn't she fought it? Why hadn't she screamed?

If she had, maybe now she wouldn't hurt so much. Maybe if she could just cry now, some relief would come, the tears flushing out the pain.

But she could not—not while she lay in the emptiness of herself, while fear still lingered in the air she breathed.

She was bleeding and trembling so violently, she vomited. She never fell back to sleep.

"You've got to tell someone," Audra said over instant messenger the next day. "He can't get away with this."

"Who can I tell, Audra? He *is* the police, and anyone else would say I made it up because I'm upset over my parents' divorce."

"I would vouch for you! I'd take the stand and tell them you called and told me everything!"

"We're best friends; that wouldn't help. You weren't here."

"You should've just come here. I knew you should have, and I didn't say anything."

"This isn't your fault. I just need to play it safe from now on."

She hardly left her room for two days—leaving only to use the bathroom, find painkillers, and grab a little food and water—and no one seemed to care. She locked her door. From now on, she would always lock her door.

She couldn't sleep anyway after that night, so she kept her

lamp on and sketched until the moon faded from the sky and her eyes became heavy and her hands were too weak to hold the pencil.

Sometime during that first night, long past the hours when the brain thinks in straight lines and even circles, her sketches formed long, spindly branches stretching through the cosmos, across the universe, where a single flower bloomed on the northern pole of a new planet. The fingers caressed the silky periwinkle blossom, wound the green stem around its knuckles, then pulled at the petals, bruising them, soiling them so that the flower shriveled and drew back its bloom. It grew a shell around its stem, stretched its head high into the sky, and raised its roots to rest above the ground, to trip up the evil tree if it ever returned. In place of petals, the flower grew needles sharper than pine on long, coarse arms. It was armed, ready to fight. Heavy with its burdensome load, the plant, which no longer called itself a flower, bent over like a weeping willow, clutching its seeds lest they fall into the cursed world.

When the wicked fingers returned, they did not bother the plant because the plant was no longer beautiful and no longer worth its time. But the plant would not be mocked. Slowly, painfully, it forced out new purple blossoms along its arms, and when the winds blew, they perfumed the air. The plant matured into a wild, thorny patch of needles and blossoms, lovely to behold but dreadful to approach.

The evil tree never returned, but one day a man wandered up the mountain to that northernmost pole and found the beautiful plant. He wanted to take a blossom and keep its beauty forever, but because he feared the armored arms and rigid roots, he extended his hand, palm upward, and waited. Hesitant and confused, the plant stretched its arm across its roots and dropped a blossom onto the man's hand. He inhaled its perfume, the scent bringing life to his eyes. With a smile, he nodded and waved and went on his way, and the plant dropped its seeds to the ground.

When Lucy awoke late into the next morning, she compiled her sketches, each in abstract shapes and strokes of pencils and chalks, and set a title page on top, on which she wrote *The Flower*, and the date. She had never titled her art before, but she needed a concrete noun for nameless feelings which now lay silent and uncertain, waiting to heal into the scar of memories she could never erase. It gave her just enough strength to unlock her door and begin the next day of the rest of her life.

Stepping outside her room on the third day felt like stepping into Oz, where everything was different from before, haunted by an evil she couldn't see but whose presence she felt growing inside herself. It was panic. It was Harold Bede. It was the ache inside her where he'd been. The heaviness in her chest made it hard to breathe, and she almost went back to her room. But she knew she mustn't cave to it. She had to move forward.

She finished *To Kill a Mockingbird* and cleaned the house to pass the time, sometimes attempting a conversation with her mother when Bede was away. She wanted to tell her what he'd done to her, but she didn't know how, and the words stuck in her throat.

To make things worse, her mother appeared sicklier each day, and Lucy started worrying when she found prescription pills in the kitchen cabinet—the same pills that she had once taken for her panic attacks. Perhaps her mother, the distant woman with the faded eyes, depicted Lucy's future. Perhaps, after years of believing that she was the apple from her father's tree, Lucy was, in fact, destined to become her mother. One day, she would keep to her room and drive everyone away. One day, she would frighten the person she was supposed to cherish. One day, she would have two children, one to love and one to bruise. She looked at her hand, which stung now with memory.

"I found your pills," Lucy said, her voice hoarse from lack of use.

The afternoon had turned cold and dark, and her mother sat in the living room, flipping between soap operas in which she had no interest. If Lucy's words affected her, she didn't show it. She kept her eyes on the television, and answered in her usual sultry voice, "You're one to judge."

Lucy sat in a recliner across from her, twisting her hands nervously.

"Why didn't you ever tell me that you have what I have?"

"Because I don't."

"I saw the pills. They're antidepressants, just like mine."

"Antidepressants are used for many things."

A commercial for toothpaste came on, and her mother turned the volume down.

"You have anxiety and panic. I have what used to be called manic depressive disorder or some such thing. They're calling it bipolar disorder now. I've been told I have quite the case, which I'm sure you don't doubt." She rummaged in the drawer of the end table beside her and pulled out a cigarette and lighter. Lucy noticed that her hand trembled slightly.

"What is bipolar disorder?"

Her mother rolled her eyes and blew out a long stream of smoke that curled at the ends. "Depression, basically, and, for me, moments of . . . passion." She glanced at Lucy, then puffed on her cigarette and watched the smoke rise to the ceiling. "My stepmother thought I acted out for attention. God knows, I did want my father's attention." She laughed and shrugged. "My mother was his second wife. Did you know he was married three times? Divorced twice. It was almost unheard of in his day." She sucked the cigarette again, this time holding it for a moment before letting it out in slow, seductive ribbons. "My mother died last year."

It had rarely occurred to Lucy that she might have living grandparents. Though she knew her mother's origins, she had always pictured her mother alone, autonomous, unto herself, with no beginning.

"She had a stroke," Linda continued. "She'd remarried and had a son. He's the one who called and told me a few months ago. He said it took a while to find me."

"Did you meet him?"

"Of course not. He's not my brother—not really." She tapped her cigarette over a glass dish. "She thought I was crazy."

"Who?"

"My mother. Aren't you listening? I was about twelve when she left. Came home from school and she was gone." She sighed and inhaled more smoke. "No one knew what to do with mentally ill people back then. They hardly know now. The truth is, we're all crazy; we just can't handle a different crazy than we're used to."

"I wish you'd told me before."

Why hadn't she? These words, this revelation, held the power to free them both. Lucy had never known another person who battled this "incurable" illness. It strengthened Lucy to know she was not alone, and it excited her to know that she and her mother could help each other.

"What difference would it have made?" Linda sucked her cigarette.

"Mom, it would have made—every difference. We're like each other."

Linda's frown filled the lines on her forehead and around her mouth. "You only understand yourself." She leaned back in the chair, sucking her cigarette.

"I'm getting worse," Lucy said quietly. "I struggle all the time. I try to pretend it's not that bad, but I'm always running from it."

"It only gets worse," Linda said. "We're all worse because Emily is dead."

It was true. Lucy's mental illness came after Emily died. If only she'd watched over her sister more closely, fought the water and gotten over to her as soon as her mother had walked away. But there was a riptide, Audra had said. The doctor had told her that she likely would have drowned, too, had she tried to swim to Emily that day. Later, she learned that the key to surviving a riptide is allowing it to carry you out, without fighting it, until the tide loses strength and dies. Then, you swim parallel to the shore to get out of its path before swimming back in.

It went against her nature, the idea of not fighting. *Fight*— that's what Lucy's mind told her every time she experienced an attack. But like a riptide, if she fought, it would only strengthen against her. She had to ride it out, tossed on the waves of fear, blinded by the salt of sorrow. Then, as if it had never happened, she must pull herself forward, swim a different path, and wring out her spirit to dry. No one ever knew she was drowning, never saw how she suffered, dying right there next to a million people, a little at a time. She didn't know how to call for help because she didn't even know what help was, wouldn't recognize it if it met her at the cafe and bought her a drink.

But now she knew she wasn't alone. She finally had a connection with her mother, a way to understand her. Emily's death had unraveled them both; maybe now it would tie them back together.

"Mom, we can help each other." She reached for her mother's hand and held it. "You can come back home, and we'll cope with it together."

"I've wished every day to go back to that day." Her mother's eyes and nose were swollen, but she held back the tears. "I should have never left her with you." She sucked the cigarette again and held the smoke for a long, silent moment, a moment that Lucy felt both united them and wedged them apart.

"It was a riptide, Mom. Even if I'd swum to her, it probably would've taken me, too."

Her mother looked at her now, her eyes pained but unreadable. She sucked the cigarette again between brief sobs.

Lucy questioned whether she could tell her mother now what Bede had done in her bed. Certainly her mother would want to save her, wouldn't let her drown, too. But before Lucy could speak another word, Bede came home, and Linda put out her cigarette.

"What's going on here?" he asked, gesturing at Linda's swollen face. He glanced at Lucy, and she felt her stomach drop, her pulse quicken.

"Don't worry about it." Linda wiped her eyes and waved him off. "I was just watching my soaps. You know how they are."

He shook his head and muttered as he headed to the kitchen.

When Lucy turned back to her mother, she was heading for the stairs, and Lucy knew she wouldn't see her again for the rest of the night.

She followed her mother upstairs, heart pounding as she went to her room, where she locked herself securely in.

17

Over the next two days, her mother became even more distant, occasionally snapping if Lucy was in the room.

She's embarrassed, she wrote to Audra. *I don't think she would have ever told me. And she has no one—but me. I'd listen to everything if she'd just talk to me.*

Her father would have listened if her mother had only talked to him. She just needed to talk things through, the way Lucy did to Audra. A person who loves you makes all the difference. Yet Lucy had told her mother that she hated her.

As her final week in Jacksonville approached an end, the heaviness in her chest grew. One night, she was sure she'd woken up because someone was shaking the doorknob.

Someone was trying to enter her room.

In the darkness, she listened for breathing that was not her own. She mentally planned her escape: She'd grab the lamp and butt it into his face, hurry to the kitchen and get the sharpest knife, run outside and just keep running.

But how could she leave her mother behind like this, with her illness and this evil man in her bed? Surely Bede had hurt her mother too. Maybe that was why her mother seemed so weak. If she didn't create some sort of catalyst for change, then Linda would only become worse, and Lucy herself would worsen.

The next morning, after a sleepless night, she knocked on her mother's door. When no one answered, she pushed the door open and peeked inside. With the blinds pulled, she had to squint to see in the dark room.

"Mom?"

She crept toward the slight bulge beneath a mauve quilt; a slit between the heavy curtains cast a dusty light over her mother's face.

"Mom, are you awake?" It was well past ten in the morning.

"What do you want, Lucy?"

"I want to talk to you about coming home with me." She sat on the edge of the bed where she could just see the top of her mother's head above the quilt, her hand clutching her knotted hair at the scalp.

"I don't have the energy for this, Lucy."

"I've thought this through."

"Lucy, please!" Her voice was raspy and weak.

"If you come home with me, you can sleep in my room. You don't have to sleep with Dad. We can help each other—I know we can—if we do it together."

"Please go."

Lucy stopped, halted by the strain in her mother's voice. She knew she needed to go, that her mother would not budge, but she couldn't leave in a couple days without telling her what Bede had done.

"I've got to tell you something."

Linda was silent, and Lucy wondered if she'd fallen back to sleep.

"Mom?"

"What?"

"Last week, I woke up in the night, and"—Linda shifted so that she lay more upright—"and Bede was in my bed."

Lucy watched her mother's eyes pinch tighter. The lines on her face deepened between her brows, at her eyes, and around her full lips. Even tired and weighted with grief, her mother was beautiful, the most beautiful woman Lucy had ever seen. Someday, she would paint her mother looking just like this.

"You always would do anything for attention." Linda pushed herself upright and held back her hair with a long, slender hand. "He was probably drunk and didn't know whose bed he was in."

Lucy felt herself grow weak. "He—he hurt me."

"You're lying."

"Why would I lie?" Her lungs were tightening, and she wanted to run. "I can show you the bruises."

Linda looked away.

Lucy stood. She wanted to say more, but panic was ensuing. She was coming out of herself. She had to leave.

"You wanted him there," her mother said.

Lucy turned and faced her. "What?"

"Don't 'what' me. I saw the way you looked at him."

"What?" She had to run. She couldn't breathe.

"Don't you dare start crying now. If he was hurting you, why didn't you scream? Or call for me—or the police?" Now her mother was fully awake and yelling.

Lucy stammered for words, but none would come, and she couldn't stop the tears rolling down her cheeks, though she had no breath to cry.

"Get out of my room!" her mother yelled. "I can't stand the sight of you!"

Lucy left the room without another word. She threw her

things in her duffel bag and called a cab. Her father wouldn't be home for another day, so she'd call another cab from the bus station to take her home. She would lie on the sand in the wind until the Gulf called her in. It was calling her now. She could hear it whispering her name.

18

Audra awoke late the Saturday before school resumed even though she'd crawled into bed well before midnight the night before. Lucy had been assaulted by a man they both despised, and now she was home alone with the Gulf in her backyard. Lucy was hurting and scared, and here Audra sat, stuck in Birmingham until summer. She thought briefly of taking the car and driving to Jacksonville in the night, snatching Lucy from the house, and taking her far, far away.

As she lay in the darkness of her room, she remembered watching a feral cat deliver kittens under the porch of their house in Maryland when she was very small. She and Levi lay quietly in the dirt and cobwebs and weeds as the orange tabby's sides expanded and fell in rapid, painful movements. Then, slowly, the first kitten came, small and wet and blind. Then another. Then three more. The kittens mewed as their mother licked away the remnants of her womb from their fuzzy fur. But one little kitten didn't move. It lay quiet and stiff. Audra reached for it, but Levi pulled back her hand.

The mother tabby scooped the limp kitten, licked it a few times, but it still did not move. She remembered the helplessness she felt in that moment, watching the mother cat learn that her baby had not survived birth. She cried all afternoon.

Now she felt the same helplessness, the same sorrow. She couldn't protect Lucy.

Sometime in the early-morning hours, when thoughts become dreams in a restless sleep that's hardly even sleep, Audra saw empty shadows on a wooded field. They were branches swaying in a cold, northerly wind. It blew south, swift and whistling through the shadow branches. She thought she saw Levi in the hall outside her room, or maybe it was his shadow. No, it was him, and he was in her room, like Bede coming in to slide his hand on the smooth of her stomach. He touched her arm, and she flailed and tried to scream.

"Be quiet, you ninny. It's me."

Now she was awake.

Levi was sitting at the foot of her bed, wearing his favorite weathered jacket, a duffel bag at his feet.

"What's going on?"

He shrugged and cleared his throat. "I'm leaving."

Audra knew from his voice that he was crying. "Where are you going?"

"Back to Atlanta. The guys there are going to put me up in a room and hook me up with a job."

"What about school?"

"I'll get my GED. It's as good as any diploma. Atlanta's my home." He wiped his nose. "I'm really going to miss you."

Audra wondered at the idea of his missing her, she who stayed silently at home, who'd long since stopped following him on his escapades under porches and up trees. How long had it been since they'd ridden their bikes through the neighborhood, one a cop and the other a bandit? It was more fun to be the bandit. Where was their last ride? Florida? Before she'd met Lucy, before Levi decided he was tired of moving from city to city. Audra knew that he missed the sister she used to be, when they were a family who didn't know better than to be happy.

"Just think this through," she said. "You don't really want to do this."

He gawked. "Uh, yeah, I do."

She tried to focus on his eyes, let her own silently plead with his. She could handle the leaving better than being left, and as with Lucy just a few years ago, she considered that if she had been a better sister, spent more time with him, or reached out more during their latest move, maybe he wouldn't be leaving.

"Take care of yourself," he said, and gave her arm a light punch. "Don't let 'em push you around."

"Will you write?"

He stood and shook his head. "Maybe e-mail, but don't tell Mom or Dad. They'll come after me."

They would go after him anyway, as soon as they learned he'd left. And they'd look in Atlanta, calling all his old friends. She found it curious that he hadn't mentioned those things.

"Come with me." The words fell from his mouth, as if he hadn't planned to say them.

Why *not* go? Would it ever truly be home in Birmingham without him? She was used to the uprooting. It was the staying put that was hard, because she never knew where she belonged.

She was tempted, but she shook her head. She knew his friends were not the crowd for her, and she knew she wasn't brave enough to leave.

"Maybe I'll visit you in Florida this summer," he said, as though reading her thoughts.

"Okay. And, hey," she said, pausing a moment, "stay out of trouble."

He grinned a little. "Yeah," he said, and then he was gone, back in the shadows.

Audra lay back on her pillow, but sleep eluded her, appearing in one moment, disappearing the next. She chased it until she finally slipped into exhaustion.

By morning, she didn't know whether she'd dreamed it or if Levi had really gone—not until she went down to breakfast. But it wasn't breakfast time anymore. It was nearly noon, and her parents were sitting at the table, her mother crying, her father stoic, with a cop.

She knew without asking that Levi had indeed left. Now she prayed that they hadn't found his body dead on the road to Atlanta.

"What's going on?" she asked.

They all looked as if they'd swallowed the pit of a peach, now lodged in their throats.

Finally, her father answered. "Levi. He ran away sometime last night."

"You're Audra, his sister?" the police officer asked.

"Yes."

"When was the last time you spoke to or saw your brother?"

When? Sometime when the sun and moon had both vanished from the sky and Levi had entered her room.

"Yesterday," she said.

"Did he tell you he was leaving and where he planned to go?"

Yes, he'd told her. Of course he'd told her. He trusted her.

"No," she said.

The officer closed his notepad and stuffed it in his pocket.

"We can't file an official missing person's report until the person has been missing for twenty-four hours. If Levi hasn't returned by then, let us know, and we'll put out the alert."

Saul nodded and extended his hand. "Thank you, officer. We appreciate it." Then he walked him to the door.

Marion was still wiping her tears, her face now crumpled and looking very old.

Audra grieved for her mother and fought back her own tears—tears of sympathy, and regret that she'd lied. If she'd told the truth, perhaps they could bring him home quickly, and they could work this out as a family.

But Levi had trusted her. She couldn't bear the thought of sending the cop after him, so she had to play the bandit. No one would ever know—no one but Lucy, whom she would call when Saul and Marion had left the house, who would also keep her secret.

That was a comfort. It's hard to bear a secret alone.

19

Lucy sat at the edge of the water after the cab delivered her to the little blue house. The moonless winter night draped the sky in stars above the dark shushing Gulf. She shivered against the cold, but she desired its pain, a pain she could control, in a way, since it was her decision to feel it. At any time, she could go inside and make a hot mug of tea. But she wouldn't. She wanted the pain.

They made it to the little blue house, up the wooden steps to the deck and through the back door.

Gladys motioned for her to sit at the table. "Coffee or tea?"

"Tea."

She set the kettle to boil and searched the cabinets, satisfied when she found instant oatmeal. In minutes, Lucy was eating and sipping raspberry tea with lemon.

"When's your father getting home?" Gladys asked. She sat by Lucy, her wrinkled hands folded, her brows furrowed.

"Tomorrow, I think." She was fairly certain that school started on Monday, and she was supposed to have returned to the Gulf tomorrow about the same time as her father.

"Well, I'm staying with you until he gets home."

Lucy wanted to tell her that this was unnecessary, and unwanted, but she was tired and felt feverish, so she nodded. After her warm breakfast, she took a hot shower and went to bed, waking later just long enough to chew two vitamin tablets and sip some chicken noodle soup Gladys brought to her, before falling back asleep.

When she woke again, she heard Gladys speaking in the hall.

"She isn't well, Frank."

"Probably the flu," he said. "Some of the band members came down with it too."

"It's more than just the flu. I found her at the water. She'd slept there all night in the cold. She should never be left here alone. You know she's not well—hasn't been right since her little sister drowned."

"She wasn't supposed to be here alone. She was supposed to come back today."

"I'm just saying—"

"She's fine. Lucy always bounces back."

Lucy heard her father saying good-bye to Gladys before falling back to sleep.

Rather than telling her father the real reason she'd returned early she told him only that her mother was unbearable, and that Bede was annoying. She had come home early to enjoy her final days of Christmas break and gotten sick instead. She was sorry.

The lie appeased him—good thing, too, because she didn't want him to worry about her and put her back on those terrible pills.

Winter slowly turned to spring in the Florida Panhandle, which brought rainy days that didn't know whether to be warm or cool. The turn of seasons always made Lucy increasingly withdrawn and irritable. Some days, she couldn't get out of bed. Depression wrapped itself like a weight around her chest, and when her father left hesitantly for school, she would cry and stare at the stain on her wall for hours. Sometimes she stuck her finger down her throat until she heaved into the toilet, as if she could vomit out the pain inside her.

Audra sent her instant messages every afternoon after school and sometimes called, and Lucy could hear the worry in her voice. It made Lucy avoid the calls and stick to instant messages, though she knew that Audra could read between the lines.

The reality was that the doctor was right: she couldn't cure her mind as she'd hoped. Maybe mental illness was her doom, and like her mother, she'd end up with a life no larger than what was found inside her bedroom walls.

Sometimes she sketched or painted—angry strokes without form. They were neither impressionistic nor abstract, but pages of scribbles that she hated. Once she pressed down so hard her pencil broke. Ms. Hooper would be ashamed of her, and Lucy wouldn't blame her.

When she did go to school, she tried to avoid Shawna and Charlie so that she couldn't hurt them the way her mother had hurt the people who loved her. But they sought her out, sent her instant messages at home, called her.

On her sixteenth birthday, Charlie insisted on taking her out for coffee. She wore tights with a too-big sweater and the same old headband she wore every day. She didn't even wear lipstick for the occasion, because it caused her more grief than gratitude for having been born. Her mother wouldn't call today. She hadn't called or written on any of Lucy's birthdays since she'd left.

This year, Lucy hoped her father had forgotten, too. She wished Charlie had.

But Charlie strolled beside her in his nicest jeans with a pressed (but untucked) collared shirt and a bit too much cologne. Had she bothered to look at him, to really look at him, she might have conjured up the sensation most girls feel in their chests when they're on the arm of a handsome beau. Instead, Lucy looked ahead, her countenance like the overcast sky above.

He was young and figuring out who he was as an almost-man, as a boyfriend. Lucy sensed his struggle and envied him for it. What must it be like to wonder who you are, rather than to know so clearly?

"I want you to get something special," he said. "It's on me, for your birthday."

"A cappuccino, I guess," she said. "Dry."

"But you always get that."

"Because it's what I like. I don't know what else I would get."

"Try something new! It's your birthday!"

"I know what day it is."

"Well, if you want the same ol' thing, go for it." His voice had shifted from excited to irritated.

"Why don't you just surprise me."

She didn't care what she drank at this point. It wasn't supposed to be this complicated.

They weaved around onlookers outside the art gallery and through the happy-hour crowd at the pub before they reached the cafe. He held the door for her, ringing a bell above them, a man with his woman.

"Hey, guys!" The barista, Vinny, waved. "The usual today?"

"Yeah, a latte for me, and—what's your most special drink?" Charlie asked. "It's her birthday!"

Vinny grinned from one large ear to the other. "Happy birthday, Lucy! Drink's on the house! What'll it be?"

Lucy shrugged. "What would you get?"

"I'd get a caramel macchiato with extra caramel." He made a swirly motion with his hand, pantomiming the addition of extra caramel.

She smiled. "Okay. I'll take that."

"All right!"

Vinny went to work on their drinks, and Charlie seemed pleased with her choice.

The earthy scent of espresso helped Lucy to focus on the place rather than the feelings boiling up inside. They needed to come out, but she couldn't release them—not yet, not in front of Charlie. He wouldn't understand. Only Audra understood. Audra would call later, and Lucy would say nothing about how she hated her birthday, but Audra would know, and she would say, "Happy birthday, Lucy. Let's talk about summer."

Charlie handed her a cup, and Vinny called a final happy birthday. She turned and smiled her good-bye.

"Have I done something wrong?" he asked, louder than he probably intended.

The sky threatened rain, and Lucy held her coffee close to her chest against the breeze. "What do you mean?"

"I mean, you've been giving me the silent treatment lately, and I want to know what I've done to deserve it."

He'd done nothing, and Lucy knew it, but she said nothing.

"Even Shawna's noticed."

"You've been talking to Shawna about me?"

He kicked at a patio chair pulled out too far onto the sidewalk. "I just asked if she's noticed a difference in you, and she said she has. Even my parents have noticed—and they mentioned it without me bringing it up."

"Well, there's nothing wrong with you."

As they strolled on, passing the statue of the pelican and Blue Herons, he let go of her hand. "If you're going to break up with me, just do it. Don't drag it out. I can take it."

Lucy crossed her arms as they rounded the block down toward the pier, where Joe's Fish Market stood, decked out in red-and-white signs for seafood and beignets. The sight of it was nauseating, evoking her memories of Bede, both past and present. How she hated him. Sometimes she lay awake at night, fearing his hand on her doorknob, breaking into her room and hurting her again. She couldn't help it now that every time Charlie wrapped his arms around her and drew her close, she thought only of the night she lay in bed, helpless against Bede's force. She couldn't help that she didn't know how to tell Charlie it wasn't his fault she shrank from his touch.

They passed the marina and stepped out on the dock that spread into the sound. Sailors and fishermen paused from winding their rigging to wave and offer them their greetings.

Charlie waved back, and Lucy forced a smile.

"I know this has something to do with Christmas break and being with your mom," he said when they'd reached the end of the dock.

Lucy looked out at the glassy water. Sea scum and sailors' unintentional pollution gathered around the thick wooden posts that bored into the ocean floor. A school of fish came to claim what could be eaten, and a pelican watched patiently from a nearby post. The gulls cried overhead.

"I know the whole situation with your parents' divorce must be hard." He leaned against the rail. "I know I'd lose it if my mom left and remarried."

"My parents never loved each other the way yours do. Not mutually, anyway."

"I guess love can be complicated."

"I guess."

He shoved his hands in his pockets, looking out at the clouded sky as if it could spell all he wanted to say. When he pulled his hand out, he was holding a long, slender blue box tied with a silver ribbon. "Happy birthday," he said and pushed it into her hand.

She pulled the ribbon loose and wiggled off the lid. She expected jewelry; men love to give jewelry, and women often love receiving it, but the idea of it made Lucy nervous. It was too intimate, too serious, too binding to receive jewelry. It makes the men expect something in return, and she wasn't ready to give it.

But when she peeked inside, she saw not a glimmering string of gold but four freshly sharpened sketch pencils.

"Since you like to draw," he said. "These are supposed to be different shades. The guy said they were H and HB and something else—or something like that—and they're good for shading." He shrugged. "They all look like lead to me. You probably already have them."

"I needed new ones." She was still looking at the pencils and not at him. "Thank you."

"I like watching you sketch when you think no one's looking."

Lucy smiled a little and rubbed her thumbs over the gray-coated pencils. Then she put the lid back on and slipped the box into her bag.

"I know you're going through a hard time, and I don't know what to do to help, if you won't tell me. But you don't have to if you'd rather not. . . . Just . . . just let me be your friend."

Lucy looked into his kind brown eyes for the first time in months, eyes that dreaded what he thought she'd say next. He suspected that she would break up with him there on the pier on that misty afternoon. She saw a tenderness she'd never seen in any man except for her father. She saw his sincerity, and she knew she loved him. Putting her arms around his neck, she pulled him close and let him kiss her long and hard. She let him wrap his arms around her waist, allowing all the love and hate and fear and confusion to roll down her cheeks and into their mouths.

"Don't cry, Lucy," he whispered, and pulled her into a hug so that she could cry into his shoulder.

At that moment, they were both old and young, foolish and wise. She felt as if they were floating above a world of uncertainty and sorrow, breathing the freshest air of young love.

For the first time, she didn't worry that she was her mother in Charlie's arms. She was Lucy—only Lucy. For a moment, the weight on her chest lightened.

Lucy worked part-time at the cafe on Main Street that summer. When she and Charlie got off work in the early afternoons, they drove Charlie's car to her house and swam in the Gulf or strolled along the shore. If he stayed for dinner, he'd amuse Frank by joining him for a piano duet, or by providing an off-key harmony to Sinatra. Her father liked him as much as she did, and, for a while, Lucy felt better. Her anxiety and the depression she'd felt since visiting her mother were more manageable.

"Is this how you spend all your summers?" he asked one day as they headed for the little blue house. The sun had tanned their skin, now sticky with salt water.

"Until Audra gets here, yeah."

"And she comes next week?"

She nodded.

"What'll I do then?"

"Maybe your old friends will take you back 'til school starts."

He laughed. "You can be real heartless sometimes."

She smiled. "I guess Audra and I can have you over once in a while."

Lucy detected the slightest bit of jealousy in his eyes and felt both pride and satisfaction.

"Maybe you'll like her more than you like me."

She regretted the words immediately because Charlie jumped on them.

"Maybe I will! You should be extra nice to me this week."

She rolled her eyes as he opened the deck door for her.

She hurried in to pour some lemonade. In her haste, and with her vision still adjusting to the indoor lighting, she didn't see the person sitting on the old green couch, waiting with folded hands and hollow eyes for her to return, nor did Charlie as he followed her into the kitchen. He sat at the table while she retrieved two tall glasses and filled them with lemonade and brought them to the table.

Lucy set his glass in front of him, planting a quick kiss on his cheek.

"Does your father know you're home alone with a boy in the house, or am I the only one who finds that inappropriate?"

Lucy spun around. "Mom! What are you doing here?" Her heart dropped as she scanned the room for any signs of Bede.

Linda rolled her eyes and fanned her face with a folded newspaper.

"Is that the welcome I get from my only daughter?"

Lucy noticed the emphasis on the word *only*.

"Didn't you get my message?"

"What message?"

"The message I left on the machine." She fanned her face more vigorously. The skin under her eyes was thin and dark and caked with an insufficient concealer. Her cheeks, hollower than ever, bore too much rouge, and her lips were too red.

"I never heard the message."

"Typical of your father. Bring me a ginger ale, would you?" She held her bony hand to her head and leaned back with her eyes closed.

"We don't have any," Lucy said. "I can make you some tea." She glanced at Charlie, who gave her a sympathetic but uncomfortable smile.

"Really, Lucy, who wants tea on a day like this?"

"Would you like some lemonade?" Without waiting for an answer, she poured a glass and brought it to her mother, who sniffed it as if it were wine, took a sip, and contorted her face from the sour taste.

"Needs more sugar," she said, handing the cup back to Lucy. "Are you going to introduce me to the young man in the kitchen, or is he just going to sit there and stare at me?"

Charlie looked away and blushed, but then remembered himself with a quick stride across the room to shake her hand. "I'm Charlie, ma'am, Lucy's boyfriend. It's nice to meet you."

Linda looked at his extended hand as if the idea of touching him insulted her.

"I'm sure it is." She shook the tips of his fingers in hers. "I hate to break up whatever you two were doing, but you'll understand—won't you, Charlie—that Lucy and I need some quality time together. All right?"

Charlie cast Lucy another uncomfortable glance. "Yes, ma'am. It was nice meeting you." He stooped for his bag in the kitchen and leaned to kiss Lucy good-bye, but stopped when he saw the warning in Linda's eyes. "I'll call you later," he said.

Lucy let him out with an apologetic smile and turned back to her mother, who sat smirking like a character from her soap operas.

"Why are you here?" Lucy asked again. "Where's Bede?" Her stomach turned at the thought of him in her house.

Linda drew back her smirk. "He's in Jacksonville, working."

"Why are you here?"

"You know, the way you keep asking that makes me think you don't want me here. At Christmas, I thought that was *all* you

131

wanted."

"I'm not playing your games. You can wait here for Dad to get home. I'm going to take a shower and start dinner."

Lucy left her mother on the couch and did exactly as she'd said, locking the door of the bathroom behind her and releasing a long but shallow breath. She stepped carefully over the cracked tiles in the small bathroom, pulling the rug over the most jagged parts to keep from catching her toes. The sink, too, had spread more veins since Linda had last lived in the house; the curtains had yellowed, and mold had gathered on the walls, even though Lucy cleaned regularly. The wallpaper in the kitchen was peeling; the windows held moisture between the double panes; the bedroom quilts had faded in the sunlight. Age had wiped its inescapable hand all over the house, but Lucy hadn't noticed until now—now that her mother had returned.

Her mother was just like the house, Lucy thought: putting on airs of beauty and perfection for so long that now she was unable to see that she'd fallen into disrepair.

If her mother had hated the house before, she would surely despise it now. She would likely blame Lucy, and Lucy wouldn't argue with her, even though she'd done her best to keep it clean. Lucy hadn't observed the deterioration with willing eyes. She'd willed herself to see it as it was before her mother left and Emily died.

Lucy turned on the water for her shower, slipped off her tank top and shorts and the swimsuit underneath, and climbed into the cool water that calmed her sun-kissed skin. For this brief moment, she could imagine she was ten years old again, and Audra was waiting her turn to shower, sitting outside the door with Emily, sorting through their newly collected seashells. Emily would take the prettiest one and give it to Linda, who would smile her only genuine smile and add it to a dish on the table in the living room.

After their showers they'd smear each other's backs and arms and noses in aloe and sip iced tea until Frank came home and the music started and the sun set everywhere but inside the little house.

It did no good to sugarcoat the past in romanticized memories that maybe never were, but they showed the life she'd always wanted, and almost had, and sometimes did before Emily died and her mother left. It did no good to remember the love in her father's eyes as he waltzed her mother to the deck, the moon on their faces and the stars in their wake. It did no good to think about what her father would say when he came home and found the only woman he'd ever loved waiting for him in the living room, sour and cold.

Maybe, Lucy thought as she dried her legs, maybe by the time she'd dressed and put lotion on her skin, her mother would be gone.

20

Lucy wanted to tell her father that Linda didn't know how to love. She had never loved him, nor had she ever loved her eldest daughter. If her mother loved at all, she loved only herself, and possibly Emily, though Lucy couldn't figure out why. If it was because Emily had seemingly adored Linda, then it should follow that Linda would love Frank, since his love for her only grew every moment they'd spent together, and then tormented him once Linda left.

Maybe her mother had loved Emily because she so resembled her—her white-blonde hair silky and straight, her cool blue eyes, her full lips. Her mother's narcissism could have easily channeled a sort of self-love through Emily. Or maybe her mother saw Emily as a chance for renewal, redemption, a chance to relive her life through an innocent and healthy-minded child. Perhaps the opposite kept her mother from loving her eldest, because Lucy represented everything Linda hated about herself.

If Lucy could have stopped her father from coming home

that evening, she would have. She'd have barred the doors, dug a moat, drawn the bridge, and chased him away with arrows. But there she stood over a pan of poorly fried cod and baked potatoes when the kitchen clock chimed six and her father came through the door.

"Hello, Frank." Her mother's sultry voice floated across the room like thick smoke.

Lucy wished she hadn't looked at his face when he saw her mother there, wished for many years afterward that she could wipe it from her mind. He suddenly looked very old.

"Linda," he managed to say, with a tongue that had surely gone dry.

In the short distance between their eyes hung a thousand words that neither said but all three of them felt. In that time, her mother's harsh features softened; her lips almost formed a smile. She looked fleetingly younger, though she was only thirty-eight, as if she'd found her twenty-year-old, just-married self again and remembered those few short months, maybe only days, of contentment, of love.

Frank broke the spell by looking down and shutting the door behind him. He cleared his throat.

"Did you get my message?" Her mother asked, somewhat frantically, to Lucy's surprise.

"I did." He pulled a cigarette from the pack in his pocket and lit it with a trembling hand. "What's for dinner, Lucy?" he asked, strolling by Linda as if her presence were inconsequential.

"Fried chicken. It's ready to eat." She wondered why her father had dismissed her mother's message and why he'd not told her about it.

"Hope there're drumsticks!" He kissed her cheek and turned down the hall to change his clothes.

"You coming to the table?" Lucy asked her mother.

Linda shook her head, her eyes and the lines around her mouth heavy. "I haven't got much of an appetite anymore."

"You should sit with us anyway. Eat a wing."

Her mother had always preferred the wings. She considered the possible psychology between her father's choosing legs and her mother's choosing wings—one the steady, marching limbs of the family, leading them through life with a song in a major key, while her mother, light and unfettered, flew away. Lucy preferred thighs, but she was tired of psychoanalyzing and let the thought die.

They ate in silence, their forks and knives scraping against the old ceramic plates.

"Very good, Lucy. Think I'll head to bed. Been a long day, dear." Her father intentionally avoided further eye contact or dialogue with her and her mother, Lucy noticed, maybe because he wanted to hurt Linda, as she had so deeply hurt him, though he'd never been a vengeful person. She wondered how he'd react if he knew Linda had let a man abuse his only living daughter and get away with it.

"Frank," Linda called after him.

He stopped, but didn't turn around.

"Frank, where should I sleep?"

Lucy felt anger surge in her chest. What a question! As if she or her father would invite her to their rooms. Frank's shoulders dropped, and he rubbed his hand through his thinning hair.

"Emily's room," he said firmly. "Good night."

No one had entered—let alone slept in—Emily's room since she had died. It was a part of the house that Lucy had almost forgotten existed, though the closed door was directly across from her own. The idea of entering that room, which had so fictionalized itself in her mind, sent a strange sensation down her spine, as if Emily's ghost had come out and breathed down her neck. Her mother must've felt it, too, because she gasped a little.

Her father paused again, then added, "You can clean it up

yourself, Linda. Sheets and cleaners are in the same closet you left them in."

He looked at Lucy then and back to her mother. "It's just a room, and we have no other place."

But it wasn't just a room, and they all knew it. It was as if that little closed-off chamber contained Emily's spirit, captured in time and place, rooted in this house. If they opened the door, she might escape, and then they would know that Emily was truly gone.

"If it's such a hassle to you," Linda said, having resumed her pride and indignation, "I can call a taxi and stay at a motel near the bridge."

"You can have my room, and I'll take the couch," Lucy said.

"I said she'll stay in Emily's room, and that's where she'll stay!"

It was the first time Lucy had ever heard her father raise his voice, and it nearly startled her to tears, but she quickly regained herself. "What's going on?" she said. Her voice was higher than she'd intended, and its vulnerability affected both of her parents.

Her father turned to face them both, shoving his hands in his pockets.

"What did Mom's message say, and why didn't you tell me about it?"

He nodded toward her mother. "I'll let you tell her."

Linda's eyes and nose swelled red, and she swallowed and coughed, not looking at either of them. "I've come home to die."

The stripes of the kitchen wallpaper, the piano in the living room, the wall hangings, the ugly green couch—they all began to spin, and in that cyclone, Lucy saw a younger version of herself watching her mother as she read *Time* magazine on the sofa, serenely sucking the smoke from a Pall Mall. She'd folded her legs beneath her favorite green sundress, a string of pearls at her neck. Lucy remembered the pretty ladies in the ads, their bright red lips and heavy dark lashes against milky skin, their hair whipped high and curled at the ears. But none, she thought, could surpass her mother. Back then, her mother could have lived forever, an ageless vision, an unmovable force.

Lucy must have looked ready to faint, because Frank took her elbow and told her to sit.

"As if you haven't hurt her enough," he was saying through the haze. "As if she hasn't had to put up with enough from you." He poured Lucy a glass of water. "You have to come back and have her take care of you—to watch you die!"

"Where is Bede?" Lucy asked.

"Where do you think?" her father answered. "Back in Jacksonville, where he can rob another idiot of his fool wife. Kicked you out when he found out you were sick, didn't he? Didn't he?"

"Frank, stop!" Her mother covered her face and sobbed.

"Who's going to pay your doctor bills, Linda?"

"I don't know," she said into her palms.

"Who's going to drive you to your appointments and pick up your pills?"

"I don't know!"

"I'll tell you who. I'll tell you who! The same idiot who put that ring on your finger!"

At first, Lucy thought he meant Bede, but then she noticed the simple gold band with the quarter-carat diamond, the same ring she'd worn for as long as Lucy could remember. Though her mother's last name had legally changed from De Rossi to Bede, the ring she wore was De Rossi's.

"The weasel couldn't even buy you a new ring."

Without really knowing the story behind it, Lucy imagined Bede's explanation: "No need for two rings that serve the same purpose." The fact that her first wedding ring signified she had belonged to another man meant nothing to him; likewise, the thought that a new ring would have tied her to him.

"There wasn't enough money," Linda said. "And you needn't drive me to the doctor or pay for my pills. I have less than six months left, with or without treatment."

When Lucy thought about that evening later on, she remembered it in circles of abstract shapes and chaotic swirls of colors. On a new canvas, she painted them—an uneven door with a lock, a misshapen ring, a broken piano keyboard. She smeared them around in aggressive motions, scribbled thick zigzags over shapeless blotches. Blacks and reds and blue-grays.

She didn't follow her mother into Emily's room that night. She carried a set of twin sheets, a feather duster, and a scented candle to the door, but she would not enter. She even ignored the sights in her peripheral vision—the pink walls, the bookshelf with Emily's only baby doll and favorite teddy bear.

"I'll be sleeping with my baby," her mother said.

"Mom—"

Lucy started to speak, but her voice broke, and she stopped. She didn't even know what she wanted to say, anyway. Too many things had yet to sort themselves out. There had been too much pain and disappointment, bitterness and anger, shock and grief. For years, all she'd wanted was for her mother to return and to love her, to tell her that everything would be all right.

Now she was back, but she was leaving again soon, and nothing would ever be all right.

Lucy didn't know what love would look like from her mother—this woman who'd allowed a man to abuse her daughter and get away with it.

What if Bede came looking for her mother here and she had

to see him again? The thought made her stomach drop.

"Does Bede know you're here?" she asked.

Her mother nodded, and Lucy felt the color drain from her face.

Her mother shrugged. "Good night, Lucy," she said. Then she closed the door.

21

When summer returned to Birmingham, so did Levi. Six long, strained months had passed, but Audra thought his face looked years older, his body much thinner and taller.

She was sitting home alone in the kitchen with a book and a glass of lemonade when she heard the back door squeak open and slam shut. She looked up, and he was there, tanned and shaggier than when he'd left.

"Hey," he said. Even his voice had changed, deepened.

"Hey." For all she'd missed him, she did not greet him with a hug or tears of joy. Too much had happened.

"Are they home?" Levi asked.

"No. They're at the church picnic." She secured the bookmark between the pages of her book.

"You didn't go?"

She shrugged. "Headache."

He smirked. "Headache. Right."

Audra almost smiled, happy that he knew her well enough to still smell a lie, but she stopped because she was angry with him and wanted him to know it.

He shifted and dropped his duffel to the floor. "Got any food?" He opened the refrigerator. "Wow! You guys on a diet?"

The refrigerator was barren compared to its former state in the Clarke home. Before, it had held pans and cartons of leftovers, bottles of cola, bags of cheese, and gallons of milk, filling the doors and shelves. Everything had to go in just so if they wanted the doors to shut and seal. Now, it had a container of deli ham, half a carton of eggs, and a jug of milk. The cheese had molded, so Audra had thrown it out the day before.

"Mom doesn't cook much anymore."

"Why?"

"She works now, up the street. She's an assistant manager at Goodwill."

Levi rolled his eyes. "For now, 'til Dad moves her again." He took out the deli ham, rolled a slice like a cigar, and bit off the end.

"They argue a lot."

"Why?" he asked, his mouth full.

"Why do you think?"

He looked hurt, his eyes lowering, feet shifting. "Yeah," he said.

Audra knew it wasn't fair or honest to put all the blame on him. No good would come from scolding him, that she knew, though she did want to make him suffer at least a little over their parents, the way she had. But who knew how much he had suffered? Besides, she knew the real anger that both she and Levi felt was toward their father, whom she'd seen almost as much as she'd seen Levi in the past six months.

"What've you been doing all this time?" She asked because she knew he wanted to tell her, and he may as well say it now before their parents returned.

He smirked a little. "My buddies didn't really come through for me." He leaned on the refrigerator and picked at the ham caught in his upper molars. "There was no room, no job. Nothing. I showed up at the guy's house, and he was all, 'Yeah, man, sorry.' I was mad. Hitchhiked all the way to Atlanta just to have a *Sorry, man* thrown at my face. So I spent that night on the street. About died from cold. Some homeless dude offered me an extra coat, though. That meant something, you know? Someone with nothing giving me something." He shook his head.

"The next day, I went to our old school. Snuck in and took a shower in the locker room. The janitor—you remember Reggie Washington, the janitor? Not the white one; the black one. With the bald head?—He caught me."

"I don't remember the janitors, either of them." She remembered places, not people.

"I told him my story." Levi laughed. "I thought he was going to turn me in or send me back here. But he didn't. He took me home—to *his* home. He's not married. Wife died a while ago. He told me his son, Ty, was in college. Georgia Bulldogs!"

"He plays football?"

"No, just goes to the University of Georgia and gets to see all the games he wants. He's studying medical engineering, or something like that."

"Wow." She sipped her lemonade.

"Reggie hooked me up with one of his friends, a guy who works with wood. Carpentry." He lifted his hands; they were calloused and red with splinters that hadn't yet worked themselves out. "Almost lost my pinkie." He held it up. "Took the tip off."

Audra cringed, but her imagination was worse than the finger itself.

"I enjoyed the work—a lot."

"Wow," Audra said again, not sure where Levi's mind was going.

"I think I got him figured out," he said.

"Reggie?"

"No. Dad."

Audra waited for him to explain.

"Reggie's a janitor, and he enjoys it because he gets to talk to high school kids and help keep them in school and whatever. All his kids are doing these great jobs they love. It's about doing what you love. Everybody's got to find their thing, you know?"

"Sure," Audra said, with a nod that said *Obviously*.

"I think Dad's just found his thing, and no one's going to stop him from doing it."

Before Audra could offer a rebuttal, the front doorknob jiggled and twisted open. In a moment, their parents would come into the kitchen, home from the church picnic. She didn't have time to prepare, to summon wit or strength to endure her parents' reactions to this unexpected homecoming, before they entered the kitchen, holding leftover deviled eggs and watermelon.

Her mother gasped and spoke first. "You're home!" The eggs were on the table and Levi was in her arms, stooped over her much shorter body as she cried and kissed and held him. "Where have you been?" she asked, pulling away from him but holding his elbows. "Are you hungry?" Then she was pulling out pots and pans she hadn't touched in weeks. "Audra, make a batch of cornbread."

Audra heard her, but she was still looking at her father, who hadn't moved since he'd entered the kitchen. Like Audra, he couldn't cry. Too much had happened. He stood with the severity of a reverend, though he'd unbuttoned his top two buttons. His face, red with sun, appeared at once ready to condemn sinners to hell but also to call them graciously to repentance. Rather than address his son, he turned to Audra.

"You always knew where he was, didn't you?"

"Yes, sir," she said.

"I told her not to tell," Levi said.

Saul started to speak, but Marion turned from the stove and lifted a hand. "Saul, it doesn't matter! He's come home."

Audra knew that Levi would never understand how much he'd damaged their parents' relationship. They had been wrapped in fear, anger, and confusion, toiling for answers until the ache inside their chests drew them into themselves and away from each other. It frustrated her when her father would forsake them with a shake of his head and lumber to his study.

Levi watched Saul go, his face betraying his longing to talk his father, yet somehow unable to follow him.

That night, long after Marion had shopped for groceries and filled their bellies with fried porkchops like old times, Audra walked by her father's study, book in hand, and saw Levi inside. Rather than standing erect in front of his father, the accused awaiting arraignment, he sat in one of the leather chairs, loose and comfortable. They each sipped root beer from glass bottles. But most of all, Audra noticed that her father was smiling, even chuckling. She wanted to linger outside the door and listen to what they were talking about, but she knew she shouldn't.

Fortunately, her father had noticed her walking by. "Audra?" His voice came loud and with authority.

She back-stepped into the study, nervous but steady.

"Tell your brother about poor Lonnie Partridge's baptism last month." He was smiling, relaxed, like the father she'd loved and admired as a child.

Then she, too, was in a leather chair, recounting the young man's baptism—poor Lonnie, fifteen and six-foot-four, straight as a stick and skinny as a beanpole. The assistant pastor, Buck Rivers, was a stout man who came barely to Lonnie's shoulder, and this was his first baptism. Watching Pastor Rivers maneuver Lonnie into the sacred waters was a bit like watching someone give a giraffe a bath in a dishpan.

Levi was in tears. "Dang! I leave, and church finally gets interesting!"

Saul gave him a look.

"Just a joke, Dad," Levi said.

The three of them sat, each careful of their next word or motion, knowing how quickly the scales could tip. Levi handed Audra his root beer, and she took a heavy swig.

"Now that you brought it up, son," her father said, "why *did* you come back?"

Levi picked at a hangnail on his thumb, a smile—sadder than he probably intended—pulling at the corner of his mouth. "Figured I better come back before you left again, and I couldn't find you."

Her father tapped the desk with his wide fingertips, looking away. He wiped his nose and cleared his throat. "I stayed so you could find us," he said.

22

By the time her mother had gone to the doctor the previous fall, months before Lucy had visited for Christmas, the cancer had already spread so rapidly that the oncologist couldn't determine its origin. It had likely started in her lungs and traveled to her breasts and lymph nodes, then, her bones. She ached from the cancer, so Lucy spent the summer drawing long, hot salt baths to soothe her mother's body. She'd quit her job the week after her mother returned, and though she tried keeping up with Charlie, she was distracted and anxious—poor company—her mind always on her mother's needs. Charlie stopped by some evenings, and when he did, Lucy simultaneously wanted to run away with him and never see him again. What he considered supportive, she found intrusive.

Her mother needed her. For the first time in her life, Lucy meant something to her mother.

Once, when her mother called Lucy to help her from the tub, Lucy saw her mother's naked body for the first time, her rib cage protruding from her abdomen, the scar spanning the width of her pelvis. She flinched at the two wide scars side by side on her mother's chest.

"When was the surgery?" Lucy asked after helping her mother out of the tub and wrapping her in a robe.

"Early October. They took the rest of my womanhood, too." Linda motioned over her stomach. "They hoped it would stop the spread after a few treatments, but it was too late. We didn't have the money to continue chemo, and I didn't want to prolong the inevitable. At least I kept my hair." She gave a sort of eye roll as if to say that it didn't matter anyway. Then she dressed and lit a cigarette while Lucy brushed her hair.

"I wish you wouldn't do that," Lucy said. "It's those things that are killing you."

"The cancer can't be stopped now," she said. "There's no use denying myself comfort in my last days."

So Lucy let her mother puff away the days until the pain became so intense that she spent most days in bed, moaning and heavily medicated. A hospice nurse told them that Linda had weeks at most.

Whether her mother was awake or asleep in those days, Lucy often couldn't tell until she heard her mother's raspy voice calling for her. Answering her call meant entering Emily's room, but Lucy did so bravely. Her mother needed her, and she would not cause her more suffering by withering at the door. She sat at her bedside, feeding her broth and sips of ginger ale in the midst of memories she didn't have the time or energy to acknowledge. Not the white metal bars of the headboard where Emily had pretended to be a dog in a crate, yelping for water and treats. Not the faded pink dresser that likely still held Emily's clothes, or the toy box in the corner. Not the ceramic piggybank, her bowl of shells, her box of bows and ribbons. Lucy fixed her attention on her mother and dammed up her emotions, including the fear.

Linda hallucinated often on the pills, and Lucy found herself protecting her from invisible demons.

"The spiders can't bite you, Mom," she said, pretending to wipe them off her mother's arms. "There's no man here to kill you. I wouldn't let him."

Lucy wondered if the man came in the shape of Harold Bede. She shook her head as if to erase the thought. There would be time for that later.

Often, Linda called for Emily.

"Emily's not here, Mom, but I am." Her mother would look at her with strange eyes, as if she'd been dealt a cruel trick, to be lying here dying without the daughter she loved.

For the first time in her life, Lucy did not have a dark tan by September, and Audra did not come.

"It wouldn't be a good visit. I'd rather you come later."

By *later*, Audra and Lucy both knew that she meant for the funeral, the days she would need Audra most—the days she dreaded now more powerfully than she had ever dreaded anything before, even the dread of the panic inside her.

"Get just one more down," Lucy said as she helped her mother swallow another pill.

"I never thought it would end like this." Her mother's whisper was hoarse. Lucy took her hand and kissed it, but she pulled it away and settled into her pillow. "Death is inevitable, I guess."

Death was coming, and it would bring an end, a finishing line to Lucy's race for her mother's affection.

"Mom, I want you to know something," Lucy said, speaking quickly, timidly.

Her mother looked like she was listening for a moment, then closed her eyes, her lashes thin and pressed against dark hollows, her forehead lined with blue veins beneath thin pale skin. Her full lips were gray. Lucy still thought she was beautiful. In this moment, she was a child again, and her mother was fastening her pearls about her neck, looking at her from the reflection of her bedroom mirror. They were together in the mirror, framed and guarded.

"I love you, Mom," Lucy said, wishing she'd said the words back then, wished she'd said them a thousand times over, that she'd had Emily's courage to say them. They were so hard to say, Lucy thought, but they shouldn't be. She said them again now, sitting beside her mother, her hands clasped and sweaty.

Her mother didn't move.

The words had hurt her throat, making it swell, yet her mother didn't move or speak. Lucy picked up her mother's hand and held it to her cheek.

"I let her die, Lucy," she said, her mind on Emily, always.

"No, Mom. It was a riptide."

Linda turned her head on the pillow to face away from Lucy. "I was here with Harold . . . when she drowned. That's why I'd left her."

The doctor once told Lucy that panic results when the mind understands that it's impossible to control a situation but still believes it must. It pushes the body to react, and when it doesn't, the panic can simulate a heart attack. Lucy leaned forward now, clutching her chest and feeling as though her head weighed a hundred pounds.

"I don't understand." She yearned for understanding and control. "He wasn't here that day."

"You didn't see him, but he was here." Her mother pushed up on the pillow. "I need a drink."

Lucy lifted the cup of water with unsteady hands and held the straw to her mother's mouth.

Linda opened her eyes but didn't look at Lucy. "We'd flirted for a while, at Joe's. I told him he could come that day at two o'clock, while you girls were swimming. I didn't expect to go so far.

I knew he wanted it, and I wanted him to keep wanting me. But he was . . . ready . . . and I couldn't stop him."

When Lucy said nothing, her mother shrugged.

"He always wanted me . . . until this." She motioned over her body of scars and missing parts.

"He—he forced himself on you? Why did you go with him? Dad wanted you, too, and he never hurt you!"

Her mother shrugged again and closed her eyes. "He was exciting . . . sometimes scary."

"He took you away from Emily, and he hurt you, and then you left with him?"

The medication was drawing her mother far from the room, away from Lucy, who was hunched over and hardly breathing. She was coming out of herself, and her chest burned to the touch. She felt as if Bede had ripped her open all over again, leaving her helpless and alone in the dark.

Her father hired a nurse when school started back up again, so Lucy wouldn't miss classes, but Lucy attended in a daze. She worried that her mother might die while she wasted time diagramming sentences or determining the values of x and y, yet she couldn't untangle the anger and pain her mother had caused her. She didn't instant-message or call Audra to talk it through.

Her resolution to run from her anxiety, to beat it to the finish line, was failing. Rather than look for the next distraction—Charlie, Shawna, Audra—to escape the anxiety, she spent most of her time in the darkness of her mind, locked in a room of worry about unseen intruders. How could she face it again and survive?

Shawna and Charlie endured her silence at lunch and her moodiness in the halls between classes. When she tried to be her old self with them, it came out as strange and unnatural. She was not her old self, as broken as that self was, and she knew she never would be again. Another tide was coming in, and Lucy braced herself for a storm.

As her mother faded each day, her father took the night shift, sitting up with her for hours, helping her sip water or ginger ale, walking her to the bathroom. He looked older and more tired than she'd ever seen him before, and she wondered if he knew why Linda had left them alone on the beach that day. If he did, the knowledge didn't stifle his tenderness.

"Take another drink," she heard him say. "Get some sleep. I'll be here when you wake up."

Lucy hated how much her mother seemed to enjoy his affection. When Lucy peeked in now and then to check on them, she often found her mother's hand in his, her father kneeling at the bedside as though in prayer. Perhaps he did pray. Perhaps he cried. Perhaps he sought atonement for a marriage that never should have happened, but did, and then failed, and then came back in the end as a non-marriage that felt more like a marriage than the one they'd had before. It was a contrived ending meant to give him something to hold on to, to give her comfort in her final days. Lucy resented the facade, but why throw the truth in their faces now?

"Take me to our room," Lucy heard her say in her old sultry voice, still able to get her what she wanted.

Frank carried her to his bedroom and closed the door behind them.

Lucy imagined her mother wrapped in her father's arms, held tightly to his chest in what could be her final sleep. Perhaps Linda was sorry about the time she'd wasted, all the ways she could have enjoyed her life as a wife and mother. Maybe she wished she'd never left Lucy and Frank.

Lucy would never know the answers, for when she woke from a fitful sleep, she heard her father calling.

"Linda! Linda!"

She heard a door open and close. Then he knocked on Lucy's door, which was locked, and she hurried to open it.

"Your mother is gone." He was frantic.

Lucy ran to her father's room and found it empty.

Maybe her mother had gone back to Emily's room? But no, it was empty, too.

"Dad! Where are you?" she called, chasing after him. "Where is she?"

He'd left the deck door open, and Lucy ran after him, down the wooden steps that whined under her weight, over the soft sand, still damp and cool from a long dark night, to the water ahead.

"Linda!" he called above the waves. "Dear God, help me!"

Lucy saw her first, bobbing a short distance away, head down, wrapped in her old silk robe. Lucy said nothing. She didn't call for her father or scream for her mother. That was what her mother wanted: to be desired even in death as she left them without word. Had she tried to look into Lucy's room once more as she left, whispering "I love you" into the darkness? Did she get to the door and turn back to look at her with something akin to regret before she walked into Death's wet arms, following Emily out to sea, leaving them once again?

When he spotted Linda, Frank dove into the water, pushing toward her in long, hard strokes to bring her back to shore. He struggled against the waves and collapsed at the water's edge, sobbing, holding her, saying her name over and over, as if speaking it might bring her back.

But she was gone. Lucy had known the moment she'd seen her mother facedown in the water, arms out and draped in her robe, floating like wings.

She had left them.

"Come on, Dad." She rested her hand on his shoulder, but he shrugged her away. "Dad, let's get her to the house and call the hospital."

He knelt over her body, holding her and weeping.

"I can't let her go," he finally said, in words so low and hoarse that Lucy could hardly hear them.

"She's not here anymore, Dad."

When he wouldn't acknowledge her, she left him on the beach and trudged back to the little blue house, which moaned when she entered. Lucy slammed the door on it.

"Don't act like you care," she said. "She never liked you either."

She pulled the cordless phone from the kitchen wall and called the hospital. "My mother is dead," she said. "Linda De Rossi—Linda Bede. We just found her; she drowned."

The hospital told her the first responders would come.

"They're not necessary," Lucy said. "She's already dead."

But they would come, nonetheless.

She looked out the window at her father rocking her mother's body on the sand. Even if her mother hadn't drowned this morning, she'd have soon taken her last breath.

There was nothing now. Her mother left behind nothing intrinsic to herself—not a single heirloom or meaningful trinket in Emily's room or the kitchen or the room she'd once shared with her husband.

Lucy took one last look in Emily's room—the unmade bed, the nightstand cluttered with bottles of pain pills and cups of half-drunk ginger ale—and closed the door. Soon, it would feel as if it had never been opened. As if it should never be opened again.

Lucy sat in the corner under the Picasso crab and hugged her knees to her chest. She rested her head on the familiar green walls and wept.

Was it grief or mental illness that made her feel as if all the happiness in the world repelled her? That she could chase a thousand rainbows and find not gold but an empty pot every time?

23

The entire Clarke family came to the funeral and stayed for a week at the motel near the bridge. Lucy couldn't quite fall into Marion's arms anymore, but she hugged the shorter woman loosely, still catching the warm vanilla scent. It was fading, and Lucy wondered whether it was Marion or herself who was changing. Saul prayed over her and her father and talked about life and work and God and faith and strength in hard times.

The funeral was short, with a small group of mourners—a mercy to her father, who'd hardly spoken a complete sentence since they'd carried Linda's body away. Lucy had feared Bede would show up—so much so that she'd hardly listened to the service as she watched for him. As far as she knew, her mother had not been in contact with him since she'd returned to the little blue house, but her father had called him to let him know that she had passed. Bede hadn't answered, so her father left a message on his machine. Would he bother showing up to the funeral? The thought of it made her ill. Were her fears unreasonable? Did they even matter now?

Afterward, Marion made them more food than they could have eaten in months, and Levi busied himself with repairing the loose, squeaky steps on the deck.

"I used some wood I found under the carport," he said. "Hope that's okay."

Lucy said that it was fine—the wood had been left over from past projects—even though it annoyed her that the new boards didn't match the remaining older ones.

That he had tried to repair an irreparable house.

Audra stayed at the little blue house with Lucy that week, and at night, the two friends linked arms, like always.

"Are you okay?" Audra asked.

"No," Lucy said.

Audra gripped her hand and said nothing because she didn't know what to say. She recognized the illness inside her friend now, and she worried that, like the last time Lucy had lost a loved one, she would try to take her own life again—and that this time, she wouldn't be able to do enough to save her.

Lucy rolled to her side and propped her head on her elbow. She seemed to draw Audra's profile with her eyes, following down the slant of her forehead, over the slightly bent nose, across the puckered lips. They were so close that they could see the short, soft hairs on each other's cheeks, could smell their shampoo, bright and floral.

Lucy's breath caught, and a cry swelled in her throat.

"What's wrong?" Audra asked.

Embarrassed, Lucy looked at the sheets and pulled at a thread. "Nothing. I was just thinking that you look older."

"I am older," she said. "I was thinking you look different too."

"How so?"

"Taller, thinner. Older."

When had they stopped looking like themselves?

Audra sighed. "Hey," she said, looking into her friend's eyes. "Hmm?"

"You aren't . . . you aren't thinking of . . . going in the water again, are you?"

A cry swelled in Lucy's throat as she recognized that Audra was the only person in the world she could know liberally, whom she could scrutinize without fear, and be scrutinized by in return. She knew this person intimately, and in turn, she was known deeply. Perhaps this alone had hindered her mother's joy? An isolation that had kept her unknown and unknowable, and unable to know others.

Audra pulled her close and wrapped her arms around her, saying, "It's okay, Lucy. Let yourself cry."

Lucy did, so hard that her throat felt raw and her breath lost its rhythm. She fell into a sleep that felt more like the dark world between dreams and awakening, where nothing makes sense and faces are distant and watery. If she started to wake, Audra would pull her close and hush her cries. If she dared slip from the dark world and into dreams, Audra reached for her there, too. They were flying together, to a place where Lucy wanted to live forever, where the ocean was far below them, the horizon at their feet.

Her father held himself together those days with the Clarke family, but Lucy could see in his eyes that he wasn't well—that he was drifting, far from sure footing. He nodded serenely and smiled weakly when Saul spoke with him, but when he himself spoke, he was loud, excitable, and unexpected.

Toward the end of the week, Marion said they'd like to put flowers on the grave.

"What was her favorite?" she asked.

"Daffodils!" Frank said. "Always daffodils! Daffodils dancing in a vase!" He swayed from side to side, pantomiming a daffodil.

Lucy took his arm and stilled him.

"Dance, my girl. Dance! Put a smile on your face!" He took her in his arms, sang the refrain from "Singing in the Rain." Lucy let him have a turn about the kitchen before she stopped him.

"All right, Dad. Let's get ready to go to the gravesite."

She would not look at Audra, or the rest of the Clarkes. She couldn't betray her father by letting them see her embarrassment.

They bought a bouquet of yellow daffodils and a bunch of daisies and baby's breath and drove in the Clarkes' van to the graveyard. A breeze whipped at their hair as they climbed the path to Linda's plot, the one next to Emily's, the dirt still dark and moist.

Marion laid the flowers on the dirt, and they stood quietly, watching the wind tease the fragile petals.

Lucy didn't like the idea of her mother's body beneath the mounds of earth, motionless and decaying, alone until the end of time. But she knew her mother's body had simply been a cage for her soul, wild, and now finally free, not in the ground, but flying over the ocean, reunited with the child she loved.

"Such a beautiful headstone," Marion said.

Frank nodded, and Lucy looked at it for the first time. Above the years indicating her life span, engraved in large block letters, was her name: Linda De Rossi.

"He gave her his name," Lucy whispered to Audra.

Audra nodded. "Of course he did."

There was no other inscription.

24

Right after Emily died, Lucy had never seen her father grieve, apart from his tears at the funeral. She had been with the Clarkes, and then, in the hospital. When she'd finally returned home, she often saw him on the deck at night, silently smoking his way through a pack of cigarettes, occasionally wiping his eyes.

Now, Lucy watched him again through her salt-smeared window. When she couldn't fall asleep, she tiptoed out and slipped under his arm, the early October night still warm. They watched the stars fade into morning, hearing nothing but the satisfied shush of the Gulf.

Sometimes he smoked, sometimes, wept, sometimes looked far beyond the water, as he had when Linda had left him for Bede. It seemed unnatural to Lucy, unfair and unjust, that she and her father had to grieve for the same woman twice, so she closed off her tears after Audra left. While her father endured the long, lonely evenings on the deck, Lucy painted with oils on canvas, experimenting with different degrees of thickness.

Charlie came over some nights after school, but Lucy no longer found comfort in the distraction from silence. His presence now made her even more anxious that she might have an attack while he was there, and have nowhere to run without causing a scene or being forced to tell him that she had a mental illness. She'd hardly been a good girlfriend over the past year, and she figured that he was too kind to dump her after all she'd been through. Surely he would break up with her soon; surely he would see that he could no longer make her happy.

As she watched her father become more eccentric, perhaps as a way to cope with his loss, she wondered if going crazy ran in her family. Would she one day lose her mind only to live in a fantasy, as her father now seemed to? Or would she keep to her room and shut out the world, as her mother had done? What was the point of living if these were her choices?

"You should go to school for art," Charlie told her one evening as they studied algebra together in the kitchen.

"I don't have money for college," she said quietly.

"Apply for grants or loans . . . or scholarships. Show them your work. I'm sure they'd take you."

"And what about you?"

"Business school. I'm getting Blue Herons one day. May as well learn how to keep it running."

"That seems fitting." She pushed away from the table to turn on the kettle.

"I'm not going to school around here," he said.

Lucy turned to him, surprised.

"I'm going to UCLA."

"In California?"

"Yeah." He grinned, but appeared sheepish and uncertain.

"Why so far away?"

"I can't live in Florida all my life. This is my only chance to

161

live somewhere really cool and do new things. My aunt and uncle live there, so I can board with them. They're only charging me a bit for food and utilities. I've already been accepted, and luckily my GPA and SAT scores were good enough to earn me a scholarship."

"Well, you've got it all figured out then." She pulled tea biscuits from the pantry and set them on the table as the kettle began to hiss.

"I've been hoping you'd come with me."

"To California?"

Why didn't he see this as a way out of their crumbling relationship?

"Yeah. We can road-trip across the country—and you can study art there."

"I can't do that." She set their cups on the table.

"Why not?"

"I don't have the money for UCLA, and . . ."

She looked through the bay window, out to the deck where her father stood with his back to the house.

"You can't leave your father."

Lucy nodded.

"I had a feeling you'd say that." He bobbed the tea bag up and down in his cup. "You're going to have to leave him at some point, Lucy."

"Why would I have to do that?"

"You've got a life! You have to live it."

"I can't leave him. He needs me. I'm all he's got, and he's not doing well."

Charlie sat back from the table, frustrated and shaking his dark head. "I'm all my parents have, too, but they aren't holding me back from living before I'm tied to this city for the rest of my life."

"Your parents have each other, and they run a successful business together."

"Your dad is an adult. He'll figure it out."

Lucy scribbled a figure she knew was not correct on her homework and closed the textbook. "What will happen if I stay here and you go?" she asked.

Charlie shook his head again. "I guess we'll break up."

Lucy nodded, certain that he would say that.

"Long-distance relationships don't work, Lucy."

But they can, she thought. They can, because Audra had been her best friend for most of her life, mostly long distance. They grew closer with every online chat, every phone call, every letter. Audra knew her better than she knew herself.

"It can work if you want it to," she said.

Charlie didn't respond.

By Christmas, she and Charlie were bickering more than anything else.

Her father sang and danced with himself, sometimes pulling Lucy in with him. He played the piano and puffed his cigarettes, put on old Fred Astaire and Frank Sinatra movies, played checkers or chess with himself, or sometimes with her or Charlie. She supposed that when a man had endured that kind of love and loss, his survival may depend on revising himself, imagining that his life was exactly as he'd planned for it to be, finding it in old movies.

She assumed that, given enough time, she might do the same.

If the ocean didn't draw her in first.

25

Her grades were suffering. That's what Ms. Northrup, the principal, told her father during their meeting. If Lucy didn't pull them up, she might not graduate.

"She's just having a bit of a hard time," Frank said, patting Lucy's hand.

"I understand that," Ms. Northrup assured him, "but frankly, Lucy isn't functioning well at all. She needs help."

"Tutors?" Frank asked.

"Doctors," she said.

"She's seen them already, and they helped her out. Gave her some pills. She's fine at home, aren't you, Lucy?"

"What kind of pills do you take, Lucy?" Ms. Northrup asked.

Lucy didn't reply.

"Are you still taking them?"

Again, she didn't answer. She could see her father mulling something over in his head. "Oh wait . . . It's her mother who took pills." He half smiled, pleased that he remembered.

"Her mother?"

"Y—yes."

"Not Lucy?"

Frank was sweating, shifting in the leather chair. "I—I don't remember," he said.

Lucy wanted to take his hand, but she too was struggling to maintain face. "I stopped taking them . . . I ran out," she finally said, lying. It had been years since she'd taken them.

Ms. Northrup looked from Lucy to her father, the frown on her face revealing concern. "I'm going to recommend that Lucy see the school therapist."

When Frank looked out the window and started humming a song Lucy didn't recognize, she finally took his hand and shook it a little. She couldn't let him fall apart in front of her principal.

"School therapist," Lucy repeated. "That will be helpful." She just needed to get them out of there. "Right, Dad?"

"Yes! Anything for my girls!"

At his use of plural *girls*, Lucy's shoulders dropped. He was losing it faster than she was.

She didn't want to talk about their deaths, and she didn't want the pills.

"I'm Dr. Preston." The school therapist shook her hand and motioned for her to sit in a large plush chair. "Tell me about school."

It was school, that's all. She was ready to graduate and be done. To stay home. Help her father. She didn't need therapy.

"Do you have many friends?"

I have a best friend who isn't here anymore. The others, I don't know why they care. When school is over, they'll move on. That's life. I wish everyone would just leave me alone.

Dr. Preston ignored her silence and moved on.

"Tell me about the pills you used to take."

Zoloft? Xanax? Both? She couldn't remember. She knew it had a Z sound in it, and she didn't want to take it anymore. *It made me feel dizzy and weird. I wasn't myself. Somehow back then, I felt . . . stronger.*

I thought I could win.

"Win what?" Dr. Preston said.

She didn't realize she'd said it out loud.

"Win . . . beat it. They said it wasn't curable, but I didn't . . ."

"Believe it?"

"Yeah."

"Are you better now than you were then?" Dr. Preston asked.

She wasn't. She was worse, and she was looking at the Gulf even when she wasn't home.

Now she was crying, wishing Dr. Preston would just leave her alone. Couldn't he see that she just needed to be left alone? She was hurting on the inside, and it wouldn't go away. Couldn't he see that?

Perhaps he could. Maybe he knew that the Gulf was calling her. But he couldn't know that she had to resist for her father's sake. She couldn't leave her father.

She looked up at Dr. Preston.

"Can you make it stop?"

26

It was only Zoloft, they said, and Xanax for the really bad attacks. She would adjust to the Zoloft once she it got into her system. Don't quit this time, they said. Let it do its work.

And she listened, because this time, feeling drowsy and dizzy was better than feeling the dread of anxiety and the ache of depression. Better for her head to ache than her chest. Easier to numb everything than to feel anything.

Dr. Preston met with her once a week, and her grades improved moderately. But her heart wasn't quite in her paintings. She had stopped telling stories with her art.

"You going to college?" Shawna asked as graduation approached.

"Yes," she answered. "Local, at the University of West Florida—to study art."

Her student loan had been approved, and she qualified for the in-state discount and financial assistance from the school. She would work at the cafe and fill in for Charlie at Blue Herons. Between all of that and her savings, she could make it work.

"What about you?"

"University of Maryland," said Shawna. "Back to my home state!"

Audra was attending a community college where her family lived now, in South Carolina. They were already planning to spend their spring breaks together.

"Keep in touch, all right?" Shawna said, but her look held pity, and Lucy looked away.

Charlie would leave for UCLA the week after graduation. His uncle had gotten him a job in the city that paid better than Blue Herons.

She pictured what would happen in the coming weeks.

He would drive his new used Camry to her house and knock on the deck door.

She would open it and step outside.

"Just packed a suitcase of clothes and a lamp," he'd say. "I'll buy whatever else I need when I can, after I've bought all of my textbooks."

Lucy would lean against the rail of the deck, her long arms already tan, her face sun-kissed.

"I . . . I probably won't be back for every break, with my job out there and flights costing so much. I'll miss you, Lucy." He would say the words in a way that would let her know he'd miss her for a long time, and she wouldn't understand why.

Her breath wouldn't catch, her eyes wouldn't fill with tears.

She would turn from him to watch the waters of the Gulf roll ashore.

"Take care of yourself," he would say, squeezing her hand.

He'd leave a kiss on her cheek that would cool and then blow away in the breeze.

Good-bye, she would say, a word familiar on her tongue. She would know it was good-bye to many things—Charlie, childhood, and, in a way, even herself.

Good-bye was a loaded word, and she would say it again, alone, with the Gulf before her and the little blue house at her back.

27

Life after high school was better. Lucy could handle college with its flexible schedule and students who didn't know about her or her family. She could slip into classes and keep to herself—no dorms or sororities or campus events for her. She didn't need them, and she certainly didn't want them. As long as she kept to herself and took her pills, she could burn the smallest light in the darkness, watch for the invisible intruder.

She couldn't think about the trade-off—that in exchange for inner stability, she'd lost her passion, her ability to feel anything.

"You have incredible talent," her art instructors told her, "but your work lacks vision."

"What do you want this piece to say?"

"What is the philosophy behind your work?"

What would Ms. Hooper say?

She saw Ms. Hooper every now and then on Main Street, but she avoided her whenever possible. Ms. Hooper cared about her former students' art, and Lucy couldn't stand the thought of disappointing her with paintings that no longer told a story.

I know what you mean now, she could say to Ms. Hooper, *about the philosophies and theories of art. I can look at my paintings and see the difference—see when my work is art, and when it's just a painting. You were right about college; I'm glad I'm going. But now I'm able to see everything my art* isn't.

I could change that, but it would require feeling, and I can't let myself feel anymore.

Then Ms. Hooper would offer to help, ask to see her work, want to talk about things. And Lucy would want to, but she couldn't, because her heart would race, and the stress would cause her faint light to flicker. It might blow out, and then she would be on the floor again, gripping her chest and hearing her name on a salty breeze.

Audra called every Thursday night, and Lucy still mailed letters because she found the act of handwriting soothing. The pressure of dark lead on parchment, the gliding of ink looped in cursive, the careful folding of the paper and slipping it into an envelope—every motion rooted her in a sense of being. Her thoughts became words in a physical reality. She started folding the paper first and sketching a picture on the front, like a greeting card. She used colored pencils at first, then watercolors. Sea turtles, pelicans, gulls. Shells, fish, silhouetted shrimp boats. Her blue house on stilts. She rarely drew humans.

So she said nothing and earned average grades and found a small internship making prints for greeting cards. The card company appreciated her work and allowed her to remain a freelance contractor with them after her graduation. It wasn't enough to pay all the bills, especially her student loans, so she continued working for Blue Herons while Charlie was in grad school.

"My parents are really glad to have you there," he texted her. "They really care about you." He'd dated someone else in college, someone named Samantha; he said she was smart, like Lucy. "You'd

171

like her," he said. But they broke up during his senior year, and he never told her why.

Couples break up. It happens. The relationship cracks, and the two partners decide it isn't worth mending. They seal the decision with words: *This isn't working out. It's not you; it's me. I think we're going different directions. I'll always care about you.*

But friendships rarely have such definite breaks. When they do, they feel unnatural, unnecessary. A romantic couple isn't required to stay together or get married simply because the relationship started out well. When the breakup happens, they often become *just friends.*

But what happens to friendships when things change?

"Let's travel somewhere for spring break next month," Audra had suggested over the phone their senior year. Her voice sounded older, like a woman and not a girl. "I want to see places and do things."

"Travel where?"

"Well . . . I was thinking somewhere neither of us has been before. Maybe Santa Fe? There's a big art culture out there, and I'd like to hike the mountains and see the pueblos."

But Lucy couldn't. She couldn't leave her dad alone for that long; he wasn't doing well. Why couldn't Audra just come to Florida, like usual?

"I mean, I want to see you," Audra said, "but I've been traveling there for, like, almost ten years. You've never traveled to see me."

But she couldn't.

"I know," said Audra. "I know, I know, I know."

Was she mad at her?

"What if I go and call you while I'm there? I can send you pictures."

That doesn't make sense, Lucy thought. Why would she go without her? Go by herself?

"I have some friends here who want to go."

Other friends—less-broken friends.

"That's not what I said."

Was she saying that she didn't want to come here anymore? Was she saying . . .

"I don't know what I'm saying," Audra said. "I'm not saying I never want to see you again."

Just not now, because Lucy couldn't leave the Florida Panhandle, because she was no longer worth a visit.

Silence filled the phone line between them until finally Audra spoke, softly, shortly.

"I'm sorry, Lucy."

She knew that ignoring Audra's texts and sending her calls to voicemail was immature. She knew she was overreacting. But she also knew that Audra deserved better friends than her, deserved to travel and do the things she wanted to do with her own life. And now she would always wonder whether Audra truly wanted to be with her, or simply felt sorry for her, or only wanted her friendship when it was fun—when the fact that Lucy was tethered to the Gulf shore hadn't mattered.

It made sense that Audra hadn't wanted to come, and it made sense to ignore her calls. It was better this way. Crying—no, that's no good. Take a Lorazepam and go to sleep. Sleep it away when it starts to hurt. Go to bed and lock the door.

It wasn't that Audra didn't want to see Lucy. It was that she wanted to see other places *with* Lucy. And she wanted Lucy to enjoy it.

But could Lucy enjoy other places if they caused panic attacks and anxiety? She didn't want Lucy to suffer needlessly. So what good was she to Lucy at this point? She couldn't stop the attacks, she couldn't help Lucy expand her horizons, and she couldn't stop Lucy from going in the Gulf.

"I'm sorry," she texted Lucy.

There was no reply.

"I know you're reading my texts."

"Come on, don't do this."

"Let's talk about this."

"Lucy."

"Please just answer your phone. I want to talk to you."

"Hey."

"I'm just going to keep texting you."

"Lucy."

"Hey."

"Heading to Santa Fe. Wish you were with me."

"Check out these mountains!"

"This inn is gorgeous."

"New Mexican food = WOW."

"I'm back! All the pictures are missing is you."

"Happy Graduation Day! Isn't yours next week?"

"How's it going?"

"Hey."

"Hey, how's it going?"

"Hey."

"Lucy."

"Lucy?"

28

Frank didn't consider himself eccentric; he didn't really consider himself at all. And why should he? Life was a dance! Jump in, folks! Sing it with me!

The school had to let him go, Lucy told him. They had to let him go so he could get better. It was okay. She had her degree and some work. It was summer, now, and all his schoolwork was done.

But the band? Who would lead the band that summer, get them ready for fall? Why look for other band leaders? No need! He was still in fine shape—pretty fine shape for a man in his sixties!

Lucy looked unhappy. He hated when she was unhappy. She was his girl. How he loved his poor brave girl. She'd been through so much.

This wasn't about her, Lucy said. This was about how he'd tried to dance like Fred Astaire on the bleachers and broke his leg. This was about how he'd swooped Kelsey, the clarinetist, into a dance routine, and her mother had nearly charged him with assault. How he couldn't remember his students' names anymore.

He was just helping them lighten up. They had a show to do. He could rest now. Why doesn't he just rest?

Rest? How does a man rest when the show must go on? He'd show her!

And he did. He sat in the middle pew at church, crutches at hand, and sang, "I'm living on a mountain underneath a cloudless sky!" as loud as his voice could carry. See the way they looked at him? He could still make the ladies smile!

"Amazing grace, how sweet the sound!" But his words weren't on the beat. The beat was off. That old gal at the piano wasn't keeping up. "If that pianist plays any slower, I'll be standing at my own funeral!" Now he had their attention. "Grace doesn't sound amazing when it's sung like that, June!" He didn't need the hymnal, Lucy; just sing! Who was Mary? The pianist? "*Allegro*, June. *Allegro*, Mary!"

He'd been a high school music teacher for thirty—forty?—however many years. When he led the parade of students and their instruments onto game fields, he danced on the tips of his toes and lifted his baton up and down, choreographed to entertain. This was living! This was how he'd won his Linda!

He lifted his crutch like his old baton and tried to increase the pianist's tempo. Mary didn't respond to his heckling then, but when they sang "Turn Your Eyes upon Jesus," even Frank struggled to keep up.

This old gal doesn't know music! "*Andante*, Jean! We can't see Him at this speed!"

They were all smiling, laughing. Just like the old times. Everyone except Lucy. She was just like her mother. Just like Linda.

Linda.

Where was Linda?

Linda? Linda!

It was hard to leave her father at home when she went to work at Blue Herons. Sometimes she came home and found him eating raw fish. He'd stopped bathing, and several times she caught him flicking his cigarette ash onto the floor.

His mental decline was rapid, and Lucy endured many nights of his crying for Linda.

But the worst night was when he thought *she* was Linda. She was washing dishes when he came in, slow-dancing and humming Sinatra. He came up behind her and put his hand around her waist.

"Dance with me, darling," he said in a low voice.

"No, Dad." She pushed him off gently, but he persisted.

He was not Harold Bede, and even in his mental decline, he would never force himself on a woman, or touch her improperly. That she knew. But the situation was too similar and the memories, too painful, and she reacted, yelled, told him to go to his room, like a bad child.

His dim blue eyes widened with fear, then pain. He fell into a chair at the table and sobbed, repeating her mother's name over and over again.

After that, Lucy worried about what he might do—to himself, and to her. An online search told her that he likely had early onset dementia or Alzheimer's disease, but she didn't want to believe it. Her father had always been strange, right? Surely this was just stress, maybe PTSD from Linda's death. It had affected him strongly.

But the doctors confirmed the online research, and by that fall he was on medication to slow its progression.

He should have come in months ago, when Lucy first noticed the signs, a doctor told her. His mind was deteriorating fast. How had the school let him continue leading the band for so long?

How could she have known? He'd always been eccentric, for as long as she could remember. He danced. He sang. He twirled her, her mother, and her sister about the deck, mimicking scenes from his old movies. She didn't know when he'd gotten this bad; she'd been in college, after all. She knew he needed her, but not this badly.

He couldn't be left alone. He needed someone to keep an eye on him so that he didn't hurt himself.

What could she do? She had to work. They didn't have enough money otherwise.

"Emerald Coast Assisted Living," a doctor said. "They offer all the care he needs, and you can fill out paperwork with the state, for financial assistance."

But he needed *her*.

"It's always great when family wants to care for their loved one, and in some cases, that's possible. But as you said, you can't be home with him all day. He's too far advanced to be left alone."

But . . . she needed *him*.

In another month, Lucy felt as if she had entered the beginning of another end. When he understood what was happening, her father notarized his last will and testament and made her power of attorney and executor. He made her an authorized user on his bank account and signed over the deed to the house. None of it felt right. She put all the paperwork in folders, dropped them in a box, and slid it under her bed.

She settled her father in at Emerald Coast, a place far less shiny than its name. His room was small and white, with only a bed, a side table, a dresser, and a green wingback chair. Lucy hung a few of her own paintings on the walls and set a potted peace lily in the corner. There was no piano, and he wasn't allowed to smoke.

Lucy hardly recognized him as he sat on the bed, hunched forward, pumping his new cane up and down as if churning butter. It hurt her to look at him.

She sat beside him, took his long bony hand in hers and kissed it.

"I love you, Dad."

He looked over at her. "Tears?" he said, and touched her cheek.

She quickly wiped them away.

"I have to go," she said as she stood and reached for her purse. She felt her light dimming, darkness rolling in. She was falling inside herself, as she had after Emily died and Audra moved away and her mother left. Loss was the wind that blew out her light, and when at last her father died, no longer knowing her name, his departure would be the last of her.

For a week, she didn't leave her house. She couldn't. Not to go to work or even to take her father to church. She felt poorly and couldn't make it, she said.

"No problem at all, my dear!" he said. "I've got to prepare for band tomorrow."

"No, Dad, you don't have band tomorrow. Tomorrow you play chess there in the rec room. Remember? The nurse said you'll play chess or checkers with your neighbors."

He fell quiet a moment, then sounded back with "Chess. Yes, that's right. I'm getting too old to keep these things straight. What would I do without my girl?"

She was his girl. That's what he'd always said, and she'd rested in confident assurance of his love. Now the words sounded off, out of tune, a song she could no longer enjoy because it was fading. She was his child, the only person in the world who accepted him and loved him, yet she'd put him in a home for someone else to care for him—but only because she couldn't be home with him all the time to protect him from himself.

Except now she was home all day and wouldn't even visit him, let alone bring him back.

She could hardly care for herself, let alone someone else, too.

Loneliness and fear settled in the darkness of her mind and bound her to the false safety of her bed for days. Audra. She needed Audra. Why had she been so foolish? Where was her phone?

She found it in the deep pocket of her sweatpants and scrolled to Audra's name in her contacts. She sent one text and then another. Then she called, but no one answered. She deserved as much; she knew that. How many of Audra's texts had she ignored with her stubborn pride? All the while, missing her so badly she could hardly breathe.

Was it morning? Noon? It didn't matter. She swallowed an extra lorazepam and waited for something like sleep to come for her.

When she slipped out of bed hours later, she was in the same sweatpants and an old tank top she hadn't changed from in days, and brewed a pot of coffee. What day was it? What time? She pulled her phone from her pocket, but it was dead. She didn't bother to plug it in because no one, not even Audra now, she figured, would try to reach her.

A look outside told her it was after midnight, when the sky is inky and dark, resisting the soon emergence of dawn. The Gulf of Mexico called from beyond the bay window as she poured a cup. Yeah, she said, I hear you. She went to the living room and sat on the ugly green couch, pulled at the worn threads, the final hairs on the balding cushions when once her mother rested Emily, her tiny body fragile, velvety, and warm. Where she and Audra had sat as Frank played the piano and sang. Where she and Charlie had found her mother.

She set her mug on the coffee table and leaned back on the chair. Would the memories fade along with the remnants of tobacco embedded in the fabrics and the walls? Would the darkness stay this time? Why weren't the pills working? She took another Lorazepam, swallowed it with coffee. They used to dull the pain and mute the water's call, but now she felt the earth shaking. Her vision was bent and distorted. Her mind told her to run and cry and rip her chest open to let in the light, but the pills, which didn't dull the pain, made her too tired to fight it. She was worn; her fabric was frayed.

She stood and moved to the kitchen, rested a knee on the ledge to look out the salt-stained bay window, her fingers on the wall where the paper peeled. The Gulf waved and knocked on the shore, retreating and reappearing, imploring her. She reached for the doorknob and slowly turned it.

Come, the water whispered.

Now the door stood open wide, Lucy filling the frame, the warm breeze teasing the curls at her cheeks.

Come.

She placed one bare foot out on the deck. It would be so easy, and no one was there to stop her. All the pain would drown with her. Her father would forget her. Audra could live without her. No one else would care. It would be her turn to say good-bye.

But as she planted her foot on the deck, pain shot into her sole, and she quickly drew it back. She hopped back to the window seat and inspected the bottom of her foot. A large splinter had inserted itself in the most tender part of her foot. The end still stuck out, and Lucy flicked it a few times before gaining enough to pinch. Then she pulled it out and watched her blood drip from the hole.

The wind blew the open door against the countertop, and Lucy jumped up and slammed it shut. Then she swiped all the dishes to the floor, where they clanged and broke into a thousand pieces. She threw over a chair and chucked the salt and pepper shakers against the wall. She reached for the peeling corner of the wallpaper and pulled. Then pulled at another. When she ran out of fragments to pull, she grabbed a butter knife from a drawer and pried up more of the paper, pulling and tearing until half the paper was striped with tears, exposing the bare, moldy wall.

She finally stopped and leaned against the wall, crying and exhausted. She screamed into the emptiness, the nothingness that couldn't answer back. On the floor, broken beyond repair, rested two of the teacups she used to sip from with her father. They'd been in this house for as long as she could remember, the same cups her father had used to serve her tea when she'd come home from the hospital.

Stooping, she gathered the pieces carefully, looking them over as if she'd wounded a small creature. There were too many pieces, the damage too great to undo. She felt as though she had no respect for living things, as if she were fully transforming into the monster that dwelled inside of her.

She set the pieces on the table and then pulled the trash bin over to throw away the rest of the damaged pieces—plates, a white bowl, and several water glasses. She swept the old linoleum floor with the same broom her mother had once used. The walls, fixtures, appliances, utensils, decor—everything in the house was like Lucy's family, crumbling and broken and abused. Time had shown this house no favor; its occupants had shown it no grace. A home should embrace its family, and the family should uphold the home. Her family and the little blue house had failed each other.

Come, the water called.

No, not so loud. Please, please go away.

Lucy.

Stop saying that! She wouldn't answer!

Lucy.

She turned away.

Lucy.

I don't want to, she whispered. Not again.

Lucy.

She picked up the chair she'd thrown and swept the floor. She would sweep until she no longer heard her name. Throw away the broken dishes. Throw out the broken things. If only she could toss herself, too. She belonged in the bag of irreparable items.

Lucy.

No, she mustn't think like that. Push the thoughts away. Take a deep breath. No, deeper than that. Stop thinking. Where are the pills? Take another one. They aren't working. Oh God, why weren't they working?

The pain seized her chest, sending shocks down her right arm. She was dying, alone. No, it was only the panic. But it felt like death. Why did it always feel like death? A heart attack, a sudden violent cancer, a tragedy. Who would take care of her father after she was gone? Who would tell Audra?

Tea. She needed tea. Chamomile tea. Get the kettle on. Use the mug that didn't break. Unwrap the tea bag. Add a drizzle of honey. Listen for the whistle. There it is. Pour it; let it steep. Bring it to the bay window. Now sip.

Finally, the pain is letting up.

Again, she sipped, trying to shut off her thoughts and feelings, to numb herself as the pills used to. This was better. Sit. Quiet. Still.

Even long after her mug was empty, she dared not move. Moving could make it happen again. If only she could fall into her bed and sleep long and hard and dreamlessly. She felt safest beneath her covers with her door locked, her consciousness someplace where it didn't acknowledge mental illness. Oh, that she could live in her dreams, where the lights shone and the darkness didn't follow. Oh, sleep. Drift. Sleep.

She woke just before dawn, hunched on the bay window seat, and as her eyes opened, the darkness sank heavily in her chest, so much so that she could hardly rise. It felt like a cry held onto for too long, that swells in the throat and down to the diaphragm. It felt as if she would never be happy again—that her happiness didn't matter anyway.

Lucy.

Why fight it any longer?

Lucy.

Why resist death's sweet release from suffering?

She stood, her back and joints stiff, and exited through the deck door.

Lucy.

She shivered. Though the October air was almost warm, the sand was cool beneath her bare feet. Her trek was slow but determined. Rain fell lightly, a cold mist floating on the wind like the lightest snow.

Lucy.

Was it Emily's voice? Was hers the sound of the Gulf?

Her feet met the water, its chill hand on her ankles.

Was it her mother calling?

She was tired, so very tired of her burden that she closed her eyes and allowed the ocean to rush up her legs. Now waist-deep in the water, her legs numb, she stumbled and slipped under the waves. She saw nothing but the dark, the shadows of forever. It tossed her over and under, burning her eyes, filling her nose and ears. Then there were stars, small pinpricks of light that at first shone dim, then bright, shaping and forming until the purple swirls of the universe appeared at her feet. She was dying. Soon, she would be free, she told herself. She was trapped in the Gulf of the universe, the ultimate riptide.

Then the water turned to space, leaving her floating among the dim distant stars. There was no air, but she didn't need to breathe. A light shone above her. It reached a glowing hand to her.

It's too cold to swim today, she thought. It was too cold. Her legs and arms had numbed; tears burned her cheek. The stars were fading.

Lucy!

It was a different voice calling her name. No longer the Gulf, but the bright light ahead of her. Was it God? Had her soul left its broken shell, free at last?

She reached for the hand.

Lucy!

It was too cold to swim, and the cold did not belong. The universe faded at her feet; the light of the stars had gone. The glowing hand took hers, and she felt herself rising from the water, the wind and rain stinging her skin. She was out at sea, no longer under the water but on its smooth surface as the light pulled her ashore. She rolled over in the sand and coughed and vomited, water leaving her chest, her nose, her ears.

She opened her eyes and saw the little blue house, standing strong and free. The sun was rising. She was calling her name.

29

Audra earned her Tennessee real estate license the summer after she graduated. She found nothing more enjoyable than scrolling online through the for-sale and foreclosure homes around Sevierville. It was the research for her clients that she enjoyed most. The Reynolds wanted a four-bed, three-bath home with an office, combined kitchen and dining, front porch, back patio, and large foyer. Three acres, preferably, and under three hundred thousand.

"You might consider building your house," she had told them earlier that day.

No, they said, there wasn't time for that. They wanted the house by summer, ready for evening parties and weekend cookouts. Oh, and they'd like an in-ground pool.

She often marveled at the contrast between the demands and the financial capabilities of her clients. The Coopers wanted a three-bedroom, two-and-a-half-bath for less than two hundred thousand, please; just a nice neighborhood, something homey.

No problem, she'd tell them, and head back to her computer to search for sales. The trick was paying her bills each month after spending more hours researching than selling.

But she had goals. Once she had established herself, she'd leave the firm and start her own, buy her own house, and root herself in. She could relax and travel as she pleased, knowing there was a place in the world to come back to.

Trouble was, she didn't know *where* to grow her roots. The Smoky Mountains didn't feel like home. In fact, she hardly knew what home felt like, so everywhere felt like someone else's place.

She pushed aside the computer mouse and keyboard and laid her head on her desk, atop the leather blotter. She was getting ahead of herself with all these thoughts of roots and travel. She couldn't even pay her parents for this month's rent without dipping into her savings.

She boarded in the apartment above her parents' garage, always telling herself that someday soon, she'd move out. Once she'd moved out, she could start deciding where to plant her roots. She could find her place. It could be here, or another city entirely— somewhere with culture but also plenty of nature to enjoy. Santa Fe was like that. It was breathtaking, and she'd loved meeting locals in their art galleries and jewelry shops, seeing the mystery staircase and sitting in Saint Francis Cathedral. But it didn't feel like a place to plant roots, just a beautiful place to visit.

If only Lucy had been with her. Lucy helped her understand her place—or at least, to feel as if she belonged in whatever place she was in. It was as if, when she was with Lucy, she was a flower dropping seeds wherever she went, leaving a bit of herself there to return to, where she could understand herself better.

Darn Lucy for not traveling with her! And darn her again for ignoring her texts and calls. Friends since childhood, and after all the things they'd been through together? Selfish, that's what she was. Selfish for thinking she was the only one who felt scared and misunderstood. Did Lucy know that she felt that way, too? Did Lucy know that she wasn't the majority shareholder on mental illness? Plenty of other people struggled with it—many in Audra's college. She didn't need to have it herself to know that it's a big deal for many women—one in three women, to be exact. She'd looked it up after they'd discovered that Lucy's mother had it, too. One in three—and Audra was sure they didn't write off their best friends just because they'd wanted to travel.

But this wasn't fair. Lucy couldn't control her illness, or just push through it, and Audra knew she'd never been selfish a day in her life. She shouldn't have tried to pressure her into traveling before she was ready.

But why did Lucy have to go silent on her? Jackass.

Maybe she deserved this. She should have been a better friend.

She should have made more friends in high school; then it wouldn't have hurt her so badly when Lucy cut her off after one silly misunderstanding. She just wasn't inclined toward having lots of friends. They took too much time and energy, especially when she knew she'd just be leaving in a few years, anyway. She should have just kept to her books and left Lucy behind in Florida. She was an idiot for thinking that Lucy needed her. She couldn't stop Lucy from trying to take her own life so long ago, she couldn't stop Bede from raping her, and she couldn't make Lucy's incurable mental illness go away.

She adjusted a picture on her desk of the two of them two summers ago during her annual trip to the Gulf. Lucy had never traveled by herself again after the one Christmas with her mother. She had tried to fly to visit Audra once, but she'd had a panic attack at the airport and called from the airport, weeping and gasping for breath.

"I can't get on that plane," she'd said. "I can't fight it."

"It's just a plane. It's just like a bus, only it flies."

But it was cramped, and she would be trapped, and Audra wouldn't be there to calm her down for the flight.

So Audra drove or flew to Florida every summer. Sometimes they drove south to Orlando, Miami, or St. Augustine. Lucy preferred to stay near the water, and Audra preferred historical landmarks and museums; they both enjoyed local seafood. She looked for adventure, novelties, the unknown, and Lucy sketched the places they visited.

She wiped the dust off the wooden picture frame and positioned it closer to her computer, then pulled out her cell phone and started to send Lucy a text, but didn't. It was too hurtful to be disregarded.

She closed out her online searches for the night and organized her paperwork into even stacks, dropped pens and pencils in a bronze cup, and tossed her empty container of Chinese carry-out in the trash bin by her feet. Levi would tease her if he knew how often she ordered Chinese. He preferred to cook rather than order out. He shared their mother's gift of food as the language of love.

When Audra's family had moved to Tennessee a few years ago, Levi stayed behind in Greenville with his carpentry business and new wife, Carla. Now they were expecting their second child. As happy as she was for him, the life he lived taunted her with everything she didn't have, and didn't know how to want. She couldn't marry a man and establish roots with him before she'd established her own. She couldn't risk living the life her mother had lived, always uprooting for a husband who wouldn't settle.

So she'd settled on work. Work was everything. Work saved her. If she could only work for the rest of her life and not deal with people who required anything more of her than her expertise, she could be happy—alone.

When Audra got back to her apartment, she tossed her saddlebag purse and phone on her bed and settled into a hot bubble bath with a book and sweet tea, allowing the next hour to slip by unnoted except when she ran more hot water to warm the cooling tub. When she finally emerged, wrinkled and soft, she pulled on her old sweatpants and a T-shirt and blasted her hair briefly with a blow dryer. No lotions or perfumes. No frills or lace. All ease and comfort as she slipped between the sheets of her bed and pulled her phone out to set her alarm.

But when she unlocked her phone, it lit up with missed messages.

"Audra," read one text.

"Are you there?" read the next.

"It's calling me, and I'm afraid."

At first, her heart leaped. Lucy needed her. How quickly could she leave town? How long could she be gone? Then she became nervous, fearful of whatever Lucy may or may not be doing. Her stomach burned. Nearly eight months, and *now* she texts? Suddenly she's worth talking to after months of Lucy's silence? And why? Because Lucy had no other friends?

"Screw you," Audra said to the phone. She wasn't her father. She didn't need to feel needed. She wanted to be wanted—wanted for being exactly who she was. She wanted to know that she was enough for Lucy, her family, herself, not just accepted because she was available.

There was a water stain on her ceiling in the distinct shape of Africa. She found the Ivory Coast on the African spot and imagined herself there, talking with locals and learning their culture. Maybe that's where she belonged.

But what about Lucy? What would Audra do without her? What would Lucy do without Audra? She could ignore Lucy now, as Lucy had ignored her, and their friendship would end, their new lives begin.

"Hey," she replied. "What's going on?"

The text receipt said it was delivered, but after five minutes, it hadn't been read. She sent another and then another. Then she called. It went straight to voicemail. Had Lucy gone to the ocean again? Was she too late to help?

Heart pounding, she felt heavy with fear. Tears rolled down her cheeks though she wasn't breathing enough to cry. She tried to call again.

"Pick up, Lucy!" She was sobbing now, imagining the person she loved most in the world face down in a glassy sea.

There wasn't time—or money—to book a flight this quickly, but Audra pulled her suitcase from the closet and haphazardly filled it with clothes, bathroom items, and her laptop. She would drive the eight and a half hours to the Gulf overnight. It was nearly eight p.m. If she left now, she could get there by five the next morning. Something inside her told her that Lucy was still alive, but she knew that time was not her friend.

30

When Lucy opened her eyes again, she was on her back against the sand. The sun was breaking over the horizon, painting the sky lavender and pink.

"Lucy," a voice said. "Come on, get up."

Lucy mumbled a reply, then the person stood, and by her height and the sound of her voice, Lucy knew her and began to cry.

"Hey," Audra said, "no crying."

"How did you get here?" Lucy said, in a low scratchy voice.

Audra sat beside her. "I got your texts and replied, but then you didn't answer."

Lucy shut her eyes. "My phone died."

Audra squeezed her hand and shook it gently. When she spoke, her voice cracked. "I was afraid *you* were dead."

Lucy looked at her friend, who was wet and sandy from pulling her out of the water, and wept. "I've been terrible to you."

"I know," Audra said, and Lucy laughed a little in the middle of a sob.

"Sit up and make sure the water is out of your lungs." She

pulled Lucy up and wiped the tears from her face. "Take a deep breath. Did it fill your lungs?"

"I guess."

"You threw up quite a bit when I first pulled you out. Should I call 911? Dry drowning is a thing."

Lucy shook her head no. "I think I'll be okay."

"Why'd you do it?"

It—a small word for what the darkness urged her to do. There was no small answer. She shrugged and shook her head. "It comes over me, and I feel like I don't have a choice. It feels like the only way."

"There are always choices. That's how we know we're alive."

"It feels like I don't want to be alive anymore."

Audra squeezed her hand tighter. "Do you still feel like that now?"

Lucy shook her head slightly. "No. It's gone . . . for now."

For now were painful words to say, and hear, and they floated between them like a curse. Neither could speak for fear of catching it. A cloud drifted across the rising sun, and Lucy shivered without its warmth.

"We need to take action," Audra said at last, "get you help. But let's not talk about that now. Let's get you inside and cleaned up and get some food in your stomach."

She pushed herself up from the sand and offered Lucy a hand.

"You deserve better than this," Lucy said.

"I do." Audra smiled, then became serious when she saw Lucy's face. "I've never once thought that, Lucy. Besides, all these years and only one major spat—I think we still have a pretty good track record."

Lucy sniffed and smiled. "Yeah. But we started off with a spat. You ruined my shoes."

"That doesn't count. We weren't actually friends then."

Not friends then? When had they *not* been friends? Audra was there even before she actually was, the shape of her a cavity in Lucy's chest, waiting to be filled.

Yes, Audra was her guide, leading her away from the darkness. For the first time in months, she felt a well of joy fill her up.

After they both showered, Audra made toast and eggs for their breakfast. The kitchen was filled with the early sun, cast in sprawling gold, bright enough to make her squint as she set the coffee to brew. When the pot gurgled and started to spit the aromatic brew into the carafe, she pulled out a wooden chair and faced away from the bay window to wait. She could see how much the sun had faded the old blue-and-white-striped wallpaper, much of which had been pulled from the walls in strips. The drywall bore left-behind glue and spots of mold. There was also a hole in the wall that she would have to ask Lucy about.

Everything else remained almost exactly where it had been when she'd first visited. The ugly green couch. Frank's piano, now out of tune. The Picasso crab on the wall. The green-and-white walls stained with smoke. The house still smelled of tobacco; the wooden floors creaked louder. It was comforting in one moment and startling in another, as if Frank were sitting on the squeaky piano bench with a steady stream of smoke floating from the corner of his mouth, smiling, singing Sinatra.

When Audra thought about this house, it made it easier to understand Lucy's anxiety. The air was thick with memories and constant reminders of the life that had been and, in many ways, never was. If she could feel it this keenly, then Lucy, who had lived here her entire life, was truly suffocating.

As the coffee brewed, she pulled out a notebook to jot down

some thoughts and ideas. Monday was coming, and Lucy needed to go back to work. If she buried herself at home, she'd never get better. Narrowing her world would only make her feel worse. When she was at the grocery store and an attack struck, she could tell herself, "I'll just go to the car until it passes. If it doesn't pass, I'll go home." But if she never left the house and an attack came, where would she go?

Audra knew the answer lay beyond the bay window, and it made her shudder. They couldn't go on this way. As soon as Lucy had showered and eaten something, she'd do some research online. One in three women—certainly they must get help from something other than just pills, which clearly didn't always work.

She poured coffee into two chipped mugs and set them on the table.

"Breakfast is ready," she called down the hall.

Lucy came out in clean cotton pants, socks, and a fresh T-shirt, her curls dripping on her bony back and shoulders. Lucy had never quite regained her appetite after her mother's death. Audra knew her own mother would be horrified by her frightfully frail appearance.

"You look emaciated," Audra told her.

"It's stress. I just can't seem to gain any weight." She slurped some coffee. "Everything goes right through me."

"Didn't need to know that."

Lucy smirked. "It's also genes. Dad is the same way."

"Your mother was also thin."

"She just didn't eat."

"You don't eat."

Lucy gave her a look and crunched into her toast. A seagull perched on the deck outside the window, and she pointed to it. "'Oh that I had wings like a dove! For then I would fly away, and be at rest.' Mom used to quote that psalm when she was in one of her moods. Funny, since she wasn't really religious."

"She went to church."

Lucy nodded and sipped her coffee.

"Where would you go?" Audra asked. "If you had wings."

"Up. Straight to the highest clouds and into that edge, where sky becomes space. And from there I'd watch the stars and call them out by name, and they would know mine, because they would have seen me before, and they would know that I'd always belonged somewhere else, beyond, where they are, and even farther."

Lucy inhaled deeply.

Audra relaxed for the first time since she'd arrived. This was the real Lucy—the Lucy who dreamed out loud.

"I hate October," Lucy said then.

"I know." Audra sighed. She knew this was coming. "How long has it been now?"

"Nine years. She would have been thirteen this year, the age I was when she died."

Lucy talked about her little sister, her long silky blonde hair in one smooth curtain down her back. Her cool blue eyes. Their mother, smiling proudly at her younger daughter.

"She would have grown up and studied something important, like medicine," Lucy said. "Maybe she would've joined the Peace Corps. She'd have done something with her life—something more than sit at the bay window and watch the tides roll in and out."

"I don't know how it feels, exactly, going through your attacks," Audra said. "But I do know what it's like to watch you go through them. I know what it's like to feel as helpless as you feel about them. We're going to get through this." She took Lucy's hand again. "Why don't you paint something? That always helps."

Lucy set her mug on the table and flicked its handle. "I don't paint much for myself anymore. Just things and scenes for other people."

"Why?"

"Same reason my work in college was trash. I just don't feel any of it."

They fell silent for a moment, and Audra searched for words to fill the void. "The highest-flying bird ever recorded only reached thirty-seven thousand feet, and it was some kind of vulture," she said. "I don't think a dove would make it to the stars."

Lucy shook her head and smiled. "How do you even know that?"

"I know lots of random trivia."

She finished her coffee and positioned the cup in the crook of her legs. "Now, let's talk about how we're going to get you the help you need."

Audra didn't regret the words, but she hated their effect. She watched Lucy's eyes darken, her smile fade.

"Do you think I'm weak for not being able to fight it?"

"No. I think you're very brave."

"It's like something inside me is trying to come out. Like I'm pregnant with fear and my body aches to push it out, but there's no birth canal."

Audra inhaled sharply. "I think you need to take charge of the problem. You can't go on living this way."

"What do you want me to do? I'm on the pills."

"But they clearly aren't enough. I think we need to do more research, to find other things to help. What do you usually do when it's this bad?"

"Dad was always here. We took long walks on the beach, even in the cold," she said. "And I painted."

"We can walk on the beach, and you can paint in the evenings. Why don't you paint that dove soaring to heaven?"

"I don't know. I could try."

"What else did you do back then?"

Lucy looked away, knowing that Audra knew the answer.

"I had sessions with the school counselor."

"Exactly." She didn't mention that Lucy should have continued therapy during college, rather than quitting after high school. They couldn't change the past, and it would do no good to add another layer of guilt onto Lucy's life. "I think it's time for you to go back to counseling with a psychiatrist or a therapist or something. It will be good for you."

Lucy nodded, but she was frowning.

"I don't think it would help at this point. It's certain to fail, just like the pills, and I would have wasted all of that time and money and emotional energy. Why can't we just walk along the shore together, like old times?"

"Why don't you get a little rest," Audra said. "Then we'll take a walk."

31

Lucy stood at the blue-gray waters, watching them roll over the white sands, leaving the shore smooth and soft. She felt her feet sink in. Don't sink, she told herself. But she could feel herself sliding slowly downward. She could hear her name whispered on the wind, and she didn't know how to block it out.

"Hey." Audra gripped her elbow and shook her gently. "Come on," she said. "It's going to rain soon."

Lucy stumbled and leaned against Audra to steady herself as she pulled her feet from the sludgy wet sand.

"Come on," Audra said.

She hooked her arm in Lucy's and led her up to the little blue house, up the battered white deck stairs. Lucy had to work the knob to get the door to close.

"Sit. I'll make you tea," Audra said. She clanked the red kettle in the sink and filled it with water.

Lucy sat on the bay window seat and looked out at the Gulf. Lightning flashed against the clouds on the horizon and thunder barked in the distance. She felt it in her gut. It weakened her, and she fought the urge to cry, because crying helped nothing.

Audra prepared the tea, joining Lucy on the window seat with two steaming mugs. "Here you go," she said, patting her leg. "Calm down."

"It's really bad this time," Lucy said. "I quit my job."

Audra stopped sipping her tea but kept her eyes on the steam. "Quit?"

Lucy nodded.

Audra sighed and set her mug on her knees.

"Lucy, you can't just quit. How will you live? Call the Flynns. I know they'd hire you back."

But Lucy shook her head. "I can't stop hearing it. It calls my name, and I'm scared, Audra!"

"This is why you need therapy. Therapy will help you get a grip on it, and going to work will help keep your mind off it."

"Not my mind."

"How will you live?"

How *would* she live? Or rather, how could she? When she left the little blue house, the panic seized her chest. When she was home, the voice wouldn't go away. She didn't want to answer, but how could she resist it? Her life was in the balance, she thought, and only the safety of her locked bedroom with Audra at her side could keep her safe. Audra wouldn't let her go to the Gulf again.

The next day, Audra brought Lucy to the library. After a great deal of research, she found a local doctor who sounded like a good fit.

"She's been to psych therapy before," she told Dr. Keith Greenfield. "At the hospital, shortly after her first suicide attempt, and then with the school counselor off and on. She says they never helped. Her sister drowned when we were all kids; her parents divorced; then her mom died; and now her dad is in assisted living and forgetting who she is. She's just been through a lot, and everything with her dad is taking a toll on her. I just need to know what to do next. "

"I assume this person is in your care, then?" he asked, in a voice like a radio commentator's.

"Y—yes."

"What kind of therapy did these psychiatrists practice? Do you know?"

"I don't, really."

Audra bit at the end of her pencil and squinted her eyes, trying to remember what Lucy had told her. "I know they talked a lot about her past and how she felt about things. They made her draw pictures and look at ink blots, so whatever you'd call that." She laughed nervously.

"Those things can work," he said, "but I'm a strong proponent of cognitive behavioral therapy. Anxiety is complex, but often it is only as powerful as you allow it to be. When patients try to fight it, it makes it worse."

"Yes, she's mentioned that."

"So, basically, we would challenge harmful thought patterns and alter destructive habits."

"And this works every time?"

He laughed. "No, not every time; it depends on the patient. But I've had more positive results than not. I also have patients work on reprogramming how they think—changing negative thoughts into neutral or positive thoughts. The key is to be believable. You can't go from 'I'm terrified at night that a burglar might break into my house' to 'That's impossible! There's no such thing as burglars!' You have to change thinking at a believable gut level."

Audra was scribbling down his words as quickly as she could. "So you've had a pretty good success rate, then?"

"Yes. But like I said, everyone is different." He paused. "You must remember that this illness, while its effects can be drastically reduced, is never really cured. It comes in varying levels of force for the rest of a person's life. Your friend may need to stay in therapy or to return to therapy again, or remind herself of the keys she used in previous sessions to unlock the panic she finds herself trapped in. Does that make sense?"

"Yes." She jotted his words in a basic shorthand she hoped she'd remember later. "This is very helpful."

They talked a bit longer, and Dr. Greenfield agreed to take Lucy on as a new patient. They scheduled her first appointment in a few days' time. Audra thanked him and ended the call.

There. Now she just needed to get Lucy to her appointments every week.

Every week? She didn't know when she'd decided this would become an indefinite stay, but now she found she wanted nothing else. Lucy needed her, and maybe she could be good for Lucy.

Or, like her father, did she just need to be needed? And what about money?

Everything will be okay, she told herself. She had enough in her savings account to survive for a few months. It would all work out fine. She made a list of loose ends in her notebook, then made some calls to her real estate clients.

"We never should've left that poor girl alone," Audra's mother said when she called to update her. "She needed us more than anyone else ever did."

"Dad would argue with that."

"He would, and does! But that's neither here nor there at this point. He has no regrets, and even if he did—regrets don't do us any good."

Her mother paused, and for a moment Audra thought she'd lost the connection.

Then she said, "He's a good man, Audra. You're more like him than you realize."

32

Getting to Dr. Greenfield's office required crossing the bay bridge in morning traffic. Lucy didn't care that they had to inch along the grooved road. She watched the water lap against the pillars, lick at the barnacles, and spray the fishermen in their boats below. It used to feel so special to cross the bridge into the beach city, filled with people who were important to her. The place where she'd kissed her first boyfriend, had her first job.

Now, it led to her father, living in an assisted living facility, which she rarely visited. And soon, it would lead her to a man who wanted to talk about her illness.

She felt a headache coming, a twist in her stomach.

"I don't feel well," she said.

Audra reached for her hand from the driver's seat.

"It's just nerves. You'll be fine. This is good for you."

She turned on some country music, but after a few minutes, Lucy turned down the volume. She wished she could turn down the volume of her mind.

"Looks like it might rain," Audra said as they finally pulled off the bridge. "We'll be there in just a few minutes."

"I feel really sick." She put her hand on her stomach. "Do you have any gum?"

"Check my purse."

Lucy rummaged until she found a stick of mint gum and then reclined her seat and shut her eyes. You're fine, she told herself. You're fine. Don't think about it. Think about good things. Think about—

But Audra was parking along the curb in front of a brick building on Old Dixie Boulevard, just a mile from Blue Herons as the crow—or heron—flies, Lucy noted and would have smiled over her wit had she not wanted to vomit.

"I feel terrible."

"You look nice, though," Audra said.

For her first appointment with Dr. Greenfield, Lucy had showered, dressed in her dark skinny jeans and loose sweater, and even applied a bit of mascara, which she was determined not to cry off. It would be fine. Her past was her past; she didn't need to delve into the emotional complexities of it all. Her sister drowned when they were young; her parents divorced; her mother died; her father was ill. Any other person in the world could have the same story. Children drown all the time, and divorce rates are high. Parents die. People develop mental illness. Life is life.

Audra pushed a few coins in the parking meter and led them in a few quick steps over the cracked sidewalk to a green door. Breathe, Lucy told herself, though she wanted to run. After caging herself in the little blue house for days, the air outside felt thick, the world, spinning too fast.

Just walk. Breathe.

They checked in and didn't have to wait long for Dr. Greenfield to greet them in the waiting room with gentle handshakes. He was

205

a clean-shaven man with kind brown eyes and one front tooth overlapping the other. Lucy guessed he was in his forties.

She followed him into his office, all faux leather and deep cherry wood, books and white sculptures of human figures.

He had an immediate grounding effect on her, helping her to relax within the first ten minutes. He established rapport by talking about his own battles with mental illness, and with his explanation of cognitive behavioral therapy.

But when he started probing further, with more personal questions, she crossed her arms over her chest.

"Lucy, no one is forcing you to be here."

She crossed her legs and sighed. "I've just been through therapy before, and I don't see the point. Mental illness is incurable." It was the truth. The doctor in the hospital had said so. She'd tried to prove them wrong before, but it hadn't worked.

Dr. Greenfield leaned back in his chair. "It's true that there is no 'cure' in the medical sense of the word, but with proper treatment, it can be very manageable."

She all but rolled her eyes. "I don't want to spend my life *managing*. I just want to live."

"Everyone feels anxiety or depression from time to time. Those are universal human emotions. The key to managing mental illness—or, if I might amend that word, *overcoming* it—is knowing how to prevent most attacks, and recover from them when they do happen. Are you willing to work toward that goal?"

What did a life of overcoming mental illness even look like? Would she still hear her name on the Gulf's salty breeze, feel the heavy darkness in her mind?

She uncrossed her arms. "I don't want to do the work and have nothing happen."

He put up his hands in gentle surrender. "You won't know until you try." He smiled. "I'm willing to try with you."

It was a big risk. If she failed, she would have nothing left but the walls of her locked room and the endless racing of her heart. She would surely end up giving in to the call of the dark Gulf, finally finding rest with her sister. She could almost feel the salt burning her eyes, her nose and throat. It gave her goose bumps and knotted her stomach.

"Are you willing to try with me, Lucy?"

She slowly nodded.

He smiled and clapped his hands. "Then let's get to work!" He shifted in his seat and leaned toward her. "Cognitive behavioral therapy is all about reframing negative thoughts. To do that, we need to know what you're thinking. What do you think triggers yours attacks?"

She hesitated.

"Your first attack occurred shortly after your sister's death," Dr. Greenfield said. "Why do you think that happened?"

Suddenly she regretted her decision to push through with this.

"The stress of it, I guess."

"What were you thinking about in the days leading up to that first attack? Do you remember?"

"Not really. I remember feeling scared."

"Scared of what?"

Lucy uncrossed her legs and pressed the soles of her sneakers into the Oriental rug.

"I was scared of what Emily's death meant for my family."

"What did it mean?"

"I didn't know. That's why I was scared."

"Fearing the unknown is normal and understandable. What gave you cause to fear the unknown? Were your parents fighting?"

"No. They were hardly talking, actually. My mom kept to her room. I think . . . I think I was afraid of losing her more."

"More?"

She looked away from him.

"She was always emotionally distant. Emily had helped her stay . . . present. I took it very personally growing up. I know now that she was mentally ill, so it's not an issue anymore. Plus, she's dead." She chuckled, hoping to lighten the mood, but Dr. Greenfield leaned forward intently.

"Why did you fear your mother's withdrawal? What was at stake for you?"

Now she looked straight into his deep brown eyes.

"I feared she would never . . . love me."

Then her tears came, and she snatched a tissue to dab them away.

He waited for her to compose herself.

"So, it's likely you were telling yourself, even subconsciously, 'With Emily gone, now I'll lose my mother, too, and all chance of being loved.' Is that right?"

She pulled at the sleeves of her sweater and tried to swallow back another cry. "Kind of. At first, I hoped . . . maybe . . . she might . . . love me . . . since Emily was gone." He handed her a tissue, and she cried into. "And then I felt guilty, like I'd possibly wanted my sister to die. And I didn't! I know that I didn't. I just wanted my mother to . . . love me."

"My question is this: Was your mother the only person left in the world to love you?"

She shook her head. "No. I had my dad . . . and Audra. But then Audra moved away."

"And now your dad has moved away, as well. You seem to have an attack whenever you're confronted with change or loss, and, as you said, you fear losing your source of love."

"Yeah." She dabbed at her eyes again. "But I don't even deserve to be loved, so what difference does it make?" She snatched more tissues.

"The very notion that you crave love is the reason you deserve it. You are human, and all humans crave and need love. It's part of our makeup." He waited while she blew her nose. "What's at stake for you if you are not loved?"

"I—I guess I won't know why I'm alive."

"I have a bit of homework for you this week. I want you to start a thought diary. First, I want you to list all the reasons you are lovable and deserving of love—this is how you start reframing negative thoughts. Then, whenever you're feeling anxious, write your thoughts in this diary, even if you know they're ridiculous or you're not really sure what you're thinking. At the end of each day, choose a fear and write out why you're afraid of it. What's at stake for you? What's the worst that can happen? Why is it important to you? Once you know the fear and what's at stake, you can reframe the thought."

Audra waited for Lucy in the cheerful lobby of Dr. Greenfield's office. She sat on a lumpy blue couch, her red sneakers clashing against the short purple carpet speckled with yellow. She stared at the framed posters on the wall: an Icelandic waterfall, and a motivational scene with a reminder: *Don't believe everything you think.*

"Well, I think this carpet is hideous," Audra said to the poster, "and I believe it."

She had scheduled Lucy for an hour-long appointment. Despite her friend's nerves and misgivings, Audra noticed that Lucy had tried to look her best, as if eager for a change, hopeful about the outcome.

Audra always felt Lucy's hope. She was also aware when Lucy lost it, those moments that drew her to the Gulf. It was these times that Audra feared most.

What would the second half of her life look like without Lucy? What would it say of her, Audra, that she could not save her best friend?

Don't believe everything you think.

The trouble with thoughts is that they rise not from the mind, but from the core, the gut sensation that validates thoughts before they're even words. To believe at all is to believe *with* all. To change your thoughts, you must change your gut feelings, Dr. Greenfield had told her on the phone. To change your gut instincts, you must prove to yourself that something else is true. Was it true that saving Lucy would make her life valuable? Was this what her father had searched for in his ministry all these years—proof that he is valuable?

When Lucy came out an hour later, her face was red, and her makeup had smeared, but she smiled a little at Audra.

"How'd it go?" Audra asked as they walked to the car.

"Fine," Lucy said, and she linked her arm in Audra's.

33

Lucy sat at the shoreline with a notebook and pencil as the sun set that evening. Rain fell in noncommittal spurts around her, leaving dimples on the sand. But the rain can't leave its prints on the Gulf; they disappear, and the Gulf rolls on.

She was the sand, pounded by waves and rain, wearing the hardened marks of too many storms. A drop landed on the page, and she wiped it away, leaving a damp spot behind. *Oh that I had wings like a dove! For then I would fly away and be at rest.* Did she need to fly away? Time would tell. If she could indeed manage, or overcome, she wouldn't need to go anywhere.

"God, help me," she prayed.

I'm lovable because I'm human, she wrote. The words felt forced. *I deserve love. Every living thing deserves respect.* She crossed out *respect* and replaced it with *love. I'm lovable because I love others.* Did loving others make anyone lovable, or was loving others the result of loving oneself? What truly gave life value? *I'm lovable because Audra loves me. I'm lovable because Dad loves me.*

Did someone else's love make her lovable? What if their love went away? What if they died and left her? She'd be back to square one.

I'm lovable because I am me. That felt strange to write, but also strangely authentic. *I'm lovable because I am the only me.* That line felt empowering, uplifting. *I'm the only me; therefore, my life has value. Whether no one else in the world ever loves me, I will love myself because I know my worth.*

She turned to a clean page and began to sketch, to really sketch from somewhere deep inside herself, for the first time since her mother died.

She outlined a woman extended in space against a sea of stars, reaching for a distant light. A sketch wouldn't do. She needed acrylics.

Pushing up from the sand, she hurried to the little blue house, past Audra's watchful gaze in the kitchen, to the easel in her room. She left only for a cup of water for her brushes, then worked in frenzied motions, creating an underpainting in light copper tones on a large white canvas. The woman was naked, vulnerable, exposed. Her eyes looked up, glossy and wide, hopeful. The light.

As long as she believed in light, she had hope for another day. Another sun to rise and fall beyond the horizon.

That night, she lay next to Audra, arms linked as if they were children again. Neither said anything. Lucy knew by Audra's breathing that she was awake yet restful. It seemed to Lucy that they were maintaining a fragile balance between a desperate past and a resolute future, each fearing how the scales might tip.

In the morning, Lucy woke with the familiar weight on her chest, the dread of another day. What did she have to dread? Audra was here, she told herself, and she had to write in her notebook. Why must her heart race and her head spin? Already she wanted to cry, and the sadness lodged under her collarbone and burned.

She looked at the tear-stain-shaped watermark on her wall. It made the sadness worse, as if it manifested itself around her tangibly, so that even the walls cried. She couldn't manage her inner chaos while living in its very manifestation. This poor old house, she thought. So loved, yet unloved, and misunderstood. Surely if she could overcome, it could, too. They could strip the wallpaper and sand the walls, then paint them new and fresh. New doorknobs that opened easily. A kitchen faucet that didn't leak. It wouldn't cost much. She'd use her small savings and stretch every dollar.

"Wake up." She nudged Audra awake. "I have an idea."

She explained everything as Audra rubbed the sleep from her eyes.

"Good," Audra finally said. "I've been wanting to fix this place up."

Lucy knew that Audra loved few things more than a good home project.

Lucy slipped on jeans and sloppy sweater and pulled back her curls with a handkerchief headband. "I'll start breakfast while you get dressed," she said. She knew her energy wouldn't last forever, and she had to get to the hardware store for supplies.

After they ate, Lucy drove them to the store in her father's old Volkswagen. She'd insisted on driving—which calmed her some, as driving always did—but the anxiety rushed in as soon as she entered the store.

"Can I help you, Ma'am?"

It was an elderly man; Lucy knew without even looking at him, because his voice sounded much like her aging father's. He wore suspenders and an old red cap.

"I need to . . . umm . . . tear down some wallpaper." She was fine. It was just a store. But it was starting to spin, and the elderly man sounded as if he were talking through a long tunnel.

No! There was no need for this! It was just a hardware store! Yet she wanted to run. The older man was now looking her in the face, holding her captive with his helpfulness.

"We want to get the wallpaper off," Audra said, "then clean the walls of any mold or glue spots," Audra said.

Sadness burned in her collarbone. Why couldn't she just do this simple thing? Her mind made the store a danger zone and begged her to run.

"Right this way." The man led them to an aisle near the paints, where he talked about more products than Lucy could ever hope to remember, or understand.

"I'll just take whatever . . . whatever you think is best." She dug for gum in her purse with a hand that felt boneless.

"You got mold on the walls underneath?"

"Yes," Audra said.

The old man started a keynote address on molds, their remedies and prevention. This was Florida, and Floridians must be proactive.

Lucy tried to remember what Dr. Greenfield had said. What's at stake . . . How did it go? What was she thinking that led to the attack? She couldn't remember! She knew only that she wanted to leave and forget the whole thing.

"White vinegar—now there's a gem!" the old man was saying.

"I'm sure," Audra said.

"You got a spray bottle?"

"I'm not sure."

"We got one here." He led her down a few aisles and handed her an empty green spray bottle. "Don't dilute it. Just spray the vinegar over the walls once you get the paper off and let it sit there for about an hour."

Breathe. What are you thinking?

She was thinking that she didn't want to be there, that she just wanted to be home. But why? Why did home make any difference? Because she felt safe there? And why, with the Gulf just beyond the rotting deck?

"Is there anything else I can help you with?" the man asked.

Lucy eagerly assured him there was not.

She felt emotionally exhausted by the time they returned to the little blue house.

"Why don't you go and write in your notebook," Audra said. "I know you were fighting an attack back there."

But there was work to do, and Lucy felt an urgency to get it done, as if her life depended on it.

"I'll do it tonight when I go to bed," she said.

Then she filled a bucket with the pungent removal solution, and she and Audra sponged it over the walls, standing on kitchen chairs to reach the high places.

"What about the furniture and decor?" Audra asked, hands on her hips as she assessed the living room.

Lucy joined her. "What do you think?"

"I think we should toss anything you don't love."

The Picasso crab went first, thrown out the front door to be hauled away with the garbage. Out went the sconces, mirrors, and shag rugs, followed by the lampshades. Lucy decided to keep the brass lamps and paint over the bases, perhaps white or pewter. The remaining wall hangings went, too. She didn't like any of them. Her mother had hardly liked them either, and her father had scrutinized them with displeasure more than once.

By the time she'd cleared the living room, night had fallen, and the wallpaper was ready to remove. Some of it had already fallen from the wall. As she pulled it off and sprayed the mold with vinegar, she imagined what her mother might say if she could see her now.

Really, Lucy—tearing the whole place apart?

"It's twenty years overdue, Mom. It was hideous, and you know it."

The strips fell from the walls like seaside grass bending in a storm. Lucy gathered and rolled them into heaps in the corner.

You can change your outward appearance, but you'll never change what you are, Linda said as Lucy scraped the walls.

No, she wouldn't think about that now.

What will your father say when he sees what you've done?

Lucy's breath caught.

You've damaged this place far worse than I ever could.

She sat in a chair and surveyed her work, her deconstruction of place and self. The deeper she went, the more dirt and mold and ugliness she found, as if her illness also resided in the walls.

You can peel the house back to its frame, but you'll still be in the same place, her mother said.

Then Lucy noticed small spots on the wall behind the table, dark spots that appeared to be moving, like chocolate syrup dripping. It could be mold, but the strange movement compelled her to look closer. Inches from the wall, she saw that the spots were not spots at all. They were holes, and the holes were growing, moving—hundreds of little bugs, crawling, spinning, eating down the wall.

She screamed and ran out the deck door and down to the sand, shaking and rubbing her body and hair, as if she, too, were crawling with bugs.

"What is it? What's the matter?" Audra ran out after her.

"Termites!"

Peeling off the wallpaper had revealed them, shortly before

216

they would have eaten through that, too. They were devious insects, hungry for destruction. Her father had warned her about them more than once.

"They lived under the rocks leading to our old porch when I was a kid," he'd told her. "My mother warned my father they were coming, but he didn't listen. The house wouldn't pass inspection when he wanted to sell. They had to condemn the old place." As a child, she'd imagined her father's boyhood home eaten from the inside out, leaving only a rotted skull—two empty window eyes, a screaming-door mouth.

She was trembling and crying. How long had they been there? How would she get rid of them? What if she dug to the root of herself and found nothing but her damaged soul, eaten from within?

The Gulf behind her rushed onshore. It lapped and fell. The wind rode upon its waves and carried her name.

"Lucy," Audra gripped her arm, "it's okay. We'll get a hotel room tonight. I'll pay for it. And we'll call the exterminators tomorrow."

Why did it have to go wrong when everything was feeling so right?

"Let's go pack a bag and get out of here." Audra said, leading them inside. "Get your notebook."

Was this how life would always be? Destruction masked in moments of peace?

She threw jeans and a sweater, sweatpants and a T-shirt into their shared suitcase, along with a few toiletries. Audra drove them to a cheap touristy motel near the bay bridge, checked them in, and led them to a first-floor room that smelled of smoke and mold.

They washed their faces and pulled on pajamas, then crawled into the queen-sized bed, shivering between the cool white sheets.

"Here's your notebook," Audra said.

"I don't know how to record my thoughts," she said. "It feels pointless. I don't know what I'm thinking or what's at stake, much less how to *reframe* it."

"Well, why don't we practice together? Why didn't you want to be in the hardware store earlier?"

"I feel safer at home."

"Are you, though?"

"I guess not. But if I'm home, it's okay if I have an attack."

"Why is it okay?"

"Because I don't want to be seen having an attack."

Audra smiled. "You know that no one can tell when you're having an attack, right? On the outside, you look just fine. I know this because I know the things you do when you're struggling. But after that first attack at school when we were kids, you've never made a public show of it. You always hide it. So, what's at stake for you if you have an attack in public?"

Lucy knew the answer. "I'd be embarrassed—and people would, you know . . . think badly of me. And not like me."

Audra took her hand. "Honey, I've got news for you: No one out there knows you well enough to like or dislike you, and no one's ever going to think badly of someone with mental illness. Well, they might, but you can't control that, and those people probably just need to learn a thing or two."

Lucy hadn't ever considered these things before. Having Audra explain it this way made her feel better, although she wasn't sure how this knowledge would affect her during her next public outing. She still felt like she'd have to fight off an attack, and she was just so tired of fighting.

"Can I ask you something?" Audra said.

"Of course."

"Are you renovating the house to sell it?"

"I don't know."

She remembered the box of paperwork under her bed. Since the house was legally hers now, she could sell it. She could be rid of it once and for all—its problems, its painful memories, and maybe, just maybe, even the Gulf. Where else would she live? What might she see out her new back window? Would it mean anything to her, and did she want it to? Could life possibly be more than the ocean in her backyard?

"I don't know," she said again.

Audra nodded, and Lucy could feel her body relax. Audra wrapped her arm around her, kissed the top of her head, then rested her head on the kiss.

After three days, they came back to the little blue house, now dusted in fallen termites.

"If you see any more, give us a call," the exterminator said.

"How bad is the damage?" Audra asked.

"Thankfully, not too bad. Looks like a new colony flew in and settled here—not surprising, given this warm, moist fall. You can probably just spackle the walls and be good as new."

Audra swept the bodies out to the deck, and Lucy caulked the holes. They stripped the living room next, watching the green-and-yellow stripes fold up on themselves as they rolled to the floor. Tobacco had infiltrated the porous walls so much that Lucy struggled to scrub away the residue.

"When you paint it, it'll go away," Audra said, hoping it was true. "What colors are you going to use?"

"I was thinking green for the kitchen—a fresh bamboo green—and white for the living room and halls."

"Just white?"

Lucy nodded. "Why not? It'll be fresh and bright." White was a fresh canvas full of endless possibilities for decorating. "It'll be a bright white—so bright it's almost blue."

"What about the furniture in here?"

Lucy surveyed the room that still held the old upright piano, long since out of tune. Her father's ashtray still rested on the top, waiting for him to light another cigarette and fill the house with song. The coffee table could go. But the ugly green couch—for a moment, Lucy couldn't decide. So much of her life had been spent on that couch, waiting for Audra to arrive, watching her mother bottle-feed Emily, listening to her father play the piano. It was as if it had been a kind of glue struggling to hold her family together.

No. Now was not the time to sentimentalize furniture and fixtures.

"It all goes, except for the piano."

Audra agreed and played an arpeggio on the old wooden keys, abruptly pulling back her hand after a few notes. "You need to call a tuner if you have any money left over. I don't know if that came out as major or minor."

Lucy laughed—a generally unremarkable act, except that she hadn't truly laughed in a very long time.

34

Lucy had never liked her hair, even as a child. Her mother had kept it short so that Lucy could manage it more easily, allowing it to air-dry into a cloud of blonde curls that were neither ringlets nor waves.

"You'll hate this hair all your life," her mother told her one summer morning. "It's just like your father's."

Lucy had just taken a bath and was sitting on a stool so her mother could trim her hair. Emily played in the hall with a hard-bodied doll with real hair to brush and style. Emily stroked its long, waxy hair with a comb.

"I want long hair like Emily's," Lucy said. The three-year-old's hair fell past her shoulders in a silky curtain of gold.

"She has straight hair."

Straight hair like her mother's, not frizzy like her father's.

"I want hair like Lucy's!" Emily said.

Linda laughed. "No, my darling. You're perfect just as you are." She stooped and kissed the small girl's wide, smooth forehead.

Lucy considered her mother's words, rolling them around in her mind like tasting a food for the first time. Lucy would hate her hair all her life, but Emily was perfect. It didn't seem fair that she must hate her hair; she hadn't picked it out in the first place, and she could certainly do nothing about it. The same was true of Emily. And what if Emily *did* want Lucy's curls? What if Lucy's hair was, in fact, enviable, and her mother simply couldn't see its beauty? Was it so bad to be like her father?

Lucy hadn't thought about Emily's doll in years. She'd had no reason to. But when she opened the linen closet and pulled out the little stool she'd sat on while her mother trimmed her hair, it brought everything back, the strangeness of it startling her.

"You okay?" Audra asked.

Lucy handed her the stool. "Yeah. Here. Throw this out."

Audra inspected it a moment as if she might protest throwing out a perfectly good stool, but she took it to the door without comment and tossed it onto the growing garbage pile.

By now, the kitchen, living room, and hallway had been stripped down to drywall, sanded, and prepared for paint. They tossed out the shower curtain with the anchor design and threw away the shag rugs and curtains. All that remained were the three bedrooms, one of which Lucy could hardly acknowledge. The sooner she did it, the sooner she could get it over with, but she felt ill at the thought.

"Which room should we do first?"

"My parents' room."

Audra knew as well as Lucy did that Emily's closed door would be the hardest to open. They passed it on the way to the master bedroom as if it didn't exist, as if it led only to a closet. They silently opted to clean out the master bedroom next and ignore Emily's for the time being.

Her parents' walls were white, almost unfinished, as if they'd been coated in primer and deprived of color. "How did I never notice these walls when I was a kid?" Lucy said.

Most of her father's clothes, his picture of Linda, and his favorite books had moved with him to Emerald Coast, leaving behind the long, low dresser where Linda had once stored her lingerie and solitary bottle of perfume.

"Not much to do here," Audra said. "Do you want to keep the furniture? We can probably refinish it."

"I'd rather sell it." She wanted it all gone—the furniture and the memories. Like the bowl of shells that Emily once collected, they were broken treasures without purpose.

"There's really nothing to do here but list the furniture online to sell," Audra said. "Let's move on to the next room." She looked Lucy in the eye. "Which'll it be?"

Breathe, she told herself. "Let's just go for it," she said.

She led them to the door across from her bedroom, closed her eyes, and gently twisted the doorknob, clutching the doorframe as if she might fall into an abyss if she lost her footing. Why was she so anxious about this? She opened her eyes. There rested the little unmade bed with the pink gingham quilt, the pink walls, the pale furniture still holding books, toys, and clothes. The nightstand still bore her mother's pain medication and an empty bottle of ginger ale. The chair where Lucy had sat to care for her mother each day still stood on the little white rug by the bed.

With a trash bag in hand, Lucy entered this time capsule of artifacts from her past. She sat in the chair and rested her hand on the bed, as if she could absorb the aura of her mother and sister. The air was so thick with nostalgia, she wondered if Emily could be standing in the corner, blowing memories like bubbles.

Lucy felt herself suffocating, her heart rate rising. Why was she anxious? Linda and Emily were dead. Gone. This was just a room.

But it was filled with the loss she struggled so hard with, the loss that left her yearning for the love she could never know.

"What are we keeping?" Audra asked, trash bag in hand.

"Nothing. We'll sell the furniture and toss everything else."

She stuffed her mother's pills and the empty soda bottle in the bag, then the bed lamp and pillow, and stripped off the bedding.

Audra's flip-flops smacked the floor as she cleaned out the closet and dresser. "We could donate these clothes. They're in great condition, considering."

"Fine." Lucy lugged her trash bag to the deck and returned with another empty one, this time filling it with Emily's teddy bear and dolls.

Audra nodded. "I'll go do your closet." She claimed one of the two remaining bags.

"Just leave the art pieces," Lucy said.

Audra rolled her eyes. "Well, yeah, I wouldn't have thrown those away."

Audra didn't throw much away because Lucy didn't have many possessions. She had far more mental clutter than material objects. Only a few weathered shirts, a skirt she never wore, and a few meaningless knickknacks went in the bag.

Then came the artwork: sketches and canvases, some framed, all collecting dust. Three nine-by-nines: a half-smoked cigarette, a chipped teacup, a sandpiper. A collection of connected sketches titled *The Flower*. Nature scenes. An impressionistic profile of her father. The silhouette of a woman Audra knew to be Linda.

And then an unfinished work: an underpainting stained in brown of a naked woman floating in space. The woman struggled above an indiscernible mass, as if the universe consisted of liquid and the woman were treading its water, hand outstretched for help toward a conspicuous light.

"Hey, Lucy?" She carried the canvas to Emily's room. "Why didn't you finish this—the one you started the other day?"

"Oh. I just didn't."

"Well, I think you should."

Lucy shrugged.

Audra carried it back to Lucy's room, where, instead of putting it with the other art pieces, she set it on the empty easel.

"I think we can use your other pieces to decorate the walls once they're painted," she called.

"At least until we have money for better ones," Lucy offered back.

Lucy hadn't forgotten about the underpainting. It had felt good to create it, and she planned to finish it when the time was right.

35

They hosted a yard sale and posted any remaining items online, garnering enough money for a small gray sofa and a new lamp, with a bit left over to repair the deck. It had been only a week since her first appointment with Dr. Greenfield, but it had felt like a month.

"I'm enjoying the thought journal," she told him at her next appointment. "But I'm not seeing how it will really help. I still have anxiety every time I leave the house."

"It won't go away overnight. The hard part—harder than dissecting and logging your thoughts—is reframing them." He shifted forward in his wingback chair. "The thoughts that fuel anxiety are frauds. They have no bearing on reality." He picked up her thought diary. "For example, your thoughts are telling you that if anyone you love dies or leaves you, you will not be loved. But that's irrational. You will always have people in your life who love you, and a healthy person should always be looking for others to love, to various healthy and appropriate degrees. Spreading and receiving love—that's what we're here for. Does that make sense?"

"Yes."

"So, this is how we reframe our thinking—speaking truth to the fraud, cutting the lies from the thoughts. You can't do this by sitting in your home every day. Reframing can certainly start there, but you have to put feet to your thoughts. Show yourself that truth is truth, to prove it, and thus change your gut instincts."

To put her truth to the test, Lucy planned her first visit to Emerald Coast Assisted Living to take her father to church. She pulled her khaki jacket high around her neck as she and Audra walked up to the entrance.

What was she thinking to make her palms sweat and lungs strain? She didn't want to see her father like this. What if he'd already forgotten her because she'd disappeared for more than two weeks? She would be a failure, a loser of a daughter, a letdown.

Reframe it, she told herself. She was ill, like her father, in her own way. She was getting help, just like he was. She loved him, and love was never a letdown. Deep breath, and push the heavy glass door open. Take the elevator up to the third floor and turn right to the first door on the left. Knock; enter.

"Dad?"

He was sitting on the edge of the bed in brown corduroys, an orange plaid shirt, and a brown knit tie. He clutched his cane and fedora between his legs and looked up to her with dim blue eyes that sought to recognize her. For a moment, Lucy couldn't breathe. Then a smile creased his face, and he pushed up on his cane.

"My girl! Come to take me to church, they told me." He opened his arms, and Lucy relaxed into his chest, wrapped in his arms.

"You look handsome, Dad." She kissed his cheek and positioned the fedora on his head. The familiar tobacco scent had long faded—for the best, she knew, but she missed it. She took his arm to lead him out. "Do you remember Audra?" She motioned toward her friend, who stood in the doorway.

227

He tried to remember, she could see the searching in his eyes, and to avoid hurting her feelings, he said, "Wonderful to see you, dear!" though it was clear he had no idea who she was.

During the service, he sang as loudly as ever and kept rhythm with his cane, but he didn't make a scene with the pianist or anyone else. He seemed preoccupied with trying to recognize people. His head slumped forward in sleep during the sermon, and occasionally, he snored.

When he woke at the end, he appeared startled and afraid, but Lucy gently reminded him where he was.

"Yes, church! Great sermon!" he said, and smiled.

Lucy couldn't tell if he was joking, so she smiled with him. "It's got me hungry. How's Italian?"

"Sounds good to me," Audra said.

"Me, too," Lucy said, unlocking the car. "Let's try Rizzo's Deli, up the street?"

He tossed his hat and cane in the backseat and bent rigidly to climb inside.

When Lucy started the car, he clapped and swayed to music that Lucy and Audra couldn't hear. He sang along with Dean Martin, "Nobody 'til somebody…"

"How are you holding up?" Audra asked.

"It's okay for now, but it's there, ready to attack," Lucy answered.

"But you're doing the work. It'll just take time."

Lucy nodded, but she found herself envying her father. Wouldn't it be easier to forget the bad things and just live in a fantasy world, filled with music?

They ate their pastrami on rye quietly, and Frank became tired before finishing.

"Let's get you home to a nap," she said.

"Home," he said, his eyes on his plate. "It'll be good to go home again."

Without hesitating, Lucy knew she'd said the wrong thing—
that he meant the little blue house, and not Emerald Coast. How
could she tell him he wasn't going home? That the house didn't
even look like his old home anymore? Sadness filled her chest,
but she took his hand. "No, Dad. To your new home . . . at
Emerald Coast."

His eyes became glossy. "When can we go *home*?" he asked.

She rubbed the skin that was spread too thin over his knobby
fingers and bulging veins. She caressed it, brought it to her lips,
and hugged it against her cheek, wishing he'd pull her against him,
stroke her hair, kiss her temple, and sing her a song. "Smile"—that
was the song he used to sing to her.

Smile though your heart is aching.

When they were back in his room at Emerald Coast, she told
him she'd be back soon and tried to hug him again, but his arms
didn't open for her. He was staring aimlessly out the window and
didn't move as they left him.

But as they closed his door, Lucy heard him softly singing,
"Return to me, for my dear, I'm so lonely." She stopped and leaned
against the door to listen.

"You did well today," Audra said, handing her a cup of tea at the
bay window.

Without saying so, she acknowledged her own triumph of
the day, too—that she had stood stalwart with her friend from the
moment they woke.

"I can't do this," Lucy had said that morning.

"Yes, you can. I'll be with you. Be mindful of your thoughts. If
you have to step out and take a breather, do it. There's no shame."

And Lucy had made it without any noticeable setbacks or
episodes. Whenever she'd felt the darkness overwhelming her, she

had reached for Audra's hand in the pew or under the table. Each time Lucy found strength in her, Audra understood the sense of purpose her father found in fulfilling someone else's needs.

Yet still, she pitied him. If only it had been enough for him to know he'd met just one person's needs, to know he'd made a difference in just one person's life.

She paused as she considered how the tables might turn if Lucy ever gained the confidence to face her mental illness alone. Would it be enough for Audra to just be a friend? Would it be enough to be wanted without being needed?

Lucy's eyes searched the water that crashed and rolled harder today, frothy from the wind and rain. "It's angry," she said.

"It's just the weather." Audra sat next to her on the white window seat, delicately handling a hot mug of tea.

"Sometimes I feel like I'll have no choice," Lucy said hoarsely. "It threatens me, and I'm just so tired."

"You always have a choice, Lucy. That's what makes you human. You made a hard choice today to see your dad, and you did great."

"It really was hard."

"That's fine. Next time might be hard, too. The point is that you survived it once, so you'll survive it again. Every time you survive, you get stronger."

Lucy leaned her head against the window and sighed. "I feel *weak*, Audra. I don't want to spend my life on a battlefield surviving but never winning the war."

Audra hated the way Lucy looked toward the Gulf.

"Hey, stop." She pressed Lucy's chin to turn her face from the window. "Don't you think there's been enough loss here?"

Lucy sipped her tea and set the mug on the tile floor at her feet.

"You'd think I'd be glad to be the last De Rossi female standing—the only one to survive the Gulf—but it actually makes me wonder what's wrong with me. Why them and not me? I have nothing to offer this world."

Audra shook her head. "Remember what Dr. Greenfield told you: You have worth because you are human. You are the only Lucy De Rossi, the only one with your DNA who will ever live. The chances of any of us being born are one in a zillion. You have your own life with your own choices in your own story. You don't have to be Emily or Linda—or anyone else in your idealized world."

The rain fell harder, punching the bay window, and Lucy shifted to look over her shoulder at the Gulf. It was obscured by the rain, but she knew exactly where it broke on the sand.

"You can be happy, Lucy," Audra said, taking both of her hands and holding them tightly. "I know you haven't wanted to talk about this, but I really want you to consider selling this house."

Lucy felt the pressure increase in her chest.

"You know it's not good for you to live here," Audra said.

"The Gulf is inside me. Moving won't make that go away. Everything that defines me is here."

"And those things will stay with you. Moving won't erase your memories or redefine you. It'll add to you. Even the Gulf is always changing. Why shouldn't you?"

Could she change? After all she'd been through?

All the changes in her life thus far had been done *to* her; they hadn't happened *because of* her. As the little blue house started to look better every day, she wondered whether she could strip away the moldy wallpaper inside herself. She had done pretty well with her father today, though she was exhausted from guarding and reframing her thoughts, from breathing through the pangs in her chests.

Perhaps Audra was right. Lucy looked into her eyes and pressed her lips together in a partial smile of resignation. "I don't know what I'd do without you."

"I know," Audra said.

"Oh, I wanted to show you something." She pushed up from the window seat, and Audra followed her to her bedroom. She opened her nightstand drawer and pulled out a trinket box. "I found it when I was cleaning out the nightstand. Open it."

Audra popped the lid open and pulled out a chain. A half-heart charm dangled at the bottom.

"Remember them?"

"B-E F-R-I-E—," Audra read.

"—S-T N-D-S," Lucy finished, smiling.

Of course, Lucy knew that Audra remembered. Those necklaces had represented true friendship to both girls—as if Lucy had truly split her heart and given one half to Audra.

"They should have put *Best* on one and *Friends* on the other," Audra said.

"I thought that, too. Do you still have yours?"

"Probably buried somewhere in my closet at home."

Lucy smiled and put the necklace back in the trinket box, back in her drawer.

Seeing Lucy's half of their shared necklaces meant more to Audra now than it had back then, now that she'd lived with and helped her best friend for three weeks. She felt more at home than she'd ever felt in her life.

As she followed Lucy back to the kitchen, she considered how they were each a broken heart that only made sense when they were together.

36

By early November, the house was done. The deck was refurbished; the carport was pressure-washed; the windows washed. They'd painted the kitchen walls as green as bamboo and on them hung black-and-white pictures Lucy had hung her sketches—a half-smoked cigarette, a chipped teacup, a sandpiper. The living room and hallway were white, with new blue-and-white-striped curtains in the windows. They decorated with Lucy's nature paintings. A new gray sofa stood in place of the ugly green one, which had worn out its welcome long ago; in front of it lay a new blue rug and a simple black coffee table. Lucy set a bowl of white seashells on the center, with two cork coasters on either side. The piano waited in the corner for Frank's return, still untuned but no longer covered in dust and used ashtrays. The old television, which Lucy rarely watched, sat on a small stand, and the new lamp was positioned on a side table they'd found in an antiques shop.

It needed plants. Some greenery. Something to give it life and keep it from feeling sterile.

"Those things will come with time," Audra said. "No need to rush your decor."

They did all the work themselves except for the outside tasks: fixing the shutters and replacing lost shingles. For these, they hired a local handyman. Lucy moved her easel to Emily's old room, now also white, along with her desk and an antique cabinet for her art supplies. She painted the walls in her father's room a light blue-gray.

Lucy's yellow room remained the same except for a fresh coat of paint and a new bookcase where her desk and easel had been. She'd always liked her room—its cheery sunshine color, the deck outside her window. Now it was even brighter and smelled fresh.

"We did a pretty decent job," Audra said one night. They sat on the new gray sofa with bowls of mint chocolate chip ice cream.

"It turned out better than I'd hoped. Hardly looks like the same place."

Audra swallowed and hesitated over her next bite. "It's in good condition now to sell."

Lucy scraped at her bowl and didn't respond.

"You said you'd consider it."

"I have considered it."

"You could rent it out."

"But I'm doing a bit better these days. Maybe I could just stay here."

It was true. After weekly sessions with Dr. Greenfield, a lot of diary writing, and a renovated house, she felt she had improved. Her mind was learning to control its thoughts and determine the good from the bad, the healthy from the toxic.

"Yeah, but you've been preoccupied these weeks. What will happen now that the busyness is over?"

Lucy's brows lowered.

"You could sell this place, or rent it out. We could travel now and then."

"You know I can't travel. I can't leave Dad, and I'll just keep having attacks the whole time."

"We could take small trips and work up to a bigger one."

Lucy scooped a melting bite into her mouth and rolled it around on her tongue. What if she did sell the little blue house? What could she do? Go back to Blue Herons? Try to find more freelance art gigs? She couldn't live off the proceeds from the house forever. The unknown future frightened her.

But that wasn't a healthy thought. The wallpaper inside her was peeling, and she needed to scrape it off no matter how badly it hurt.

"You could always put it up for sale and see what kind of bites you get on it. No sale is final until you say so."

Lucy mulled it over and, finally, gave in. "Okay."

Audra's spoon stopped halfway to her mouth. "Okay, what?"

"Okay. We can list it and see what happens."

Lucy expected Audra to cheer, but instead, she calmly sucked the ice cream from her spoon. "There's something else I've been wanting to talk to you about."

"Umm, okay." Now she was nervous.

"Just tell me if you think it's a bad idea." Audra shifted, looking into her ice cream bowl instead of at Lucy. "I've thought about this for a while, and it makes sense to me."

"Just tell me. You're making me nervous."

"I'm thinking of staying in Florida and getting my real estate license here. So, unless you have any objections, I'd like to be your roommate and pull my weight financially."

"Objections? This is everything . . . I've wanted this for so long . . ."

Audra wiped a tear from Lucy's cheek.

"I don't know how to handle so much . . . so much happiness," Lucy said. She set her bowl on the coffee table and put her face in her hands. "I mean, this makes me *so happy*," she said, her voice muffled. "But now it'll be even worse the next time you leave! I won't be prepared!"

Audra pulled Lucy's hands from her face. "Stop, now—dry your tears. Look at me." She took Lucy's face in her hands and squared it with her own. "Don't think about the future. All the troubleshooting in the world can't predict life's changes. Enjoy what we have together now. It could last years, or decades, or a lifetime. Not knowing is part of the adventure."

Lucy nodded. "It feels really dangerous to let myself be this happy."

Audra laughed. She empathized with Lucy's struggle. Was there anything more vulnerable than happiness?

"I grew up never wanting a place to feel like home because I was so afraid of losing it. Now I think home isn't a place. It's why I've never really felt rooted to any house or state I've lived in. I think home is a person. That person may change, but it's always a person." She looked into Lucy's eyes. "When I think of home, I think of you. I'm willing to be happy and rooted with you here, for however long that might be."

Getting back to work was the next step. As Audra began working on shifting her life from Tennessee to Florida and earning her real estate license, Lucy painted a few greeting cards and prints for her usual clients. The work kept her busy with the holiday season rolling in, but the money wasn't enough to sustain them.

With a hollow feeling in her stomach, she called Beatriz, who assured her there was still a place for her at Blue Herons. For the first time in nearly two months, she parked around back and shoved her hands in her jacket pockets as she walked around to the white door at the back.

"Lucy!" Beatriz pulled her into a tight hug. "It's so good to see you again. Are you sure you're ready to get back to work?"

"Yeah, I think so," she said, smiling, telling herself the room wasn't actually spinning. "Thank you for holding the job for me."

"No problem!" Beatriz said. "Everything is the same, but Henry has a new job for you." She led them to the front of the store, where Henry was laying out fish in the display case.

"Tell her about our idea," Beatriz said.

"Yes," Henry said, with a warm smile. "We'd like to use more of your art around here to improve our signage." He pointed to various pictures of fish on the displays. "This art was done way back when Charlie was just a kid. It needs to be updated."

"I'd like that," she said.

"And, if you're interested, we thought you might like to sell some of your greeting cards and prints here. We have some shelf space in the grocery area. If it doesn't work out, it's no loss."

"That would be worth a try, I think," she said. Their kindness, thoughtfulness—it was all overwhelming.

"The biggest news," Beatriz said, with her hands clasped, "is that we're opening a restaurant!"

Lucy's eyes widened. "Oh my goodness! Where?"

Henry pointed at the wall across from the display. "We got the burger place next door. We're going to offer shrimp and grits, crab patties, lobster bisque, and fish and chips to start with, and of course, fish platters of all kinds."

"And we'll need menus and pictures for the walls!" Beatriz cut in.

"Plenty to keep you busy, if you're up for it," Henry said. "Charlie's excited about it, too. It's his buddy coming to be the head chef."

Lucy shook her head. "I can't believe it. This is all—it's so great."

Soon, Blue Herons would more than triple its staff, and though the idea of working with so many people for so many customers overwhelmed her, she focused on the Flynns' kindness, and let the gratitude wash over her.

That was her key: *gratitude.* She was grateful for her best friend who had literally saved her life, for her psychiatrist who was weekly helping her to retrain her troubled mind, for the Flynns, for happiness. She only feared that she was on a high tide which would soon start to recede. From a point this high, the drop would be devastating. It wasn't healthy thinking, she told herself, but the old fear was lodged deeply in her mind. She couldn't help but brace herself for the fall.

Since she didn't know how to reframe the inevitability of a fall, she focused on her work. By day, she cleaned, filleted, and weighed fish. By night, she designed menus and greeting cards with Gulf themes, and painted pictures of fish and other marine life to decorate the new restaurant.

Then December came, and with it, visitors to the little blue house, potential buyers who'd long eyed the quaint little house on the sea. Audra said she expected visitors throughout December and January, but no one would likely make an offer until February, when the financial dent of Christmas had smoothed back over and people started thinking about tax returns.

Lucy kept mostly to her easel even as agents showed off her house. She painted a fish market so familiar it startled her. She'd sketched it without a photo, filling in its red siding and people leaving its doors with brown paper packages of fresh fish. She painted a gray sky, the way it was on her birthday when she'd kissed Charlie, really kissed him, for the first time. She painted a slight break in the clouds, just enough for a single ray of sun to warm the dock.

"Where did you get these paintings?" Lucy heard a woman's low, raspy voice coming from the living room.

"Lucy, the owner of the house, is an artist," Audra answered.

Lucy stepped out to the hall to see who was inspecting her work. The woman was wrapped in a European shawl, a hat on her short dark hair, with heavy dark lashes and liner on her upper eyelids. Lucy wanted to paint her standing there, looking at her paintings.

"They're mesmerizing," the woman said. "I collect art, you know. Look at this one, Robert. I can hardly look away from it."

"Mmm, yes, very good." Robert didn't look at the paintings. "How old is this flooring?"

The couple followed Audra and their realtor to the hall, and Lucy stepped back inside Emily's room to resume painting.

"You must be the artist?" The woman had entered the room. "Your work is really lovely."

"Thank you. I appreciate that."

"Oh, and this one!" She pointed to the unfinished painting of the lady extended in space. "I feel as if I know her."

Lucy cleared her throat. "My prints will be for sale soon at Blue Herons, on Main Street."

"The fish market?"

Her tone made Lucy blush. "It's becoming a real landmark in the city."

"Hmm," the woman said. She pointed to the lady in space. "I'm especially interested in this one."

Such a simple painting, yet Lucy felt proud the woman valued it. She seemed to value all of her work, and, by association, her. It was hard to take in this unexpected feeling—this joy, this lightness.

They didn't buy a Christmas tree. After all the money they'd spent on the house, neither wanted to purchase a tree that would just be thrown out in a couple of weeks. Instead, they bought an artificial evergreen wreath and trimmed it with a few bulbs and tinsel, and a star at the top.

On Christmas Eve, they ate two cans of tuna fish on toast with mayonnaise and melted cheese, a pickle on the side. While Audra cleaned the kitchen, Lucy pecked out a few clumsy Christmas carols on the piano, sometimes singing a line or two. In an hour, they'd leave and pick up Frank to attend the Christmas Eve service at church, where the choir would sing of Christ's birth and the children would perform a nativity skit. They would all hold candles and think about the meaning of this holiday—peace, joy, hope, love, life.

Audra called her family—first Levi, who'd stayed in Savannah for the holiday with Carla's family, and then her parents, who'd spent the day ministering at a nursing home. They spoke for only moments before they had to go to prepare for Saul's evening service.

On Christmas Day, they sat with Frank at Emerald Coast rather than bringing him home. Lucy feared that seeing the house in its renovated state might upset him, or, at the very least, confuse him. Her concern likely worked in her favor that day, because Frank enjoyed himself more than usual, singing along with all the Christmas songs on the radio, and occasionally dancing with his cane.

"We've been working on the house, Dad," Lucy said. They were sitting at a little round table in the cafeteria, eating stuffed ricotta shells with overly acidic marinara and dry parmesan.

"Excellent!" he said, but Lucy wasn't sure he knew what she meant. "I worked on a house with my father when I was a boy. One of the best times of my life."

Lucy smiled. He so rarely mentioned his life prior to Linda.

"We took off all the wallpaper and painted. I'd like you to come see it sometime, maybe after New Year's."

He smiled, a tomato stain on his smoothly shaved chin. Lucy wiped it clean.

"Your piano is still there. Just needs to be tuned."

They finished eating, and Lucy led her father to a couch in a large sitting room draped in artificial evergreen garlands and lights. Frank leaned back and closed his eyes, breathing a long, quiet sigh.

"You okay, Dad?"

"Yes, yes. Just a bit tired."

"We painted the kitchen green, the living room, hall, and Emily's room, white, and your bedroom, blue-gray—the color of your eyes." Lucy took his hand and held it in hers, and his blue eyes seemed to understand that the house in question had once belonged to him.

"Emily," he said calmly. "Emily's room was pink."

"Yes," Lucy said, worried he would be upset that she'd changed it. She looked at Audra, who shrugged as if to say *It is what it is*.

"And your room was yellow."

"Yes!"

"It's still yellow," Audra said. "We gave it a fresh coat of paint."

"Yellow for daffodils," he said softly and smiled.

Until that moment, Lucy had never noticed the correlation between the color of her room and her mother's favorite flower. She took a breath and asked the question that had haunted her for her entire life.

"Why didn't she love me? Why didn't Mom love me?"

He fell silent, and from the distant look in his weak blue eyes, Lucy thought the conversation was over. Oh, well. Some things were best left unanswered. Maybe it was best not to know why her mother hadn't loved her.

"She never liked herself," he said slowly. "Perhaps she saw something of herself in you? He took her hand and squeezed it lightly. "She was sick, Lucy."

That old refrain again.

Yet Dr. Greenfield had alluded to something like this just last week. "We can't love others until we love ourselves," he'd said. Even the Bible says to love your neighbor *as yourself*.

Surely her mother had tried. Surely the trying and the failing and the intensity of her feelings was the reason she'd hidden in her room for hours—not because she didn't love her eldest daughter.

"Daffodils, Lucy. Remember the daffodils."

37

She was high, and she knew there was nowhere to go but down. Audra, the Flynns, Blue Herons, her dad, her art—so much goodness and joy. A person can't live like that. You don't get to live on the waves; you have to crash down with them at some point.

When would the inevitable crash come? What would cause it? Reframe the thought—no, there's no reframing the truth. There will always be crashes, and the higher the wave, the harder the crash. Just crash and get it over with!

With sneakers squeaking on the linoleum floor and hands cracked from the cold, she carefully laid out fillets of pink salmon and white flounder on curly leaves of kale over diamonds of ice. Sprigs of rosemary separated the fish from the scallops, and a row of lemon wedges divided the scallops from the shrimp. Her new labels included hand-lettered descriptions and true-to-life sketches of each fish, shrimp, scallop, and so forth. Beatriz praised the display with sincere enthusiasm. No matter, though. Yes, she was grateful and pleased with her own work, but the crash was coming.

When work ended at five o'clock, the winter day had turned to dark, hovering over her walk to her car. She bent her tired legs into the seat and ignited the engine, which greeted her with a gentle ding to indicate an empty tank. Why didn't she pay better attention to these things? She'd have to stop at the Shell station before the bay bridge.

The station was busy with others who knew better than to cross the bridge in high traffic with a low tank. She waited behind a new Ford Taurus, sleek, black, and reflecting the oranges, reds, and yellows of car lights and neon signs. It pulled forward, past the first pump to the second, so Lucy pulled in behind it and rummaged in her purse for her credit card. There it was. Pop the gas cap, make this fast.

She pushed her card in the machine and pulled it back out, punched in her zip code, selected her grade. Then the pump went in the tank. The gas moved slowly through the pump, and she leaned against the car with arms crossed over her chest, teeth chattering.

If she hadn't looked past the pump to the other side, she'd never have seen him. His hair was longer, and his thin lips were now shrouded in a mustache and goatee peppered in black and gray, but she knew him immediately, and he knew her. How long had he been watching her before she'd looked up?

Bede took a deep breath as if they'd been in conversation and pulled up the sides of his pants. "So, how've you been?"

The gasoline flowed, the numbers on the tank ticked, the Taurus in front of her car was reflecting the lights, but Lucy was alone in the dark, hearing nothing but the sound of her breathing, feeling the clenching in her chest.

"Fine," she heard herself say through a fog.

His pump clicked, and he turned and clenched the handle to squeeze out a few more drops. "You still living in the blue house?"

"No, I sold it." She hadn't, but she didn't want him to know where to find her.

He capped his gas tank, but rather than get back in his car, he came around to her side of the pump. Get back in the car, she told herself. What was he doing? Calm down. Breathe. Don't crumble. No, swallow that pain your chest. It can't hurt you. Cry if you must. It's okay to cry.

But crying is weakness. Don't let him see you weak.

"I'm sorry about your mama," he said.

She pulled the pump out of her tank but didn't sheath it. Holding it felt safer. "What brought you here now?" she asked.

Bede shrugged casually. "Just . . . uh . . . I'm just passing through on the way to New Orleans." He pulled up on his belt again and leaned an arm against the pump. "You're a beautiful woman, Lucy. Your mama would be proud."

Showed how well he knew her mother.

He didn't know how to know a woman by anything but her body, something he was too vile to love, understand, or value. Did he love himself—a man who spreads darkness and dread? Did he loathe himself as much as she loathed him? Asking would do no good. Antagonizing him would only increase her own pain. There was no justice for her younger abused self. There was only the power she held now.

"I think every woman is beautiful in her own way." She sheathed the gas pump and looked him square in the eyes. "If I were you, I'd stay away from beautiful women."

He understood the flash in her eyes, for he took a step back and cleared his throat. "Good seeing you again, Lucy." He lumbered back to his car, and Lucy kept watch until he pulled out of the station and onto the busy road, disappearing into the nameless masses.

Her hands felt weak on the steering wheel as she inched over the bay bridge. The old familiar pain burned in her chest and down her arms. It was there when she'd stood her ground, and it was there now in the quiet space of her own car.

Yet she breathed. One breath in, another breath out.

She lowered the windows and let the cold air smack her face and pull her hair. The wind stung her eyes, and she let them burn her cheeks with salty tears.

Lucy.

Her name drifted from the Gulf, familiar, like an old tune her father might sing.

Lucy.

It was louder, and for a moment when the traffic halted, she closed her eyes and listened, inhaling and exhaling on the syllables.

Lucy.

Now she turned off the bridge on the road to her house. There it was, the one light in the carport glowing yellow and hazy, the streetlights dim. Audra's car was gone. She didn't walk upstairs to the front door, or even around back to the deck. Rather, she kicked off her socks and sneakers and carried them through to the carport, over the grassy dune, and across the sand to the moonlit Gulf. It reached for her toes and dampened the hem of her jeans. The waves crashed, rolled, receded, and rose up again. It was the rhythm of the Gulf, of mental illness, of life. Roll with it. Draw back as you need to, then rise up again.

Lucy.

Dropping her shoes and purse in the sand, she knelt and stretched her palm, trembling, over the water, letting it rush between her hand and the sand.

Lucy.

"No," she whispered.

The Gulf rushed at her harder, nearly knocking her off balance, but she braced on her hands and knees, the pain in her chest rushing up in sobs that rose and ebbed with the water.

Lucy.

"No more," she said, louder this time. If it took her, she would ride it out until the storm passed, then swim back to shore. If it rolled her under, she'd hold her breath until it was safe to breathe. It could crash over her, but she would never let it crush her.

Not anymore.

"Lucy!"

Lucy looked up at the water, then over her shoulder. A light was growing brighter, growing closer to her.

"Lucy!"

Lucy stood when she recognized the voice, the flashlight of a cell phone, the smaller figure. In a moment, Audra held her in her arms, her chest heaving.

"You're—you're still here," she said.

"Yes," Lucy said, "and I'm staying."

38

The little blue house sold in February, just as Audra had predicted, to a couple looking for a vacation home. Nearly every house on the street was a rental now. They'd likely rent it out for most of the year, and Lucy recognized that her disappointment stemmed from a subconscious fantasy of a family of four, a mother and father and two daughters, moving in and loving the house, the grassy dunes, the silky sand, the emerald coast.

But a new family couldn't rectify her broken one, she told herself. The house was moving on, and who knew all the families it would meet, all the stories it would hold.

They didn't have a lot to pack, but they ended up with more boxes than either had expected. How strange to see a life summed up in boxes. This must be how Audra had felt her whole life, like a softshell crab, vulnerable—yet somehow, Audra didn't fear the vulnerability; she rode it like another wave, feeling its movement, accepting its unpredictable but inevitable break, knowing she would survive it.

The week before moving day, Lucy sat in her art studio, Emily's old room, finishing the painting of the lady extended in space. A brush of bronze on her bare leg, spits of dim blue stars on a dark universe. Swirls of midnight blue and sinister green for the Gulf at her feet. Gray for the eyes looking upward, squinting. White for the light extended, touching the hand that was reaching, ever reaching.

"Who is she?" Audra asked, watching over Lucy's shoulder.

"Me. Some woman I'll never know. The inside of every person with mental illness, I guess."

Audra studied it, lips pursed, and Lucy took her hand.

"You're the light," Lucy said.

"Not for everyone."

"For me."

The light that comes to everyone in different forms—human, spiritual, material—if one only looks for it. It was the hope that precedes all the help and prayers, therapists and friends, medications and thought diaries.

Audra squeezed her hand and rested her head atop Lucy's.

"You're your own light, Lucy."

"You saved me," Lucy said.

"I just helped you save yourself. You're doing the hard work of living and fighting every day."

For the first time in her life, Lucy felt more like the hero in her own story than the victim on the sidelines. It *did* take a lot of courage to get out of bed some mornings, and some days she simply couldn't, but other days she would again, and it was okay that other people might think she was ridiculous. Her battle wasn't theirs, and theirs wasn't hers.

"It's your best yet. What will you call it?"

"I don't know. Some things are too hard to put into words," Lucy said.

"I think the anxiety is at her feet, and the hope is in the light where she's reaching. It seems more like—"

"—like that moment after an attack, when you don't know whether to be depressed about it, angry that you have them, or glad it's over. You feel naked, exposed to the worst of yourself. You feel humiliated, even though you're all alone."

"Just call it *Anxiety*."

Lucy shook her head. "That feels too on the nose, and not authentic. It's more than anxiety; it's someone surviving mental illness."

"Call it *Courage*."

Lucy smiled. "That'll do."

Lucy wrapped and slid her paintings carefully on the backseat of her car the morning of the move. The movers loaded their furniture and boxes into a truck, leaving the blue house barren but for the sunlight, Audra, and Lucy, who stood at the bay window.

"You okay?" Audra asked.

Lucy nodded. She wasn't ignoring or discrediting the pain in her chest, the urge to run to the Gulf, away from it, anywhere the attack would lead. She was letting it be. Who would she be without her little blue house on the Gulf?

I am Lucy.

The Gulf, the mental illness, the loss—those things no longer defined her. They were simply a part of her ever-changing, ever-surprising story.

"Let's go," Audra said. "The movers will be waiting for us."

Lucy followed her through the kitchen and then the living room one more time. As Audra descended the front steps, Lucy turned back once more.

There was no use being sentimental. No use thinking about Mom, Dad, Emily. No point in memorializing the storms or happy summers with Audra. No good saying good-bye because she couldn't say good-bye to something that was already gone. She would take a deep breath, pull the door shut, and go. She would hold the doorknob as if it were a hand, then hold it just a little bit longer and whisper thank you—for everything.

When she drove across the bay bridge, it was with faith and courage to meet the next part of her life. She rolled down the windows. Wasn't the wind wonderful? So free and wild.

They hung the portrait in their new living room in a small house with yellow siding, just a few blocks from Main Street, in a neighborhood occupied by young families, elderly couples, and newlyweds, with plenty of diversity—locals and natives rather than tourists. There was stability in a community of consistent neighbors, Audra said; she was already planning a late-spring barbecue.

The yellow house was a two-story with two bedrooms, two baths, a living and dining area, a small kitchen with all new appliances, and a den for a shared office and studio. Lucy chose gray for the walls, a cheery gray, she said, that softened the sunlit rooms and accented the many plants Audra had potted and positioned around the rooms.

Outside the kitchen window was a tall privacy fence guarding a small flowerbed and patio with a glider, table, and two chairs where they sipped coffee or tea in the cool spring mornings. Lucy strung lights from the fence to the roof of the house for evenings of reading, painting, chatting.

"Congrats on your new house," Charlie texted her. "I'll be home in June to start working with the parents again. Looking forward to seeing you again."

"Thanks!" Lucy replied. "And same."

What would it be like to work with him full-time in his parents' market and restaurant? The thought made her queasy, but she reframed it: Being with him had always been fine, and she'd roll with the changes.

When Charlie returned in June, he was broader, darker, but still grinning that boyish smile. They met up at their old cafe for old times' sake and talked about college and grad school and all the things that had happened since he'd left.

"I have a mental illness," she told him, feeling it pit her stomach as she spoke the words. "I've had it for a long time, since before high school. I've been getting help, and I have a friend looking out for me. But I wanted you to know because I think you deserve to."

He stopped smiling and looked away, then down in his empty cup, and shifted a little.

"Thanks for telling me," he said. He took her hand and looked into her eyes, as if seeing her for the first time. "I wish you'd told me back then. My mom battled mental illness when I was a kid."

"She's never told me that." Of course, Lucy knew it was often embarrassing to talk about.

He shook his head. "She went through a lot of shame over it—not from me or my dad, obviously—a lot of self-imposed shame. I think talking about it and finding other people who also have struggled with it takes away a lot of the shame. I'm glad you told me, seriously. A lot of people I went to school with have mental health issues; it's not as rare as you might think."

No, not rare, because she'd read the statistics and knew that plenty of people were on antidepressants and had regular appointments with therapists. She just didn't think they were around her, walking the streets with her, standing at work with her.

How much better could she have felt, how much stronger could she have become if she'd opened up about it sooner and found a community of support?

Audra obtained her real estate license in Florida and already had a job with an agency a few blocks from the yellow house. She had a handful of clients, and sometimes the work required long nights, but Lucy always waited up for her with a kettle of hot water or a pitcher of sweet iced tea. Even after ten o'clock some nights, Lucy helped her wind down from the day, sitting with her on the patio under the lights.

"Are you sorry you sold your house?" Audra asked her one night, the heat forming condensation around her glass of tea.

"No, I'm really not."

"Are you ever . . . mad at me, for making you sell it?"

"You didn't make me sell it. You gave me the courage to do it."

Audra took a deep breath. "There's something else I'd like to give you the courage to do."

"Okay."

"What do you think about going on a trip somewhere?"

She didn't miss the way Lucy stiffened or the hesitancy in her voice when she finally replied. "Like, to where?"

"Anywhere that you're comfortable. We'll build from there. I'm thinking one or two trips a year, depending on money and time. We can start with short flights in the US, like to New York, and then maybe go overseas someday."

Lucy sat, breathing and swinging and sipping her tea.

"What about my dad? I see him twice a week, and I take him to church every week."

Audra chose her words carefully. "Do you think he'd be okay for just one week?"

She fell silent again.

"You can call him from wherever we go. He won't forget you, Lucy—not in a week."

"What if something happens to him while we're gone?"

Audra took her hand. "You can say good-bye before we go, and if something happens, we'll come right back."

Lucy breathed again and looked up past the lights that obscured the stars, to the dark night sky. What if she had an attack on the plane or in a taxi or a bus or the subway, and couldn't get out to breathe and calm down? What if the attack was the worst one yet, setting her back after all of her progress? Why couldn't they just enjoy their peaceful, manageable life here?

But she knew this meant something to Audra. She craved the adventures to be found in new places, with new people and cultures, always with the promise of home awaiting her at the end. Lucy couldn't deny her this—not after all she'd done for her.

"What sounds good to you?"

"Well, I was thinking, if we wanted a calming vacation, we could visit the mountains in Colorado, or California, the Pacific Coast. Or if we wanted a big city, which obviously would be less peaceful, we could visit Chicago or New York."

"Let's see Colorado. I'd like to see mountains and lakes. I'll bring my sketchpads and pencils."

Audra's breath caught. "Are you sure?"

Lucy looked at Audra, whose face reflected the lights, and nodded. "Positive."

TO THE READER:

Because one in three people has mental illness, and woman are twice as likely as men to suffer from it, I'm sure many of you identify with Lucy. However, some of you may not relate with her journey at all.

Whether you suffer from depression and anxiety or not, it's important to remember that every journey is unique unto itself. Relief comes to every person differently and in multifaceted ways. Some people find healing in natural, herbal remedies; some in medication and therapy; some in lifestyle changes and relationships. This book is not meant to show anyone how to live, heal, or deal with their mental illness, but rather to encourage others in their own journeys. It's meant to further destigmatize mental illness, which is not a struggle for the weak and pathetic, but for whomever it strikes. Those who suffer are some of the strongest and bravest among us.

It is also meant to honor the Audra Clarkes in our lives— those patient friends who love us not in spite of ourselves but because of ourselves, who shine their stabilizing light on us in our darkest times and help us breathe when we feel we're drowning. You are heroes.

If you're struggling with any form of mental illness or thoughts of suicide, please reach out to the National Suicide Prevention Lifeline at 1-800-273-TALK and tell someone in your life. You don't have to struggle alone, and your life is worth saving.

Acknowledgments

First and foremost, my sincerest thanks to Sarah Eshleman, to whom this book is dedicated. She heard multiple versions of this story and let me know what was good and bad and sometimes awful. She was always right.

Thanks to Woodhall Press and my editors for believing in this book.

I'm forever grateful for my parents, Chris and Paula Allnutt, for loving, supporting, and cheering me on always. They believed me when I was child saying that I wanted to be an author when I grew up, and they strangely always assumed I would be.

I owe enormous gratitude to my mentors, Kim Dana Kupperman, Eugenia Kim, and the late Da Chen. Their guidance and instruction in the beginning days of this novel helped it find its footing.

A huge thank you to all my readers through the years, who read parts or whole versions of the book and offered invaluable feedback, and especially to Kathleen Herald, Sonja Lyle, Kaycee Simpson, and my wonderful cohort in Fairfield University's MFA program.

And thank you, readers, for selecting this book among the hundreds of options on the shelves.

ABOUT THE AUTHOR

Laura Allnutt holds an MFA in creative writing from Fairfield University and teaches writing and composition. She has been published in *Chicken Soup for the Soul: the Power of Yes, Long Island Literary Journal,* and *Lost River Literary Magazine.* Visit Laura's blog at:

ThinkingWithMyMindFull.wordpress.com.